Countdown to chaos . . .

There were last-minute reports from CIC, Lieutenant Colonel Jensen, and the battalion commanders in the 7th Regiment. Lon set up a command conference channel with the battalion commanders in both regiments. The order to begin the offensive would go directly to each unit. Seven battalions would attack simultaneously. There would be little air cover.

Two minutes. Lon glanced to his left, in the general direction of 1st Battalion's positions, though it was too far away for him to see anyone there. That was where Junior was, with the two platoons he led— on the left flank, with no friendly troops to guard it.

Will we both make it through the day? Lon wondered. Hidden deeper in his mind, Lon was almost unaware of *What would I tell his mother?* nagging at his subconscious defenses. He squeezed his eyes shut, trying to force his thoughts away from that unpleasant prospect. *I can't allow myself to be distracted, not now.*

One minute. Time for a last hurried call to CIC for the latest updates. One of the enemy artillery units had—apparently—been hit by the Shrike IIs and put out of commission. The shuttles carrying the three remaining battalions of the strike force were on their way in and would soon be out of reach of the weapons aboard the New Spartan transports.

Time . . .

Ace Books by Rick Shelley

COLONEL

RICK SHELLEY

ACE BOOKS, NEW YORK

COLONEL

An Ace Book / published by arrangement with the author.

PRINTING HISTORY
Ace mass-market edition / November 2000

All rights reserved.
Copyright © 2000 by Rick Shelley.
Cover art by Duane O. Myers.

This book may not be reproduced in whole or in part, by mimeograph or any other means, without permission. For information address: The Berkley Publishing Group, a division of Penguin Putnam, Inc., 375 Hudson Street, New York, New York 10014.

The Penguin Putnam Inc. World Wide Web site address is http://www.penguinputnam.com

Check out the ACE Science Fiction & Fantasy newsletter and much more on the Internet at Club PPI!

ISBN: 0-441-00782-1

ACE®
Ace Books are published by The Berkley Publishing Group, a division of Penguin Putnam Inc., 375 Hudson Street, New York, New York 10014. ACE and the "A" design are trademarks belonging to Penguin Putnam Inc.

PRINTED IN THE UNITED STATES OF AMERICA

10 9 8 7 6 5 4 3

COLONEL

The year is A.D. 2830. The interstellar diaspora from Earth has been in progress for seven centuries. The numbers are uncertain, but at least five hundred worlds have been settled, and perhaps well over a thousand. The total human population of the galaxy could be in excess of a trillion. On Earth, the Confederation of Human Worlds still theoretically controls all of those colonies, but the reality is that it can count on its orders being obeyed only as far as the most distant permanent outpost within Earth's system, on Titan. Beyond Saturn, there are two primary interstellar political groupings, the Confederation of Human Worlds (broken away from the organization on Earth with the same name, with its capital on the world known as Union) and the Second Commonwealth, centered on Buckingham. Neither of those political unions is as large or as powerful as they will be in another seventeen decades, when their diametrically opposed interests finally bring them to the point of war. In the meantime, humans who need military assistance, and do not want the domination of either Confederation or Commonwealth, have only a handful of options. Those who can afford it turn to mercenaries. And the largest source of those is on the world of Dirigent. . . .

1

Although Christmas was a week past, a decorated tree still sat in one corner of the Nolan living room. Each of the three strings of lights was guaranteed to include bulbs of 120 distinct colors. They twinkled in unpredictable sequences and combinations—"Like snowflakes, no two patterns will ever be exactly alike," the advertisement had promised. The only other light in the room came from the screen of the entertainment console. For the past three weeks, Dirigent City's special-events channel had been offering holiday music of the last thousand years. Although there was video to go with most of the selections—performance, dramatic, or simply mood—Lon had muted the monitor to leave only the dark blue background of a vacant screen.

Lon Nolan and his wife, Sara, were sitting on the sofa, snuggled close. For the moment, their attention had been diverted from hypnotic staring at the tree lights to watching the timeline on the entertainment console as it counted down the seconds of the final minute of the year 2829. Lon, Junior, stood leaning against the mantel of the room's decorative fireplace, a bottle of beer in his left hand. Junior had been nursing the same bottle for nearly an hour. When the countdown reached twenty seconds, he set the beer on the mantel and straightened up. Although he was not in uniform, Junior stood almost at attention. He was nearly two inches taller than his father now, and perhaps five pounds heavier. As a boy, Junior had appeared to be the image of his father; now he seemed to favor his mother more, at least through the face. His complexion was lighter than his father's, even though his face was tanned and beginning to show the weathering of a life spent largely outdoors.

The screen of the entertainment console came to life then, programmed earlier by Lon, Senior. The several hundred couples who were seeing the new year come in at the grand ballroom of Corps Headquarters had stopped dancing. They were counting down the last seconds. The band on the stage at the east end of the ballroom was ready to jump straight into the traditional music for welcoming the new year.

"Happy New Year!" the master of ceremonies shouted at the appropriate second. Balloons, streamers, and confetti filled the air at the grand ballroom. The band launched 2830 with "Auld Lang Syne," a song whose origins had been partially lost in the mythology that had grown up around it when the song had been chosen as the accompaniment to the start of the journeys of early colony ships leaving Earth.

Lon and Sara welcomed the new year with a long kiss. Sara twisted around on the sofa until she was almost sitting in her husband's lap. Junior turned half away, as if distancing himself from the demonstration of parental emotion. He occupied himself by finishing the beer on the mantel. It was almost room temperature by now.

The new year was a full minute old when Junior cleared his throat and said, "I've got a taxi on order for quarter past."

That interrupted his parents. Sara got up from the sofa and took a step toward her son. "Your sister won't be home yet," she said.

Junior shrugged. "I promised some friends I'd meet them in Camo Town. They'll be more than half plotched by now, but they'll remember enough if I don't show up at all. Besides, they'll need someone around who's going to stay at least halfway sober to get back to barracks by dawn."

His father was slower to get up from the sofa, but put his hands on Sara's arms as if to keep her from going to their son. "I appreciate you seeing in the new year with us," Lon said.

Junior shrugged again. "There haven't been all that many years when we've all been together for the holidays." He grinned. "And this time it's Angie who's missing, after all the times she moaned when you were away on contract, and she sure let me know how she felt when I was off on contract last year."

"Oh, it's not the same," Sara said. "Angie's just out for a few hours. We were all together for Christmas, and all your grandparents as well."

"I know, Mama," Junior said, crossing and giving her a serious hug—picking her off the ground with ease. "But you can bet I'm going to use it just the same." He grinned as he let her go.

"Stay out of trouble, Junior," Lon said.

Junior's grin threatened to become a laugh. "Don't worry, Dad. I'm not about to do anything you'll have to convene a court-martial for. They don't call me 'Old Sober-sides' for nothing." The two had quit hugging the day Junior had put on the uniform of the Dirigent Mercenary Corps. He had enlisted as a private shortly after his eighteenth birthday, seen combat, then been chosen for officer training. Eleven months earlier, he had earned his lieutenant's pips after seeing combat as an officer cadet. Now he was a platoon leader in Delta Company, 1st Battalion, 7th Regiment. His father was the regimental commander, a full colonel and member of the Council of Regiments that governed the DMC and the world of Dirigent. The Corps was full of cases where more than one member of a family served in the same regiment. Over many generations a set of rules and commonsense traditions had grown to make sure that nepotistic favoritism did not weaken the fabric of the Corps. Every man wearing the uniform had to earn his own way, and being related to a senior officer had at least as many drawbacks as advantages.

"Will you be here for dinner tomorrow . . . today?" Sara asked.

"One o'clock?" Junior replied. When his mother nodded, he said, "Sure, I'll be here. Now I'd better get my coat. On busy nights, the cabdrivers start their meters when they honk to announce they've arrived."

"There are times when I think it's all a conspiracy against the women of Dirigent," Sara said when the taxi's tail-lights blinked out as it turned the corner.

"What are you talking about?" Lon asked.

"You finally get to the point where I don't have to worry about you going out so often and I've got to start worrying about Junior off on contract." Regimental commanders only went off-world on single-battalion contracts under the most extraordinary conditions. If two battalions—half the regiment's line companies—were involved, the commander might go *if* it were an especially important contract, or one including considerable ancillary forces; otherwise, his executive officer was more likely to draw the assignment. Only if three battalions or the entire regiment went off-world on a contract was the commander certain to go, and contracts that large were relatively infrequent.

"I tried everything I could to convince him not to enter the Corps," Lon whispered. There were still moments when he found his mind trying to decide what more he *might* have done to prevent Junior's enlistment.

Sara turned away from the picture window at the front of the house and walked toward the Christmas tree. "I know," she said, so softly that Lon hardly heard. "It was a losing fight from the start. This *is* Dirigent. The Corps is what we're all about. We send our men off to war, and sometimes all that comes home is a box and the official regrets of the General."

Lon went to Sara, stood behind her, and put his hands

on her arms, resting his cheek against her hair. "I know it can't stop the worrying—it doesn't keep *me* from worrying about him—but he *is* good. He's one of the coolest junior officers in the regiment. He keeps his head in combat and he's careful, with himself and his men. He's got good people around him and they take care of him, the way Phip and the others took care of me when I was in the same position."

"He could have gone into the technical end, become an engineer, and worked in the munitions side of things," Sara said. "He's got the brain for it. He's got the brain to tackle any job he could dream of. No one on Dirigent would have thought the worse for him. The Corps can't take *every* boy, and he could have done a lot more good for the world developing better equipment."

Lon swallowed the sigh that wanted to come out. Nothing about this conversation was new. Alone or together, Lon and Sara had gone through every phrase, every word, uncounted times, spoken or thought.

The romantic holiday mood was gone, and Lon saw little chance of recapturing it that night. When Sara got fixated on this, there was seldom any cure for it but sleep and—sometimes—crying. It was holidays more than anything else that could bring this mood out in her. It didn't happen often, and it had rarely happened before Junior neared the age when he could enlist. The Corps was so integral to the existence of Dirigent that the need for young men to become soldiers had to be the highest priority, and schooling and social pressure had always been used to impress everyone with that need. *Dirigent is the Corps. Without the Corps there would be no Dirigent.* The truth of that was unfortunately easy to demonstrate. Without the Corps and its ancillary munitions industry, Dirigent did not have the resources to support 10 percent of its current population at anything beyond the subsistence, everyone-a-farmer, level. It certainly wouldn't be one of the dozen most prosperous colony worlds.

"You know his argument," Lon said after a long silence. "He figures he'll have time to do both, learn first-hand what soldiers face on the ground, then continue his education and find ways to make things better for them. Look on the bright side. He doesn't plan on spending his entire working career in the Corps. He talks about five or ten years, and if he gets some idea that really catches his imagination, he might cut even that short, anxious to get involved in the research and development end of the business."

"If he lives long enough," Sara said. Then she expelled a sigh and turned to face her husband. "I know, I'm making a botch out of the holiday and I shouldn't."

"You worry because you care," Lon said. He knew it was a cliché, but he had learned years before that clichés were the safest way to handle a situation like this. "You wouldn't be much of a wife and mother if you didn't worry about us. We might get to thinking that you didn't love us."

Sara buried her face against his shirt. To avoid a show of tears, Lon changed the subject. "What time is Angie supposed to be home from that dance?"

"By one-thirty," Sara said, pulling away from Lon. "The dance ends at one o'clock." It was a well-supervised affair, chaperoned by teachers from the high school on base that Angie attended and teachers from the three civilian high schools in Dirigent City that also were taking part. "The bus will have the kids back on base by one-twenty, and it shouldn't take her more than ten minutes to walk home from the bus stop. And, no, I don't think you should walk over to meet her there. She'll have friends with her."

Lon chuckled. "I wasn't going to suggest that. The only thing I was thinking was that I might stand on the porch and watch."

"Not even that," Sara said. "Angie is sixteen years old now, and you know how touchy she is when she thinks we're still treating her like a little kid."

"I can't help it. Where I grew up on Earth it wasn't

safe for a cop to be out alone after dark, let alone a teenager. My hometown had more crime in any given week than the entire world of Dirigent has had in the past quarter century. I still think about that at some level."

"The kids think you're making that up, you know, even after they looked up the statistics on the net. Besides, Angie probably won't be alone. She's got a new boyfriend, and I imagine he'll walk her home."

"New boyfriend? Not that Bobby anymore?"

Sara laughed. "You're way behind times. There have been two others since Bobby. Three with this latest boy."

"Who's she seeing now? Someone from her school?" Lon did not even notice that Sara had come out of her funk.

"His name is Gordon Aruba. His father is a battalion lead sergeant in 10th Regiment."

Lon closed his eyes for a moment, trying to make a connection to the name. He shook his head. "I don't think I know him."

"No, you probably don't, but Gordon knows who you are, so you can bet he'll be a perfect gentleman. Now, let's get back to the music. We don't want Angie to come home and spot us standing around looking like we're just waiting for her to check in."

2

Dirigent City and the DMC's primary base woke on New Year's Day to a fresh coating of snow, slightly more than two inches in most places, which made it the heaviest snowfall of the winter. So far. The snow had started falling, lightly, just after one o'clock that morning, before Angie Nolan got home from her New Year's Eve dance. By the time Angie and her parents got to bed, near two o'clock, there was already a dusting on the lawns and streets. The snow showers peaked at about four, and started to taper off less than a half hour later. By dawn the skies were clearing. The temperature was in the mid-twenties, and there was just the hint of a breeze coming from the northwest.

Despite his late night, Lon was out of bed by seven o'clock. He had already been awake for an hour. More than a quarter century as a soldier had made it virtually impossible for him to sleep past dawn in garrison. Lon avoided moving or getting out of bed as long as he could, not wanting to wake Sara. Eventually, though, he could take immobility no more. He got up, showered, shaved, and dressed in comfortable civilian clothes, then went to the kitchen to fix his own breakfast. When he heard Sara moving about, he doubled everything. There was little chance that Angie would rise before nine, and even then she would probably eat no more than a single slice of toast . . . if that. Angie had given up on breakfast about the time she reached puberty.

"One of these days I'm going to learn," Sara said when

she came into the kitchen wearing robe and slippers.

"Learn what?" Lon asked.

"Learn to stick a sleep patch on you when you don't have to be up before the chickens," Sara said. She sat at the table in her usual place—nearest the stove and food replicator.

"I tried not to wake you," Lon replied. "Breakfast will be ready in two minutes." He set a cup of coffee in front of her. Sara closed her eyes while she took her first sip. Lon always made the coffee too strong, but—this morning—that was just what she wanted. Sara had only had three drinks the night before, but that was more alcohol than she usually drank in a week. There was no headache—no hangover. She had applied a patch, what men in the Corps called a killjoy patch, to avoid that before going to bed, but she still felt a little sluggish.

"You called the officer of the day yet to make sure the whole regiment didn't move without leaving a forwarding address?" Sara asked as she set the coffee cup back down.

"No, I haven't called the OD yet," Lon said. "All I did was check the complink to make certain there were no important messages. And I'm not planning on going in to headquarters at all today."

"I noticed you weren't in uniform," Sara said.

"Come on," Lon said, starting to dish up the eggs and sausages he had cooked. "I have learned to relax a *little*."

Sara smiled. "A little," she conceded.

"We've got snow on the ground," Lon said. He put one plate in front of Sara and took his around to the other side of the table and sat across from her.

"I know. I looked out. Enough snow to look pretty, not enough to be a nuisance if we want to go anywhere. A few hours and the streets will all be clear." There were few wheeled vehicles on Dirigent. Most automobiles and trucks were ground-effect vehicles—floaters. The passage of one floater's fans normally left clear pavement behind, except when there was wet, heavy snow. Then it might take considerable traffic. It had been twelve years since the Corps had needed to put snowplows on tracked vehicles to clear streets in the city or on base. This time, the snow was not excessively wet and the temperature would probably climb above freezing before noon. By sunset there might be almost no evidence left that it had snowed at all.

Lon and Sara ate silently for several minutes. The years had made them both comfortable with long silences. Neither one felt the need to fill every moment with sound. When they had finished eating, Sara got up and put the dirty dishes and pans in the dishwasher, then went back to the bedroom to get dressed.

Lon went to the living room and turned the entertainment console on to get the news summaries. The night's snow was the major story, which was a relief, since that meant that nothing more . . . traumatic had happened on Dirigent and no dire news had come in from elsewhere. After a few minutes he keyed in a filter command for news about the Corps. New Year's Eve had passed without major incident. There were notes of a couple of minor fights, but nothing more serious. The fights had both been between soldiers, and none of the participants had been injured. Had civilians been involved, it might have been different.

"Anything world-shattering on the news?" Sara asked when she came out dressed for the day.

"Maybe thirty thousand soldiers went out to drink in the new year last night, and all that happened was two minor fistfights," Lon said. "You'd think they were monks instead of soldiers. Sometimes I think we're the most peaceable bunch of humans in the galaxy." Even after more than twenty-five years on Dirigent, Lon found himself occasionally astounded by how little crime, how little violence, there was. It had been five years since the last killing on the world, and the killer had been a recent immigrant, not a member of the Corps. The stern discipline within the Corps was reflected to a large degree within families—the tradition of obedience and duty. Also, there was little economic distress due to the almost constant influx of revenue from off-world. The police force, with the best preventive and investigative equipment made, was also a deterrent to crime; the odds of escaping detection—and punishment—were slim.

Lon got up from the sofa and stretched. "I think I'll take a walk. I need to get a little exercise. It's been three days since I went to the gym."

"Just don't get carried away. It's cold out. And your parents might be here before noon."

"Just a quick turn around the neighborhood," Lon promised.

The houses for married personnel had been laid out with military precision. The sizes of houses and lawns varied in strict proportion with the rank of the soldier each was designed for. The most senior officers, colonels and lieutenant colonels, were along one street, nearer Corps headquarters than the rest. Majors and captains were quartered in the next blocks. Farthest off were the few lieutenants and senior enlisted personnel who were married. At all ranks below major, married men were the minority in the Corps. Marriage was—unofficially—discouraged until the soldier had at least ten years in uniform and had reached the rank of captain or lead sergeant . . . for officers and enlisted personnel respectively.

Lon had set himself no route before leaving the house. He turned right and started walking. The sidewalks had not been cleared, so he left a clear trail in the snow, the ridged soles of his boots crunching snow underfoot, giving a muted sound track to his walk. The air was crisp, bringing a tingle to his face and ears before he had gone a single block. He kept his hands in the pockets of his overcoat, out of the cold. He had gloves with him but did not bother to put them on.

He walked, at something less than a normal marching gait. Even five years earlier he might have felt compelled to jog. He still ran, perhaps three days a week in garrison, but not as far or as intently as he had when he was younger and considered himself a distance runner. He was not constantly trying to meet his best recent times for the mile . . . or any other distance. It was enough for him to maintain a significant edge over the time he would have to meet when he took his annual physical fitness test. No one in the Dirigent Mercenary Corps could let himself get flabby or out of condition. Even the General, commanding officer of the Corps and head of state for the world, had to meet the same physical conditioning standards as any private just completing recruit training to remain in the DMC.

When Lon eventually increased his pace, it was strictly as a response to the cold. It wasn't enough to turn him back toward home immediately, but a little more speed did help offset the nip in the air. A brisk walk helped to keep stray thoughts from intruding as well. He was as off-duty as a regimental commander ever could be. Unless the communications link in his pocket beeped, he was free. He looked around, enjoying the snow-covered scenery, the antiseptic look of fresh white covering everything. The residential area was set far enough from the rest of the base that there was nothing overtly military about his surroundings. He saw children playing in a few yards, some attempting to build snowmen . . . without marked success. The snow wasn't wet enough for that. At least no one tried to use him as a target for snowballs.

Lon walked three blocks, then turned to his left and walked a block over to the next street of houses, then turned left again and, unconsciously, increased his pace a little more. It was cold enough that he felt no desire to prolong the morning walk. He found himself whistling, some unidentifiable mélange of partially remembered songs strung together in a way guaranteed to offend the ears of anyone who appreciated good music, but Lon had the sidewalks to himself. There was no one to scream in agony at his efforts.

He went two blocks beyond the corner he would have turned at to go directly back home, then finally crossed back to his own street. His exertion had him feeling a little warm, except for the persistent chill against his exposed face. He intentionally turned the wrong way on his street, away from home, and went two more blocks before he crossed the lane and reversed his course.

Sweating and freezing at the same time, he thought as he kicked snow from his boots on the front porch of the house the family had moved into when he won his promotion to colonel. This one had more room than they could possibly need. *That's about standard for an infantryman.* He took his hands from his pockets and rubbed vigorously at his cheeks. They were more than a little numb after a half hour in the below-freezing air. Before going inside, he turned and scanned the street in both directions. There was no one else in sight.

"You look like a lobster just pulled from the pot," Sara said when she saw Lon's face.

"I'd almost trade places with one," Lon said, rubbing at his cheeks again. They had started to tingle. "Very nippy out. You catch the forecast, by any chance? Our 4th Battalion is due to go out on overnight maneuvers tomorrow. The colder it is, the more bitching there'll be." He stomped his boots on the rug in the entryway a couple of times to get rid of any vestiges of snow and to warm his feet.

"No, I haven't checked the forecast yet, but I've heard some of the things *you* said when you had to go out in the cold, or in the rain," Sara said, turning away to hide her grin. "Serve you right to be on the other end of it."

Lon took off his coat and hung it in the closet. "I never get to hear any of it since I made colonel. Everyone's too careful for *that.* But the looks." He laughed. "Especially since I won't be out with them. It's not the whole regiment."

"Well, you could always go out with them just to show the men your heart's in the right place," Sara suggested, more in jest than earnest. "Suffer with them, be the stalwart campaigner you always claim to be."

"And listen to you complain about me being away when I don't have to?" Lon asked, falling into the same bantering tone. "I don't have three layers of men keeping me from hearing the awful truth at home." Both of them were comfortable with it after the twenty-three years they had been married. It had helped carry them through some of the more difficult days in those years. "You'd remind me of it for months. Besides, I've been in the army long enough to know not to volunteer for anything I don't have to."

"Me, complain?"

"You know why Napoleon always had his hand inside his tunic, don't you?" Lon asked as they moved from the foyer into the living room. "It was because Josephine's nagging gave him ulcers."

"Are you two at it again?"

Angie's parents hadn't seen or heard her come into the room. Her unexpected question startled both of them.

"We're just talking," Sara said. "We do that now and then. It helps pass the time between meals."

Angie wrinkled her nose at her mother. At sixteen, Angie Nolan was a beautiful young woman with a trim figure. Even just a few minutes from sleep, her face looked fresh and clear. There were no dark circles around her eyes, no hint of sleepiness in her face. Her shoulder-length blond hair had not been combed yet, but there were few visible snarls to it.

"You want breakfast?" Sara asked.

Angie shook her head, which dislodged most of the tangles in her hair. "We'll be having dinner in a couple of hours. I'll just have some juice and maybe a piece of toast."

"Too many cookies and chips at the dance last night?" Lon asked.

"No," Angie said, drawing the word out like stretching a rubber band. "I'm just not hungry. I don't like to eat right after I get up. Makes me feel bloated. Is Junior going to be here for dinner?"

"He said he would be," Lon said, nodding. "But I wouldn't count on it until you see him. He was going out to meet friends when he left here last night. They might not have found their way back from Camo Town yet."

"Lon!" Sara said, a world of admonishment in the word.

"What did I say?" Lon asked.

"Mother, I'm not six years old. I do have *some* idea what goes on in the world. Nothing Daddy says is going to shock me senseless."

Sara took a deep breath. "It had nothing to do with you, dear."

Angie looked from her mother to her father, then back. That response was not what she had been expecting. "I've got to shower and get dressed," she said then. She didn't wait for a reply. Sara watched Angie until she turned into the hallway and the stairs leading up to her bedroom. Lon started chuckling as his daughter went out of sight.

"I never know *what's* going to come out of your mouth," Sara said when she turned back to Lon. "Honestly! Barracks talk."

Lon's chuckle threatened to get completely out of control. "If you think *that* was barracks talk, then you've never heard the real thing . . . and I know better. You grew up in a pub. You probably heard worse before you were half Angie's age."

"That's beside the point. Anyway, my father never let the soldiers who came to the pub get too far out of line. He could tone them down in a hurry, and you know that."

Lon moved to Sara, put his arm around her, and led her toward the kitchen. When she started to resist a little, he tickled her side.

"Stop that," Sara said, but there was no protest in her tone. "I've got to get this place ready for dinner. Your parents could be here in an hour." They kissed quickly, and Sara pushed Lon away. "Go watch cartoons or something."

Lawrence and Maddie Nolan both looked younger after living on Dirigent for six years than they had when they arrived. It was something Lon and Sara talked about occasionally, and even their children had noticed the change in their grandparents. The stress lines had disappeared from their faces, making them look softer, younger. The voices and movements were more relaxed. It was rare for either of them to even mention Earth any longer, though Lon's father admitted that they kept track of news from there. Filtered by distance and time—the "latest" news from Earth was always at least a month old before it reached Dirigent—the information was rarely more . . . emotional than lines from a history text.

Despite the quarter-century difference in their ages, Lawrence and Lon now looked more like brothers than father and son. Lawrence was a little heavier, a little softer in appearance, but with the help of his implanted nanotech health maintenance system he was maintaining his apparent age at about fifty, close to Lon's real age. Lon's hair was beginning to show a little gray, since he did not have his HMS programmed for cosmetic effects. Few active members of the Corps did. A semblance of age lent authority. Most waited until they resigned or retired before having their systems reprogrammed in that fashion. Then they might shed apparent years in weeks. Molecular repair units could even carry melanin out into hair to remove gray.

"You figure this will be the year you make General?" Lawrence asked his son as soon as they were alone in the living room. Maddie had gone to help Sara in the kitchen. Angie had come downstairs just long enough to greet her grandparents, then had disappeared upstairs again to resume a complink conversation with one of her friends from school.

"We've been through this before, Dad," Lon said. "I

don't *ever* expect to become General." There was only one General at a time in the DMC, elected for a one-year term by the fourteen regimental commanders from among their own number. "It would break too many traditions, and the Corps is almost as tradition bound as any army on Earth. No first-generation Dirigenter has ever held the post, no one whose father wasn't an officer in the Corps has ever held it. And on and on."

Lawrence snorted. "I've done a little research. Only one man who wasn't born on Dirigent has ever commanded a regiment. You. Only one man who didn't have any ancestors in the Corps has ever commanded a regiment. You. And on and on. There's no reason to think you won't be elected General before you retire."

"I'm not so sure. Maybe if I hang around another twenty or thirty years and everyone else on the Council of Regiments has had a turn or two already, they might decide the only way to get rid of me will be to let me play General for a year, but I don't expect to stay on that long. Staying fit enough to pass the annual physical fitness test gets harder every year. Even if I don't decide to pack it in and take over Sara's parents' pub sooner, I can't see me staying in the Corps more than another decade. If that. Once Angie graduates from high school, I might decide enough is enough just about anytime."

"The kid who kept saying, 'All I ever want to be is a soldier'?" Lawrence asked.

Lon frowned. "You don't know how many years I've spent having nightmares about that sentence. Ever since Junior started saying the same thing. Anyway, I've been a soldier more than half my life. I've seen more than enough of what that can mean."

"Sorry. I didn't mean to raise ghosts. Let me ask you something else, then. Who do you figure will be the next General?"

Lon smiled. "*I* don't have a clue, but Sara's back-fence gossip circle says it'll be Bob Hayley of 15th unless he's off-world when election time comes around in March.

And 15th Regiment is at the top of the rota for regiment-size contracts, so that's possible. And if Bob is off on contract, there's no favorite for second choice among the wives."

"Not electing someone who's off-world . . . is that another of your hidebound traditions?"

"Pretty much. It's not a written rule, but it's never been done. I don't know. It might just be superstition, afraid to jinx a man who might be in a combat situation, or fear that he might be killed or captured. But, once elected, the General doesn't leave Dirigent during his term. Ever. Any diplomatic travel is generally done by civilians, usually career bureaucrats or retired senior officers."

"So if Colonel Hayley is off on contract when election time comes around and there's no clear second choice, then your chances are as good as anyone else's, right?" Lawrence asked.

Lon laughed. "You got a bet on with someone?" He didn't wait for his father to respond. "No, if Hayley isn't here, it'll probably end up with Murtaugh, Mills, or Dumbrovski. They've all been on the Council longer than me and haven't had a shot at the top job yet."

"None of them has a record to match yours, and the word I've been hearing is that Murtaugh hasn't got a shot at ever becoming General. Something about a contract on Aurora."

"That was a long time ago, his first time out as a company commander. He's completed a lot of good contracts since then." Lon knew about the Aurora contract. He had heard it mentioned several times by senior officers, and had eventually looked up the record. Murtaugh, then a captain, had commanded one company on a battalion-size contract. Exactly what had happened was still a matter of dispute despite the video and audio recordings from the battle helmets of the officers and noncommissioned officers involved, but Murtaugh's company had suffered 20 percent casualties and had failed to fulfill their part of the operation, which had led to serious casualties in the rest of the battalion. Another battalion had to be sent to Aurora to fulfill the contract.

"Maybe you're right about Murtaugh," Lon said after thinking about it for a moment. "Memories can be long for something like that. The Corps lost money as well as too many men on that contract. It still leaves Mills and Dumbrovski. Mills's father and Dumbrovski's grandfather each served as General at least once."

"Don't you *want* to be General?" Lawrence asked.

"I've never let myself give it much thought," Lon said. "Getting my own regiment always seemed to be right at the very edge of possibility. I never had the time or the inclination to look much beyond that. Do I *want* to be General?" Lon paused, then shook his head. "Not especially, not now. Oh, I wouldn't turn it down if by some miracle the job was offered to me, but I don't need the title to validate my life. I don't have any driving urge to have it. Does that surprise you?"

Lawrence was slow to reply. "In a way. I'd think that going as far as you could in your chosen career would be more important to you."

Lon closed his eyes for an instant before he spoke again. "Dad, I've got too many ghosts haunting my dreams now. I've seen too much death, buried too many friends. The way conditions are in the galaxy, we do a lot of good. I can see the need for the Corps, despite the cost in lives. As long as I'm a field commander, I can make a difference. I have to believe that fewer of our people die with me in command than might under someone else. But the General isn't a field commander. He never goes on contract. He just has the final word on which contracts we accept and sends men out where he can't personally affect what happens."

"I don't think it's quite that simple."

Lon shrugged. "Maybe not, but the point remains. It's bad enough for me now sending a battalion off, or a company, and not going along to oversee the contract personally."

"You oversee training. You have some say in who gets promoted. You affect things, just at one remove. You're not God, Lon. You're human, just like the rest of us. All we can do is the best we can."

"I'm a soldier. When the best I can isn't good enough, men die. There are rows and rows of men who have died on contract under my command, so many that sometimes I can't remember all of their names. That's part of the nightmare."

3

Although Dirigent used the same names for its months that Earth did, they had been synchronized with the seasons on Dirigent's primary continent, putting Christmas and New Year's Day in the two weeks past the winter solstice, and bore no intrinsic relationship to the calendars of Earth. When Dirigent was settled, directly from Earth, its calendar was "out of phase" with Earth's by ten weeks. Over the centuries, slight differences in the length of the year between the two worlds had taken it nearly one more week out of alignment. It was a common problem, and the lengths of day and year on Dirigent were closer to Earth's than many other colony worlds' were. Every complink had automatic functions for converting the local calendars of hundreds of worlds to the month and year of any of the three "standards"—those of Earth, Union (for the breakaway Confederation of Human Worlds), and Buckingham (for the worlds of the Second Commonwealth).

On January 2, 2830, Lon's staff car pulled to the curb in front of the house at two minutes before seven o'clock in the morning—0658 hours in military time. Sunrise had occurred just six minutes earlier. Night was retreating west. Shadows were long. The temperature was slightly below freezing, and there were patches of ice where the snow of the day before had melted and frozen again. Sergeant Jeremy Howell got out of the gray floater and held the passenger's door open for Lon when he came out of the house.

"How'd you draw the duty this morning, Jerry?" Lon asked when they were both in the warmth of the floater. "Where's Dorcetti?" Frank Dorcetti was Lon's usual driver.

"Not due back from leave until tomorrow, sir," Howell said. "And I was the only sergeant around HQ this morning." One of the "honors" a colonel in the DMC was "due" was to have a sergeant as his assigned driver. Jeremy Howell was Lon's aide, one of the people Lon had brought along from 2nd Battalion to 7th Regiment headquarters when he was promoted.

"That's right. I guess I forgot," Lon said, nodding to himself. "How about you? You have a good New Year's Eve?"

"Holidays are always good when we're home, sir." Jeremy, his two brothers, and their father were all on active duty in the Corps. "We've got enough stripes among us to shame a zebra," he had joked once. His brothers were both corporals in the regiment's 1st Battalion, and their father was 4th Battalion's lead sergeant. "I could count the number of Christmases and New Years we've all been home on one hand . . . and still have a finger left for an obscene gesture."

Lon laughed, and Jeremy started the floater down the street.

"Never yet been a year when the four of us and my uncle and all my cousins were all home for the holidays," Jeremy continued. He had six first cousins in the Corps. Another uncle had been killed on duty ten years earlier, in a training accident on Dirigent. The rest of those relatives were in 5th Regiment. It was currently out on contract, not due back for at least another six weeks. And he had more distant kin in two other regiments—a not unusual situation in the DMC. "Just as well. Get too many of us together at one time and there's sure to be trouble."

"Your whole clan gets together at one time here and it pretty much means the Corps is out of work, doesn't it?" Lon asked.

"Oh, it works out sometimes, sir," Jeremy said. "Some of us on planetary defense, some on training routine, everybody either just back from contract or due to go out soon. Sometimes. Not often. We were all on-planet about four years back for a couple of weeks in the summer . . . no, five years come August. That was the last time."

The drive to 7th Regiment did not take long. When Lon's car came around the side of the headquarters building he could see each of its battalion HQs lining the regimental parade ground. No one was standing out there at this time, and there were only a couple of men crossing it. Reveille was past, and most of the men would be at breakfast or getting ready for their work formations at 0800 hours.

"You figure you'll need the car before quitting time this afternoon, Colonel?" Jeremy asked as he held the door for Lon to get out.

"Not that I know of, Jerry, but that's always subject to change without notice. We've got a Council meeting at ten, but I'll walk over to Corps headquarters for that. I need the exercise. Check with me after lunch. If I can get away I'm going to spend a couple of hours in the gym this afternoon."

"Yes, sir." Jeremy saluted. Lon returned the salute, then went into the building.

All fourteen regimental headquarters buildings had been built to the same plan, inside and out. They were three-story stone and plascrete buildings with the sizes of individual offices tailored for those who would use them. Unlike company or battalion headquarters, which might be left empty if the unit was on contract or simply at one of the Corps' secondary training bases, a regimental headquarters was always manned, even if the regiment and all its ancillary units—armor/artillery, transportation, and maintenance—were away, and it was extremely rare for all of the secondary services to accompany the regiment on contract.

At the front of the first floor, the orderly room, domain

of the regimental lead sergeant and his clerks, was on the left, and operations was on the right. The executive officer had his office behind, and connecting to, operations. A conference room was across the hall from that. Lon's office was on the second floor, above the orderly room and connected to it by a private lift tube. The intelligence officer and his staff were across the hall. There was a coffee room for officers at the rear of the second floor. The third floor was given over to other administrative offices.

Lon glanced into operations, then went into the orderly room on the other side of the corridor. Only the duty sergeant from the night shift, Brian Kespean from 3rd Battalion, was in the orderly room, waiting for the regimental lead sergeant to arrive and relieve him.

"Morning, Colonel," Kespean said, standing to attention and saluting. "Quiet night, sir. Not a bit of trouble on the log."

"That's always good to hear," Lon said as he returned the salute. "Good way to start the new year."

"Yes, it is, sir," Kespean agreed. "Nothing much on the log for the whole weekend." New Year's Day had fallen on Monday, which meant that there had been a long holiday weekend. Only those units serving a tour as part of the planetary defense system had kept more than a skeleton staff on duty.

"Tell Phip I'll be in my office when he gets here," Lon said, continuing across to the door leading to the private lift tube. Phip Steesen had been another of the men Lon had brought along from 2nd Battalion. Phip was the regimental lead sergeant now. "He can wait until his people get in before he comes up. Tell him there's nothing pressing on the docket."

"Yes, sir. I expect him in the next couple of minutes. He's in the area. He stopped by and said he was going to have a look around at the mess halls. I think he wanted to see how many hangovers he could spot."

Lon smiled. "He seem to have one himself?"

"Not that he was showing. Probably not. His wife

wouldn't let him have one even if he did get drunk and
forgot to put on a killjoy patch soon enough."

"I think Phip lost the taste," Lon said. *The way I did,*
he thought. *Drinking was more fun when I was young and
single.*

Lon had never gone in for excessively decorating the various offices he had occupied during his years in the Corps.
There were holographic photographs of family members
on the desk, a small lump of rock gathered in the Great
Smoky Mountains of Earth, near his childhood home, on
top of the single filing cabinet in the room. The wall directly across from his desk held a manning chart for the
regiment, showing each officer under his command. He
could call up a more complete manning chart on his desk
complink, showing each man in the regiment, with links
to complete service records and photographs. Even after
two years, Lon spent at least a few minutes every day
with that when possible, still trying to get to know all of
the men under his command. At the regimental level, that
was an almost impossible task. With four line battalions
and the auxiliary units assigned to 7th Regiment, he had
five thousand men under him. There was a constant, if
slow, turnover in personnel, as well as promotions and
changes of assignment for those who remained.

There was a fresh pot of hot coffee on the cart next to
Lon's desk when he got there, almost certainly prepared
by Jeremy Howell before he left to pick Lon up. Lon
poured himself a cup, then carried it to the window and
looked out over the parade ground while he sipped at the
liquid. He hardly noticed the taste, strong and unadulter-
ated by cream or sugar. Lon slipped into a blank stare,
something near the mental numbness of a soldier too long
in combat with too little sleep. He was scarcely aware of
what he was seeing outside; the movements of his coffee
cup were automatic, unnoticed. There were no pressing
problems waiting for his attention, no special worries carried over from the past year. Lon could afford the luxury

of a few minutes in something approaching a trancelike state, his mind idling. There were too few opportunities for this sort of passive escapism in Lon's life. When they did come, he abandoned himself to them completely, knowing the respite never lasted.

What brought Lon out of his reverie was an empty coffee cup. He had continued to drink automatically until he brought the cup to his lips and there was nothing left in it. Lon blinked several times, then looked into the cup as if he thought he might be mistaken, that there still might be coffee lurking in a hidden corner, reluctant to be drunk. Walking to the cart to get more coffee was too much bother. Lon simply set the cup on the windowsill in front of him and put his hands behind his back.

The blank did not return. Lon was too aware of people moving outside, and the slight sounds filtering through to his office from other parts of the building. His office was supposedly soundproof, but that insulation was not as thorough as it might be . . . or might have been when the building was new a century and a half before. Renovation of all fourteen regimental headquarters buildings was a perennial topic in the budget planning of the Council of Regiments, but it carried a low priority even though the fourteen colonels who decided on the budget would each get refurbished offices from the renovation. It might be another dozen years before the project would be started . . . after the last barracks and battalion headquarters had gone through renovation and remodeling.

The knock on the door was welcome. Lon turned away from the window and said, "Come in." Phip Steesen opened the door and entered, carefully closing the door behind him.

"Happy New Year, Lon," Phip said. In private, they could still indulge in the informality of longtime friends, even when they were both on duty. It was only when others were present that they had to observe all the protocols of military life. Phip was ten years older than Lon and had spent more than that number of years in the

Corps—not rising above the rank of private—before Lon arrived as an officer-cadet. Since then, Phip's rise in rank had paralleled Lon's, going from private to regimental lead sergeant in the same time that Lon had gone from lieutenant to colonel.

"Happy New Year, Phip," Lon responded automatically. "You manage to stay sober?"

"Unfortunately," Phip said, grinning. "Jenny and I shared a bottle of wine and were both asleep before midnight New Year's Eve. The kids were probably both awake later than we were." Jenny was his wife. Phip shook his head. "Makes me feel like an old man."

"Hell, you're not sixty yet. Still in your prime," Lon said.

"For some things, maybe," Phip said. "But there are only three men in the regiment older than me, two lieutenant colonels and one major. I've been in the Corps longer than half the officers have been alive. If I had half a brain I'd get out. That'd save me the aches of all the exercising I do to stay fit enough to pass the annual test. And maybe I'd have time to do a little serious drinking now and then."

Lon went behind his desk and sat, gesturing for Phip to sit on the chair at the side of the desk. "I know how you feel," he conceded. "When I was a kid I was a fanatic about physical training. Used to think that if I invested enough sweat I'd get that little bit faster and get my name in the record books for the fastest mile. I won a few races when I was in high school, and even while I was a cadet at The Springs"—the military academy of the North American Union on Earth—"but I never even tied the existing record for the mile, let alone set a new record. And as the record times got faster after I came here, my times were already getting slower. Now it's been a dozen years since I came within a minute of the record, and four years since the last time I broke four and a half minutes."

"Hell, I couldn't break four and a half minutes for the mile when I was twenty," Phip said. "And making the six minutes I need to stay qualified for duty gets harder every year. There's only one reason I don't hang up the uniform right now."

"What's that?" Lon asked when Phip didn't go on to explain.

"I'd kind of like to be here when you make General," Phip said after a snorted chuckle. "Be nice to retire as Lead Sergeant of the Corps. You've dragged me along every time they changed the pips on your uniform."

"Another optimist. You've been in the Corps long enough to know they're never going to elect me General."

"Back when you got your commission, I might have agreed with you, but now I can get even odds on you being elected General within the next five years at any betting parlor in Camo Town."

"I thought you gave up gambling when you got married."

"I did, pretty much, but I still check the sheets every day. Make mental bets if nothing else, just to keep my hand in. Oh, by the way, there's nothing special on the program for today, not that's come to my attention, anyway."

"Normal routine, no changes to the training or work schedules that I know of," Lon said, nodding. "No disciplinary problems over the long weekend. I've got the weekly council meeting at ten o'clock." He glanced at the timeline on his complink. "And it looks as if it's about time we got to work."

The building that housed the headquarters of the Dirigent Mercenary Corps and served as Government House for the world was H-shaped, with the crossbar on a north-to-south axis looking across a parade field large enough to hold seventy thousand soldiers without looking particularly crowded, toward the main gate of the base. The wings of the building were two-thirds on the west side of the crossbar. The facade was of polished white marble covered with a transparent preservative that added a sparkle to the stone. In front of the north and south wings, on the side facing the parade field, were rows of artillery pieces—many brought from Earth—showing the development of artillery from the earliest extant bronze cannons to the most modern self-propelled howitzers and rocket launchers.

The meeting chamber of the Council of Regiments was in the central portion of the building, on the second floor, with floor-to-ceiling windows overlooking the parade ground. A circular table in the chamber had built-in complinks at each of the fourteen places. Seating was in regimental order, clockwise beginning at the north. The General, whoever he was during a particular year, presided from the same seat he had held as regimental commander. The only visible distinction his place showed was a small gold gavel and a red bokka wood pad to bang it against. Several small curved tables sat behind the main table, with seats for aides or guests.

The colonels who made up the Council started gathering in an antechamber about fifteen minutes before the scheduled beginning of their regular weekly session. All wore the dark blue "working dress" uniforms that had a minimum of decoration and lacked the high, stiff collars of "formal dress" uniforms. They drank coffee and chatted among themselves. With nothing pressing on the agenda, the talk was mostly about the holiday weekend or family gossip. Two minutes before ten o'clock, the General's senior aide opened the doors to the meeting chamber, and the colonels started filing in. All were present by that time except the General. *He* came in thirty seconds after the last of the others had taken their seats.

Jules Lecroix of 1st Regiment was serving his second term as General, not consecutively. He had already announced that he would be retiring from the Corps after completing this term. His sixty-eighth birthday would fall three days before his successor was elected, and on the day of the change-of-command ceremony, he would mark fifty years in uniform—a rarely achieved length of service; few men stayed in the Corps more than forty years.

"Good morning, gentlemen," Lecroix said before taking his seat. "I trust you all had a pleasant holiday weekend." The General was slightly below average height for Dirigent, built stocky. He had been a champion boxer in his younger days but showed none of the injuries he had received during his "career" in the ring. "Coming just after the first of the year, I had intended to keep this session perfunctory. What little old business we had on the calendar was all pushed forward until next week. We do have one new item to consider, but I don't have details for you yet. There is a delegation from Elysium inbound. Their ship came out of Q-space less than ten hours ago, so it will be Friday morning before they land. Since the delegation is headed by their chancellor—the number-two man in their government, as I understand it—we'll have a formal welcoming ceremony at the spaceport. I'll get details to all of you as early as I can. The short message I had from the head of the Elysian delegation suggested that a large contract might be in the offing." The General shrugged. "As I said, no details yet. Colonel Ruiz, you will chair the contract committee. Colonel Hayley, you and Colonel Nolan will complete it. I'll make sure that everyone receives any pertinent information as quickly as possible, but the Elysians expressed reluctance to say much before they can do it face to face."

"Elysium, the university world?" Lon said, making it a question.

"More than a university world," the General said, smiling, "though that was the first thought that came to my mind when I received the initial call from the ship. Their university is still important, drawing students from more than a hundred colony worlds according to the data we have, but they've gone far beyond teaching and abstract academic research. They are also heavily into medical and industrial research and development, marketing their discoveries as freely as we market our services—perhaps more so. The last major advances in Nilssen Generator technology came from Elysium, which makes them important to us and to every other world that builds ships or depends on interstellar shipping . . . which means almost every settled world in the galaxy. And they are heavily into R&D in military ordnance. Anything that threatens Elysium threatens us." He turned to look directly at Jorge Ruiz. "Which means that we aren't necessarily out to obtain every last coin in their treasury. I know how hard a bargain you can drive, but while we don't expect to give our services away or lose money on the project— whatever it is—we will have to be prepared to cut the philosophers a little slack if necessary."

"I understand, General," Ruiz said. He had served for several years as head of the Corps' Contracts Division. "We don't demand a Nolan from the eggheads." That brought a laugh from most of the men at the table. Lon managed a slight blush at the allusion. More than fifteen years earlier he had negotiated an addendum to a contract that brought the Corps a "piece of the action"—a percentage of the looted precious metals and minerals his company recovered for the contracting government. It had been an unprecedented coup, rarely repeated since.

4

"No one _ever_ wants to talk about a contract by link," Jorge Ruiz said. The three members of the contract committee appointed to deal with the representatives from Elysium had decided to eat lunch together in the Officers' Club. They had ordered their food and were waiting for it with drinks. "It's as if they're all afraid they'll lose some bargaining chip if they let us know what they're here about before we're physically eyeball to eyeball with them." He chuckled while he shook his head, then took a sip of his martini and set it back on the table.

"It sure would be nice to have _some_ idea what this is all about," Lon said. "What drives a world like Elysium to look for mercenary help? They have a pack of renegade intellectuals or something?"

"I can imagine a lot of possible scenarios," Bob Hayley said. "A lot of worlds might like to control the practical knowledge coming out of Elysium's R&D labs. Better Nilssen Generators than anyone else, more powerful beamers, new ship designs. I'm more curious what they consider a 'large' contract."

"Well, if they want a full regiment, yours is number one on the list," Ruiz said. "Lon, I think 7th is second on the rota, isn't it?"

Lon nodded. "If Elysium is so important to everyone, I'd think that there would be a sort of balance. If one major power tried to take it over, the other two would be in a hurry to get involved to make sure it didn't happen. Earth. The Confederation. The Second Commonwealth.

And it would almost have to be one of those three trying to make a grab . . . if that's what this is all about. None of the independent colony worlds would dare. That would leave some sort of internal problem, but . . ." Lon stopped and shook his head. "I sure can't think that there could be anything as big as a regimental-size contract coming, not from Elysium."

Ruiz spotted the waiter coming with their food. "Maybe not, but it doesn't do any good to speculate. We don't want to build any preconceived notions that might get in the way later."

After lunch, Lon returned to his office for an hour to work his way through the inevitable routine reports—incoming and outgoing. Then he informed Phip and Lieutenant Colonel Tefford Ives—Lon's executive officer—that he was going to the gym.

Lon put himself through a full routine on several of the exercise machines, then ran two miles, forcing the pace on his last half dozen laps of the indoor track—so much that he felt almost ready to drop by the time he finished. After a ten-minute rest, he got into the swimming pool and swam laps for forty minutes. By the time he climbed out of the pool, his arms and legs felt as if the muscles had turned to jelly. He sat in the locker room for five minutes before he felt recovered enough to shower and dress.

Three times a week, in garrison, Lon put himself through such a rigorous workout, and on the other days he tried to get in at least a little "light" work, even if no more than a mile's jog and a half hour of hand-to-hand combat drill with other officers. And, at least one day a week, he took morning calisthenics with one of the battalions in 7th Regiment, rotating from one to the next. "A soldier is his own first weapon," an instructor in DMC recruit training had told his charges the first day. "You have to keep that weapon in first-rate condition, just as you'll be expected to keep your rifle and every other weapon the Corps entrusts you with ready for action at all times."

It's a lot easier to keep a rifle serviceable than it is a body, Lon thought as he left the gym—limping a little because of a strained muscle in his left calf. His body's health maintenance nanobots would need a little time to repair the damage, but Lon did not consider calling for his car to take him back to regimental headquarters. *Walking's better therapy than riding,* he told himself, but he walked slowly, favoring the sore leg as much as he could, and the discomfort had faded to insignificance before he reached the orderly room.

"Phip, is 4th Battalion ready to go out for its night training?" Lon asked, stopping just inside the lead sergeant's office on the first floor.

"Yes, sir. They'll form up in about fifteen minutes, due to leave the area at sixteen hundred hours." Phip's clerks were in the room, so the niceties of protocol had to be observed. "I spoke with Colonel Watson about a half hour ago." Lieutenant Colonel Parker Watson was 4th Battalion's commander. "He called to make certain there had been no schedule changes."

Lon chuckled. "You mean he was hoping for a reprieve so he wouldn't have to be out in the cold."

"He never actually *said* that, sir," Phip said, carefully suppressing a laugh of his own.

"I'll stick around to see them off," Lon said. "Just to keep you informed, I'm going to be serving on a contract committee. We have a potential client coming in to offer what might be a large contract, so my schedule is apt to get a bit busy the next week or two."

"Yes, sir. I'll make a note. When does the client ground?"

"Not until Friday morning. Details will be coming from the General's office as available. And make sure I see any messages from Colonels Ruiz and Hayley."

Phip nodded and keyed in notes on his complink.

●   ●   ●

Lon stood off to the side as the men of 4th Battalion came out of their barracks and fell in for their night training session. There was no skin visible in the formation. Cold would not be any real problem, and should pose no more than a minor inconvenience to the men. Insulated battle-dress uniforms over thermal underwear with well-insulated boots and gloves were all that would really be necessary for their protection, since the predicted low temperature for the night would be no more than ten degrees below freezing. Battle helmet faceplates would protect faces from most wind-chill effects. Still, the men of 4th wore field jackets as well; the fleece collars of those would keep the chill from necks and help close off the gaps at the edges of their helmets.

Soldiers had to be ready to fight in any weather. No winter training exercises would be canceled for less than subzero temperatures and blizzard conditions—circumstances that might be severe enough to halt real combat. The battalion formed up by platoon and company. Sergeants made their "all present or accounted for" reports to platoon leaders, who echoed the reports to company commanders, who repeated them once more for the battalion commander—all with exchanges of salutes. Lieutenant Colonel Watson gave the orders, and the battalion started to march off toward their assigned training area some six miles away.

As he passed Lon, Watson gave him a casual salute. Lon returned it with a smile, but waited until the entire battalion had passed before he returned to the office.

"Unless something's come up in the last twenty minutes that needs immediate attention, I'm going home," Lon informed Phip.

"Nobody's said anything to me, Colonel," Phip replied. "No important messages have come in. Sergeant Howell just went to get your car. It should be outside in two minutes."

•　•　•

Sara Nolan opened the front door of their home before Lon reached it. Lon started to ask if something was wrong but stopped when he saw the smile on her face. In the doorway she put her arms around his neck and gave him a long kiss. Lon half-carried her inside and closed the door with his foot.

"Okay, what did you see that you think I'm going to say we can't afford?" he asked when she finally let him break the kiss.

"Come in and sit down," Sara said, dragging him toward the living room and the sofa. "Relax. I'll fix you a drink."

Lon started to speak but shut his mouth again, realizing that the fastest way to learn what had his wife so happy was to go along with the scenario she had obviously planned. He sat on the sofa and loosened the collar of his shirt. She *skipped* off toward the kitchen, her red hair bouncing lightly. Lon just shook his head, having difficulty keeping a smile from his face. *She must have a real beaut cooked up this time,* he thought.

Sara was gone less than a minute, and came back with a scotch and water on ice—Lon's usual home-from-the-office drink. She handed it to him, waited for him to take a sip, then sat at his side—pressed right against him. He set the drink on the end table.

"Okay, what's got you smirking like the proverbial bird-eating cat?" he asked, turning toward her.

Sara hesitated for a moment, fidgeting against Lon, then it all came out in one long breath. "I saw the doctor this morning. I'm pregnant."

Lon was not aware of the seconds of shocked silence before his mind processed the information thoroughly enough for a reply. To his credit—and *almost* making up for the delay—his first words were, "That's great" . . . even though his voice did not show the proper level of enthusiasm to underline the words. Luckily for him, Sara was too excited to notice.

"It is great," Lon said after he had a few more seconds

to recover. He hugged her tightly while his mind fought to catch up. *That's the last thing I expected,* he thought. Sara did not see the frown that accompanied her husband's next thought: *If it's a boy I'm going to get out of the Corps before he's old enough to start thinking about being a soldier.*

5

Alberto Esteban Berlino was an imposing figure. Seven feet, three inches tall, he had to duck to get through the passenger door of the shuttle. But it was not his height so much as his hair styling that caught the attention of the members of the official welcoming delegation—which included the General and the three colonels who had been tapped as contract committee for the Elysians. Berlino's hair, dyed an impossibly bright yellow, came down to his shoulders in three distinct sections—over each shoulder and several inches below the base of his neck in back. Those tresses were stiff with some sort of styling spray. On top, the hair was curled up into an outlandish pompadour that added another two inches to his already considerable height. His hair had been stiffened so much that there was not the slightest hint of movement, even though there was a fifteen-mile-per-hour breeze blowing. His clothing was almost as startling to Dirigenters, a one-piece, form-fitting jumpsuit—mostly a reddish plum color with luminous blue accents, vertical stripes of almost random width and separation—that extended from his neck to his toes. The outfit seemed a bit . . . thin for the season. The temperature was below forty degrees Fahrenheit, and the wind made it seem far chillier.

Berlino paused near the top of the ramp and scanned as much of the port as he could see. A man and a woman waited behind him, the woman unable to get out of the shuttle until the other two started moving down the ramp. The General and the rest of the welcoming contingent moved closer to the bottom of the ramp as soon as the Elysian chancellor resumed his descent. Berlino was a foot taller than the tallest of the Dirigenters present.

Berlino timed his descent carefully. The band playing music for the ceremony ended a song when he was a single step from the ground. Jules Lecroix, the General, made the welcoming remarks, as he had a number of times before. There was no real "set" speech, but there was little variation between one arrival and another. Those standing with him listened more for the end than for content. The chancellor replied with equal platitudes, somewhat more flowery.

Introductions came next. The man with Berlino was Thomas Beoch, Elysium's minister for external affairs. The woman was Flora Chiou, treasurer. In appearance both seemed subdued, even plain, compared to the flamboyant coif and bright dress of the delegation's leader, as if they wanted to be careful not to upstage him. Neither said anything other than polite responses to the introductions.

No one seemed upset at the brevity of the welcoming ceremony. The official parties moved to limousines that took them across Dirigent City to the DMC's main base and Corps headquarters. The visitors would stay in guest suites in the north wing. Berlino rode with the General. Berlino's companions followed in the second floater, with Colonel Ruiz. Lon and Colonel Hayley were in the third vehicle.

"Quite a dandy, the Elysian chancellor," Hayley said as the convoy cleared the aerospace port. "I was afraid I was going to bust out laughing there when he first came out of the shuttle, and that would have been . . . embarrassing. And I know I heard a few sniggers from the spectators."

Lon chuckled. "If someone stuck a big round ball on the end of his nose he'd make a fine clown. He's no buffoon, though. The man is a physicist, apparently one of the best on Elysium. And we're going to be facing him a lot over the next few days."

"If he represents high fashion on Elysium, I'm damned glad I don't live there," Hayley said, shaking his head. "What a nightmare! The clothes were bad enough, but that hairdo. He must have three pounds of glue holding that concoction together. I may have to suck lemons to keep a straight face."

"No one ever promised us that soldiering would be easy, Bob. Maybe he won't be so . . . extreme when we get down to business," Lon said. "Especially now that he's had a chance to see that fashion is a lot different here."

"Once he realizes that we're just poor country bumpkins with hay in our ears and pig shit on our boots?" Bob Hayley asked.

"Whatever. Just hope that it's not the normal regalia of his office, something Elysium's laws force him to wear."

"We've had people attend their university," Hayley said. "And we maintain diplomatic and industrial contacts with Elysium; have to, with the kind of research they do. I don't recall seeing anything that bizarre in our files. I've been back through the lot in the last three days."

"So have I," Lon said.

There was a short meeting at DMC headquarters shortly after the convoy arrived. The General and the three members of the contract committee met with Chancellor Berlino and his two senior companions. There were several other Elysians in the delegation, but they were aides and technical support people—staff members whose contributions to the mission would come later.

"Basically, this is our situation," Chancellor Berlino said once the meeting started. He had not changed out of the bright jumpsuit or . . . eased his hairstyle, but he had put a somewhat more subdued mauve tabard over the bright clothing. "For some years now, a series of representatives from Union have been pressuring us to 'acknowledge the sovereignty' of their Confederation of Human Worlds. That would entail paying taxes to Union, and it would also—and more significantly—mean giving them unacceptable levels of control over the direction and products of our research programs. I don't just mean first option on new technology. They insist on the right to totally control distribution, who we could sell to and when.

"We have refused, repeatedly and with a certain, ah, intensity, especially in the last year. Union's diplomats urge us to accept their 'protection' against any threats, internal or external, and warn that we might be opening ourselves to conquest or raiding from other powers.

"Nine months ago we did experience two rather minor raids, causing minimal destruction and resulting in the loss of some defensive assets. We were unable to determine the identity of the raiders, but we have little doubt that the raids were commissioned if not conducted by Union. They, of course, deny any connection to those events and tell us 'I told you so' and renew their arguments that we should concede their sovereignty and save ourselves from any further armed depredations.

"We have continued to refuse. Then, four weeks ago, we were invaded by a large contingent of mercenaries from New Sparta, and more of them landed just hours before my ship left the system. Had they known I was aboard and my destination, I don't doubt that they would have attempted to intercept the ship to prevent my, ah, escape. We have confirmed their identity but not who hired them, though we assume their orders and pay come from CHW headquarters on Union, though perhaps with one extra . . . step between them. By this time, I assume that our government has received Union's latest protestations of innocence along with another, ah, sales pitch for joining their empire so that they could come to our assistance.

"We prefer to retain our independence. It is important, and not merely as an abstraction. I assume Dirigent's independence is similarly important to it. We both need to be seen as operating freely, without hands tied by external allegiances. Were we to submit to the Confederation or—on the other hand—apply for membership in the Second Commonwealth, we would give up much of what independence means for us. We would lose our undisputed neutrality, which would impact on our university and our research and development industry. Joining the Commonwealth would be less onerous than accepting the overlordship of the Confederation, but would not satisfy anyone on Elysium. And joining the Second Commonwealth would be the only way we could obtain military assistance from them. We would accept that, as the lesser of two evils, only if it were the only way to avoid falling under the dominion of Union and its idea of the Confederation. So I came here."

"Can you give us a rough idea of the assets that New Sparta has sent against Elysium—men and ships?" the General asked.

"The last assessment I had before our ship made its first jump into Q-space, New Sparta had landed about thirty-five hundred soldiers. There were five troop transport ships overhead, two smaller transports, and one heavily armed weapons platform that also carried at least a dozen aerospace fighters. Obviously, I cannot report on anything that happened after we entered Q-space the first time."

"What defensive assets does Elysium have?"

This time Berlino hesitated. "You must understand, we have never felt the need to maintain a massive defensive capability. We have relied primarily on our diplomatic corps. Our neutral status has always been observed, if not officially recognized, by Earth, Union, Buckingham, and the few other worlds prosperous enough and populous enough to pose a serious threat. We have dealt with Dirigent, New Sparta, and most of the other worlds that are the primary sources of mercenaries. Our position has allowed us considerable freedom because of the counterbalancing interests of our various clients. Our independence has been important to a lot of different worlds." He paused for a few seconds, but it was clear that he had not finished.

"Elysium has maintained a planetary militia for more than two centuries, a small active force and a much larger reserve, but we have never had universal training or a requirement for every young Elysian to, ah, participate. In part, the militia served as an adjunct to the university, allowing us to offer military training to students from other colony worlds who could then go home and establish home defensive systems. Over most of the last hundred years we have maintained additional defense assets, heavy weapons systems, but more as, shall we say, marketing displays for our munitions and research and development industries—evidence of the variety and capabilities of our products. That means more breadth than depth. We don't have a *lot* of any particular system. Defensive missile systems, artillery, aerospace fighters, and two ships that are capable of operating as weapons platforms in space. Most of these advanced systems are capable of being operated with minimal human staff."

How did they stand up against real-life enemies? Lon wondered when Berlino paused again.

"When faced with a massive attack, the results were mixed," the Elysian chancellor said, as if he had heard Lon's thought. "The systems themselves appear to have performed admirably, but none of the defenses were fully staffed at the time, and delays and confusion in human control limited their effectiveness. Our ground installations destroyed three shuttles carrying invading troops, and two of their aerospace fighters. But neither our ground- or space-based systems were able to destroy or seriously damage any of the New Spartan ships, and we lost one of our two ships in the initial assault, and the other was damaged so severely that it had to, ah, leave the area to effect repairs and had not returned as of the time my vessel jumped to Q-space."

"How many ground troops did Elysium have under arms at the time of the attack?" the General asked.

"Approximately four thousand men were on active duty, of whom perhaps eighty percent could be called battle-ready. The rest would be support personnel and the cadre needed to train the militia's standing reserve. Those reserves were being called to duty but were not yet organized and had not been put through the two weeks' refresher training called for in our strategic planning," Berlino said. "Our training system can handle fifteen hundred at a time, which means it would take two months to fully mobilize our reserves and have them ready to face an enemy."

"So, assuming that has continued on schedule since your departure, there would be about fifteen hundred of those reserves processed and trained by this time?" the General said.

"Approximately that," Berlino conceded. "We obviously never foresaw a situation in which we might need the entire reserve so . . . quickly. And with enemy troops on the ground, the speed with which we can mobilize might be, ah, seriously compromised."

And men pulled out of civilian jobs and put up against a professional army with only two weeks of training can't be counted on to be worth a hell of a lot, Lon thought. *Confusion, heavy casualties, and rapidly deteriorating morale. They might be more of a liability than an asset.*

"The situation is most distressing," Berlino continued, "and our government decided that the fastest and most efficient method of dealing with it is to bring in professional soldiers in sufficient number to deal with the threat and minimize the damage to our infrastructure and people. I do, of course, have full authority to negotiate a contract."

"We'll have our technical people go over your requirements in detail," the General said, "but—in a preliminary way—just what assets do you estimate you will require from us?"

"Since I have no way of knowing if New Sparta has put additional forces in-system, we feel it necessary to bring in a force sufficient to deal with those we know about and those who might well have been sent in as reinforcements—say, eight thousand men plus the space assets to deal with their capital ships and aerospace fighters. I believe that would work out to two of your regiments. You *do* have that many men available for a contract at present, do you not?"

"Two full regiments of infantry, support troops—including armor and artillery, transports, and probably two weapons-platform ships. This looks as if it will be the largest contract the Corps has had in a decade or more," Lon said while he and Sara were dressing for the state dinner that evening. "If it goes through the way it looks." He shrugged. "This early, that's not completely certain, but, altogether, it could mean more than ten thousand men for a minimum of three months, with possible extensions."

Sara stopped what she was doing and turned toward Lon. "This could be a bad one, couldn't it?" she asked. "You'll be facing mercenaries from New Sparta, troops every bit as professional and well trained as our men are." Two regiments: She knew that meant that Lon's regiment would be included, and since it was the entire unit, he would be going along.

"It could be," Lon conceded with a reluctant nod. "On the other hand, it might not be. The one thing we know we won't face is irrational fanaticism. Professionals aren't going to go into action with a 'do or die, fight till the last man drops' mentality. If we go in with clearly superior numbers, establish a solid perimeter on the ground, and stymie their forces in orbit, it could all be over in a relatively short period of time. Once the commander of the New Spartan force sees that he's in a no-win situation, he will look for a way to end the conflict as quickly as possible, just as we would."

Sara sat on the edge of the bed. "What I really dislike about this is that it will be the first time that you and Junior are both off on the same contract."

Lon sat next to her and took both of her hands in his.

"I know," he said very softly. "But you have to figure that it's unlikely that the situation will ever come up again. By the time 7th Regiment gets back to the top of the rota for regimental contracts, I'll probably be in Bascombe East tending bar at the Winking Eye, and Junior may well have had his fill of military life and be working a civilian job, or continuing his education. He might even want to take an advanced degree on Elysium." He continued to hold her hands. When she didn't reply, he added, "I suppose there's even a fairly good chance this will be my last off-world contract, even if I spend another five or six years in the Corps. Jobs large enough to require a full colonel in command just don't come along that often."

They sat together in silence for another minute before Sara pulled her hands free and stood. "We'd better get busy or we'll be late to the General's dinner," she said.

"I know this is going to be bad timing for you," Lon said a moment later. "I wish I wasn't going to miss any of the next months, while you're pregnant, but at least I'll be here when the baby is born, and through the holidays."

"I hope so," Sara said, too softly for Lon to hear.

The state dinner at Corps headquarters was purely social, with no talk of the pending contract or Elysium's difficulties. The commanders of all fourteen regiments were present with their wives, along with a few senior officers from the headquarters staff and ancillary branches of the DMC, as well as the mayor of Dirigent City and his wife and a few other civilian notables. There were toasts and short speeches. There was music. The food was the finest that the chefs at Corps headquarters could provide, almost everything grown or raised naturally, not fabricated by a nanotech replicator.

Chancellor Berlino dressed less flamboyantly, in light blue, but his hairdo remained exaggerated. He and his companions received as much attention as they could handle during the cocktail hour before dinner and in the informal mingling that continued after the meal and speeches had been concluded.

Lon and Sara got home shortly after eleven o'clock that night. "I hope that hair doesn't start a new fashion among the women here," Sara said. "It looks as if it would be uncomfortable, at least to sleep in."

"It won't be a fashion in the Corps," Lon said. He ran his fingers through his own hair. He didn't keep his as short as many in the Corps did, but he knew he would need two years to let his hair get long enough for the sort of arrangement the Elysian chancellor wore . . . and that would *never* happen.

"I think the mayor's wife might try it," Sara said. "The way she stared at it."

"Bessie Macklin?" Lon laughed. "She's a hundred years old if she's a day."

"Don't tell her that. She'd slap your face." They both laughed. "Bessie's kind of nice, in a way," Sara said. "A little pompous sometimes, but usually quite friendly."

"She has a great-grandson in the Corps," Lon said. "And a daughter who's younger than Junior."

"Not younger, six months older," Sara corrected. "Six children, nine grandchildren, and twenty-six great-grandchildren. I think she talked about every one of them this evening." Sara put her hands over her face to hold in a laugh. "I think Chancellor Berlino was about ready to pull that plastered hair out by the roots before he was able to get away from her."

"*That* would have been a sight to remember," Lon said. "I think if he bent his hair hard it would break off in huge chunks."

There was no weekend off for Lon. The contract committee met with the three Elysian politicians twice Saturday and once Sunday. Support staff on both sides were in almost continuous session through the weekend. Chancellor Berlino was in a hurry. Between open negotiating sessions, Lon spent most of his time either in conference with Colonels Ruiz and Hayley or reading the voluminous documentation and evaluations being assembled by the Corps' Contracts Division. Saturday evening, it was nearly midnight before Lon got home.

Sara was waiting up for him.

"How soon?" she asked after a quick hug and kiss.

"Very," he said, knowing what the question referred to. "We could have a contract ready for signatures as early as Monday morning and ship out Thursday or Friday. Berlino is extremely worried about the situation on Elysium, and he is conceding virtually every bargaining clause in short order."

They went to the kitchen. Lon sat at the table. Sara fixed him a drink and set it in front of him before she sat. Lon closed his eyes as he drank down half the scotch and water.

"I talked with Junior this evening," Lon said as he set the glass back down. "He's got OD duty at 1st Battalion tonight. I told him not to make any plans for the next few months but to keep it quiet until he heard the official word."

"What did he say?" Sara asked.

" 'Does Mom know yet?' " Lon said, not meeting her look. "I told him you had a pretty good idea something was coming up but that we didn't have anything plascrete yet."

"There's no chance this will fall through?"

Lon shook his head. "I don't think so. The Elysians came prepared with enough gold, platinum, and transfer credits to hire twice the force we're talking about. The transfer credits are drawn on Buckingham banks with the guarantee of the Second Commonwealth. They've also brought diversion orders for other materials we don't produce on Dirigent—shipments that will come here instead of to Elysium."

"It sounds as if they're desperate," Sara said. Lon nodded. "Could it be that Berlino knows the situation is much worse than he's admitted to?"

A weak smile flickered across Lon's face. "That's the sort of thing we expect on any contract, but my own guess is that his evaluation was closer than most, as of the time he left Elysian space. And he hasn't tried to hide the fact that he expects to learn that the situation has gotten worse since he left."

"What happens if you get there and find that the war is over, that Elysium has been conquered and occupied?"

"We evaluate the situation. If it appears that we have an edge on the New Spartans in men and matériel, we go in and start the work of liberating Elysium. If it appears that we are outnumbered, we wait for additional manpower from Dirigent—a third regiment and one or two additional battle cruisers." He paused. "It's been something like sixty years since the last time the Corps mounted a three-regiment contract, and there's never been one larger than that."

At 1023 hours, Monday, January 8, A.D. 2830, the contract between Elysium and Dirigent was signed in the chamber of the Council of Regiments, five minutes after that body voted to accept the terms that the contract committee had negotiated. The largest deployment of Corps personnel in twelve years would begin seventy-five hours later.

6

Lon briefed his battalion commanders and executive officers as well as company commanders and his senior staff officers Monday afternoon, immediately after lunch. The conference room across the hall from his office in regimental headquarters was crowded. The order to release men from duty for the next three days had already gone out, so everyone knew that the subject of this briefing was the contract.

"Thursday afternoon we leave for Elysium," Lon said without preamble once he came into the room. While others were eating, he had been making notes for this briefing. "This is probably the largest contract any of us here have been on . . . or will be on in our careers. The initial deployment will be two complete regiments, ours and 15th, along with the heavy-weapons battalions of both regiments, battle cruisers carrying two squadrons of the new Shrike II fighters, and several freighters to carry munitions and other supplies. Colonel Hayley will be in overall command of the contract, and I will serve as second-in-command. Depending on what we find when we arrive, there are circumstances in which a third regiment might be added to the force. There will be an operational briefing for senior officers at Corps headquarters Thursday morning. That will be battalion COs and XOs and senior staff. By that time you should be familiar with all of the background data available." He gave them the file codes.

"Naturally, we will have to wait to see what we find

when we emerge from our final Q-space transit in Elysium's system before we can settle on a final deployment plan. The information we have will be more than a month out of date by then and the situation on the ground could be . . . just about anything. One thing we know is that we are going to be facing professionals, mercenaries from New Sparta, and twenty days ago they had a regiment or more on the ground, with all of the backup from aerospace fighters that we would use in similar circumstances. We need to keep that in mind. We're not going to be facing amateurs, but well-equipped, well-trained career soldiers.

"The contract is open-ended, but if it lasts more than six months, 7th and 15th can expect to be relieved by other units." Except in the most extraordinary circumstances, the Corps tried to limit a unit's continuous contract time to six months—seven months, including the transit time in each direction. "Because of the opposition, I think we had better all hope that the contract does not last that long.

"You will find detailed information and maps of Elysium in the briefing files, but I'll give you a few basics." This was the point where Lon had to start referring to his notes. "The planet is slightly smaller than either Dirigent or Earth, surface gravity .956 Earth Standard, not enough less to be significant. The total population is about fifteen million, of whom approximately three hundred thousand are students drawn from perhaps a hundred different worlds. The largest concentration of people is in and around University City, which is the planetary capital in addition to being the location of the main campus of Elysium University. The population of the metropolitan area is roughly three million. There are two other metro areas with populations topping one million, a half dozen with at least half a million. The rest of the populace is spread out in smaller cities, towns, and rural areas.

"There are three primary continents. Eighty percent of the inhabitants live on Athens. Most of the remainder live on Rome, with just a few scattered research outposts on the continent the Elysians call Carthage.

"Athens, and more particularly University City, is the focus of the New Spartan attack, or—to be more accurate—was the focus as of the time the Elysian delegation left on its way here. University City has to be the focus of any attack. Essentially, whoever controls it controls the world. The government is there, the university, the center of its communications nets, and more than thirty percent of the planet's industrial capacity, including several of its primary research and development laboratories.

"University City is located near the west coast of Athens, about sixty miles from the ocean, primarily on the north shore of the river the initial colonists called the Styx, an allusion to classical mythology for those of you who might not have encountered it before. There are two bridges across the river serving University City and the few sections and suburbs on the south shore, which may or may not still be intact. The Elysians were debating whether to blow the bridges when the chancellor and his party left. The New Spartans landed forces on both sides of the river, outside the metropolitan area."

Lon talked for another ten minutes, then dismissed his officers. The briefing would move down the ranks, with company commanders telling their platoon leaders and senior noncoms. Except for those men who might have already left base for their three free days before deployment, everyone in the regiment would know the basics of the contract within an hour. A few officers stayed to ask questions afterward, but those were related to preparing for departure, not about the mission itself. Lon passed the questions to his executive officer, Tefford Ives, and retreated to his office across the hall.

Alone, finally, Lon noticed that his hands were trembling. He had started sweating halfway through the briefing, and the temperature in the conference room could not have been the cause. He stood just inside his office, leaning back against the door, taking deep breaths, trying to relax.

It's too soon to get tied in knots over this contract, he told himself. The nightmares had started coming after him Friday night, as soon as it was apparent that this would be a two-regiment contract, that he—and his son—would be going. Finally, he had resorted to sleep patches to keep the dreams from surfacing and disturbing his nights . . . but nothing could keep the thoughts away when he was awake.

I've been away from action too long. The last time I came under fire was . . . the second Bancroft contract, before I made colonel. He took a deep breath and moved to his desk. He sat, but not for long. After less than a minute he got up and went to look out the window. *There's no reason to think you'll come under enemy fire this time. Not yet.* But Junior would be a lot closer to action. As a platoon leader, he would likely be on the front line of any combat. That was the real source of Lon's nightmares now.

How could I come home and tell Sara and Angie that Junior had been killed? In all the nightmares—asleep and awake—he had never found an answer to that question.

The general Corps policy that everyone should have seventy-two hours' leave prior to shipping out on a contract could not apply to a regimental commander. When a battalion shipped out, the necessary preparatory work could be conducted by regiment. When the entire regiment was going, only so much of the preparation could be handled by the civilian staff, the people who would not be going, and by Corps headquarters. Lon and his senior staff officers had to be available to make decisions, to see that necessary steps were taken, to make sure there were no snags that could delay the departure. The ships and supplies. Additional information about the contract. One afternoon was not long enough for all of the conferences. Lon did not leave his office until after five o'clock

Monday afternoon, and planned to be back at eight the next morning.

"A contract this big is a logistics nightmare," Lon told Sara at supper that evening. He winced a little over the final word. "Dirigent is going to be short on ships and soldiers until units get back from some of the current contracts. A couple of battalions of men who should still be on training routine are going to have to move to planetary defense assignments early to cover the gaps." He gave a laughing snort. "This is one of those rare times when we've got as many men off on contract as we like to have. Even a little more once our two regiments leave. For the next couple of weeks, at least, we won't be able to send out more than a single battalion on contract, and even that would strain our resources."

"Anything else in the offing right now?" Sara asked.

"Not that I know of."

"Then it doesn't make much difference, does it? You all must have taken that into account when the Council accepted the contract."

"Yes. But if the situation is bad on Elysium when we get there and we have to call in a third regiment, it could be damned hard to find ships to move them. We're going to have to be awfully picky about accepting any other contracts until we know what the situation is on Elysium and get the word back here."

"Don't borrow trouble," Sara said, knowing that her words would have no effect. "It'll be a month before you get there and have time to send a message rocket back. There must be enough contracts over or nearly over to get the situation in hand."

"Theoretically." Lon shrugged and pushed his plate away, even though he had eaten almost nothing. He had started with little appetite and had lost that. "*If* everyone gets back on schedule. *If* none of the units got torn up too bad. If, if."

"The Corps isn't going to leave anyone hanging, Lon. You know that."

He sighed. "I've got five thousand men I'm responsible for, Sara, lives and well-being as well as how they perform. I've got to think about anything that might possibly go wrong, look for ways to deal with . . . whatever happens."

A million details to keep track of. Ten million things that could go wrong. Lon sat in front of the complink in his home study—the study was one of the perks of the house he rated as a full colonel. It was past eleven o'clock Monday night, and Lon was tired. He had been smothering yawns for an hour. Sara had just gone to bed. Angie had gone to bed hours earlier.

Bed. That's where I should be, Lon told himself, but he did not move. It wasn't just that he still had a lot of data he needed—or at least *wanted*—to review. Nor was it the inertia of a tired man. *Bed. Sleep. Nightmares.* Lon did not like to rely on sleep patches all the time, but he knew a patch would be the only way to keep the nightmares away, the only way to get restful sleep with a combat contract coming up.

More than once this night he had thought, *I don't have to go to Elysium. I could retire now and that would be that. There would be talk, but my record is good.* But that would not end the nightmares. Junior would still be going on this contract. There was no way to talk him out of staying in the Corps. For now. Two combat contracts had taken the fantasy out of soldiering for Junior but had not robbed him of his desire to *be* a soldier . . . to *continue* being a soldier, and he seemed excited by the size of the Elysium contract.

He's good, probably better than I was at his age, Lon conceded, but he had seen too many good soldiers die to take any comfort from that. Circumstances and conditions. One brief lapse of judgment. Bad luck.

I have to believe Junior has a better chance with me in command than with anyone else running the regiment. In the end, it came down to that. No matter who might get the regiment next, Tefford Ives or one of the battalion commanders, Lon still thought he could do a better job.

Lon squeezed his eyes shut for a moment, then blinked several times and tried to focus on the complink screen. He clicked the NEXT tab and stared at the first screen of the next file on his queue: "Flora and Fauna of the Western District of Athens, Elysium," a thesis on the ecology of the area, including the impact of imported Terran species. The Corps had unusually detailed and up-to-date information on the world of Elysium, most of it highly reliable. There were fairly frequent contacts between the two worlds—as a result of students going to study at the most renowned university off-Earth, as well as industrial deals with Elysium's R&D corporations. And Chancellor Berlino had brought along extensive database updates that had been integrated into the data the Corps already had.

He only scanned this file, looking for key words such as "toxic," "dangerous," and "predator"—plants and animals that might pose a hazard to people—glancing quickly at photographs. Key entries could be studied in more depth later, on the journey to Elysium. There were no snakes—one of his routine checks—but there were several carnivorous lizards, two poisonous species and one that was larger than the extinct Komodo dragons of Earth. The Olympic Dragon, the name of the Elysian variety, was warm-blooded and known to reach as many as eighteen feet in length and more than two tons in weight. The entry said that they were "rare" in the vicinity of University City but did not quantify their numbers. Lon flagged the entry so his officers and noncoms would be sure to see it. He shook his head. *That's all we need, lizards big enough to eat a man in one gulp.*

Trees whose bark could produce a nasty rash; a flowering plant that triggered allergic reactions in 3 percent of humans exposed to it, and anaphylactic shock in 1 ½ percent of those who were sensitive to it. Lon keyed that entry to the regiment's senior medical officer. In transit, the health maintenance systems of every man would have to be upgraded to deal with the threat.

Lon continued to scroll through the file until he started to doze, nodding off as the lines of print climbed the complink screen. He jerked his head up and blinked rapidly several times, then yawned—his eyes watering.

"I can't do much more tonight," he said softly, then yawned again. But he stretched and turned his attention to the screen once more. He rubbed his eyes and tried to focus, scrolling back a hundred lines to make certain he had missed nothing important. Twenty minutes later he dozed off a second time and didn't awake until his chin hit his chest. He stared at the screen then, hardly aware that there were words on it.

After several minutes he pushed his chair back and stood, not even bothering to put the complink console in standby mode. The room lights went out when he left. There was no help for it: He had to go to bed, and sleep.

The last thing Lon did before he lay down was to stick a four-hour sleep patch on his neck. It was well past one o'clock, so he could not afford to use a longer-duration patch. The medication worked quickly, and knocked him out before he had time to start a new round of futile worrying. For four hours he slept deep and dreamless, but as soon as the patch wore off, the dreams started to intrude. At first, his sleeping mind was troubled only by vague images, a growing sense of foreboding. Soon, however, the nightmare that had been dominant the past couple of nights forced itself forward. He saw himself kneeling on some unidentifiable battlefield, holding the broken and dead body of his son, the boy's blood covering both of them. Dream sobs seemed to bring real physical discomfort, but the nightmare progressed. Lon felt himself being riddled with bullets, feeling each impact, seeing each wound and the blood spurting from it. But Lon did not die in his nightmares. He was denied that escape. He saw himself looking out of a trauma tube still—somehow—

holding his dead son. He would not be able to escape his final excruciating duty, that of going home to tell his wife and daughter that he had failed to keep Junior alive. *It's your fault! Your fault!* his mind screamed at him, over and over, louder and louder.

No! NO! "NO!" The screamed denials in his nightmare finally escaped his lips . . . at their loudest. Lon woke almost as quickly as Sara did.

"It's just a dream," she said, leaning over him, one hand on his shoulder, gripping firmly. She could feel the way Lon was shaking, almost out of control, the way he might have with an extremely high fever. He was also sweating profusely. "Just a dream." Sara was used to Lon's troubled nights, though he almost never shared his nightmares with her. They came—most often when a contract was near, or expected, or in the first nights after he returned from a combat contract—and then they went away . . . until the next time. She kept her hand on his arm until the trembling faded and some semblance of recognition appeared in Lon's eyes. He was gulping in air, his eyes open in a wide stare, only slowly able to focus on Sara.

"A bad one?" Sara asked, her voice barely a whisper next to his ear. Lon closed his eyes, then opened them again. His heart started to slow toward normal, but he continued to breathe deeply, greedily, for another minute before he was able to reply.

"A bad one." He took in one controlled deep breath, then rolled onto his back, looking up at Sara. "What time is it?"

She glanced at the clock. "A few minutes to six."

Once more, he closed his eyes briefly, working to control his body. When he opened his eyes, he said, "Time for me to get up, anyway. I need to get to the office as early as I can today. There's still a lot to do before we leave."

"The work will get done even if you're a little late. You're pushing yourself too hard. You've got a good staff. Ease up a little before . . ." She couldn't find a way to finish the sentence. She didn't have to. Lon could put a variety of endings to it.

"I'm responsible for my regiment. I can't delegate that. It goes with the pips." Lon sat up, then stood. That was easier than continuing the conversation.

A driver from 8th Regiment picked Lon up and took him to his office. To allow all of 7th's enlisted personnel and junior officers their allotted three days off before the contract, a dozen people had been borrowed from 8th. That was a routine courtesy in the Corps.

Regimental headquarters was busy, but not nearly as busy as it would have been without the pending contract. Most of Lon's senior staff officers were in before he arrived Tuesday morning. They had the civilian staff and temporary help from 8th hard at work well before the usual start of the workday at 0800 hours.

Lon went straight to his office. With Jeremy Howell off, Lon had to brew his own coffee. While that was in the works, Lon turned his complink on and scrolled through the list of messages that had been logged in since he had last checked from home the night before. There were half a dozen he would have to read right away, so he sat down and started . . . tried to start. Halfway through the first message, though, he pushed away from his desk, stood, and walked to the window.

He stared out at the regimental parade ground—virtually deserted. There would be no formations until it was time to muster the regiment for the ride across Dirigent City to the spaceport Thursday afternoon. Elysium. Contract. Fighting. Professionals. The words clicked in Lon's head, but there was no continuity, no expansion. His mind felt numb, rejecting work. He squeezed his eyes shut, trying to force concentration. It didn't help. Minutes passed before he realized that his coffee had finished brewing. He poured himself a cup and drank it black, so hot it nearly scalded his tongue.

After he emptied the cup, Lon set it down and went

back to his complink. Instead of continuing to work at the overnight messages, he made a call.

"Doc, you have a few minutes for me this morning?" he asked when a face appeared on the screen.

There was only a brief hesitation before the man on the other end of the call nodded. "I'll be right there, Colonel."

Major Dan Norman had been 7th Regiment's SMO, senior medical officer, for a dozen years. Despite the sophistication of nanotech health maintenance implants and the efficiency of trauma tubes, the long-standing predictions that highly trained physicians would "soon" be redundant had not come true. The computerized equipment that dealt with physical problems had to be updated periodically, especially since new worlds were being opened up every year with new toxins and diseases. There were rare cases, mostly neurological, where HMSes and trauma tubes were not entirely sufficient without guidance from a human specialist. And every physician was now, by definition, an expert in treating psychiatric disorders, particularly those that were not caused by chemical imbalances.

In civilian practice, where the physician's primary function was delivering babies, one doctor per one hundred thousand people was considered adequate . . . except on newer colony worlds, where birthrates were generally extremely high. In the Dirigent Mercenary Corps there was one physician for each regiment and one for each ship in the fleet. A regimental SMO did not function alone, though. Each battalion had seven medical technicians assigned to its headquarters detachment, and there were also two medtechs attached to every line company. They were qualified to perform basic medical tasks to stabilize casualties' conditions, operate trauma tubes, and administer updates to individual HMSes. In addition, every man in the Corps received training in combat first aid—the techniques needed to keep a wounded soldier alive until he could be put in a trauma tube or treated by a medtech. Among colony worlds not affiliated with either Commonwealth or Confederation, perhaps only Elysium had a better medical school than Dirigent.

Major Norman reached Lon's office in less than two minutes. The SMO was in his early forties, black hair and eyes, trim and athletic. He was one of the best tennis players in the Corps.

"I've been expecting a call from you, Lon," the major said after he closed the office door behind him.

"Have a seat." Lon gestured at the empty chair at the side of his desk. "Am I that predictable?"

Norman shrugged. "I've been treating you for most of the last decade, Lon, and I know your medical history back to the day you joined the Corps. If there was ever a situation designed to aggravate your anxieties, this would be it. The whole regiment is going out on a major contract. Your son will be going along. And your wife is pregnant." In garrison, the senior medical officers also staffed the base hospital and dealt with dependents as well as soldiers. "By the way, congratulations."

Lon squinted, and shook his head mildly. "To tell the truth, Doc, I've been so upset over the nightmares and all, that the pregnancy really hasn't sunk in yet."

"You're exhausted because you're afraid to go to sleep at night. The only halfway decent sleep you do get is with a patch, which affects the body's chemical balance, especially when you use them frequently. The nightmares drain you and wake you soon after a patch wears off. In addition, you have all the normal stresses of any commander readying his unit for a combat contract. You're probably not eating decently either. Have I missed anything?"

"I'm not getting my work done. My mind just mutinies, like this morning when I came in. I couldn't even deal with my mail. I just had to get up and go stare out the window. I'm not thinking straight. I can't concentrate. I can't get the worries out of my head. The way I'm going, I'm afraid I'll be a basket case by the time we get to Elysium, and I can't afford that, even though I'm not going to be in overall command on the contract. There's too much to do between here and there."

"Okay, Lon, we've been through this before, so you know the routine. "I'll start by running a chemical assay to see how badly you've managed to get your brain chemicals out of whack and make sure there are no anomalies that might indicate an organic problem your HMS hasn't been able to diagnose and treat. Then we'll talk. Mostly, you'll talk and I'll listen. I'll ask a few questions and maybe spout a few platitudes you've heard before. Then we'll see where we are and what we need to do next."

Lon nodded. Norman pulled a small black case from his trouser pocket and opened it. He extracted a medpatch about a quarter inch in diameter from the case and peeled the backing from the adhesive side. The patch went high on Lon's neck, over the spine, just below his hairline. Norman smoothed it in place, then took out a portable complink and spent half a minute keying instructions. By the time he had finished, the nanoagents in the patch had established communications with the molecular computers that regulated Lon's HMS and were beginning to feed out strings of numbers and chemical formulas.

"Okay, Lon. Tell me about the latest dreams," Dr. Norman said, setting his complink on the edge of the desk, where he could continue to monitor it.

There were no outside interruptions. Lon had set his complink to take messages but not to signal any calls, and he had told the duty sergeant downstairs that he was not to be interrupted for anyone less than the General. Lon talked—with assorted prompts and comments from Dan Norman—for nearly two hours. Norman took a final reading of the numbers on his complink screen, then removed the patch from Lon's neck and tossed the patch in the trash can.

"Well?" Lon asked. Although it was January and the temperature in the office was kept at seventy-two degrees, he had been sweating through most of the ordeal.

"Your brain chemistry is the worst I've ever seen it, Lon," the doctor said. "And your blood is almost outside normal parameters. Much more and I'd suspect multiple malfunctions in your HMS controllers . . . and *that* doesn't happen. You're not going to like what I have to say, but it isn't a suggestion. You and I are going to leave here together. Tell your sergeant that you'll be back after lunch and can't be reached. We're going to the hospital and I'm going to stick you in a trauma tube—"

"*What?*" Lon shouted.

"You heard me. In a trauma tube. I suspect that it will only be for two hours or a little more, but that's up to the tube. If you're going to lead 7th Regiment on this contract, we've got to get your body—and your head—back in . . . balance as quickly as possible. While you're in the tube, I'll have the lab prepare special medpatches for you to use until just before we make our last Q-space transit en route to Elysium—sleep patches that will guarantee you eight full hours of undisturbed sleep every night, with added agents calculated to make certain your chemistry stays as close to proper balance as we can manage. We'll also spend an hour or two together like this each day, and—depending on your progress—there might be another tube session before that final Q-space transit."

"Doc, with all the work that has to be done between now and Elysium, I don't have that much time to waste. I'll get by, the way I always have."

"Lon, I told you it wasn't a suggestion," Norman said, his voice getting softer, almost a whisper. "You'll have to make time. Either we do this my way or I report you medically unfit for deployment and you stay behind."

Lon moved his gaze from the doctor to the top of his desk. He didn't speak, though he wanted to shout protests. He knew that the doctor's threat was not idle, and he also knew the potential consequences. It could mean the end of his career. *Maybe that would be the easy way out,* he thought.

"You're not the first commander to suffer this sort of

problem, Lon," Norman said. "You might be surprised to learn just how common it is. It's something we can handle, but I've got to have your full cooperation or I can't let you command on a combat contract. It's that simple."

Slowly, Lon nodded. "We'll do it your way, Doc." *If I do leave the Corps, it can't be* this *way,* he told himself.

7

When 7th Regiment fell in at 1300 hours Thursday, only one man was missing from the formation. His bus had been damaged by a landslide between Rainbow Falls and the airport, and he had missed his flight back to base. He would, however, arrive in time to leave with his battalion. Rainbow Falls was a popular resort, and it had frequent shuttle service. The later flight he had caught would arrive at Dirigent City's public aerospaceport twenty minutes before the convoy of buses carrying the regiment was due to leave base. He would join his unit at the port.

Lon took the manning reports from his battalion commanders, then dismissed the troops—sending them back to barracks to complete their preparations for deployment. When they fell out again, in ninety minutes, it would be to board the buses. The regiment's heavy equipment, mostly the self-propelled guns and rocket launchers of the Heavy Weapons Battalion, had already been ferried up to the ships. The personal baggage of the troops would be going up to the ships shortly.

"They look good, Colonel," Lieutenant Colonel Ives said. "Raring to go." He knew that Lon had been seeing the SMO, and—like most of the people who came in close contact with the commander—he had been able to tell that Lon was having some kind of difficulties. Seeing improvement in his boss was a major relief to Ives.

Lon grunted. "Contract pay and the chance for a big bonus at the end, Tefford. I think that's how we developed

67

the tradition of giving the men three days off before a contract, so they could go out and blow all their money and be looking forward to earning extra."

Ives laughed. "Wouldn't surprise me a bit. Of course, it could be that they just want to bathe in the intelligence of all the eggheads on Elysium."

Lon grinned and shook his head. "I only wish smarts rubbed off that easily, Teff. We could rotate everyone in the Corps through Elysium, a battalion at a time, starting from the top. Make life a lot simpler for all of us." That morning, Lon had conceded to Doc Norman that he felt better—"almost one hundred percent," was how he put it, followed by a suggestion that perhaps they could forget about the rest of the course of treatment the SMO had prescribed. Norman had laughed and suggested that the rest of the treatment would remove the "almost." Lon still had his worries—about Junior and about not failing his men—but he was managing them with less stress than before.

The night before, an MR—message rocket—had arrived in-system from Elysium. The news the MR carried was mixed, but more good than bad. The New Spartan mercenaries had destroyed all of Elysium's orbiting communications satellites and its fighters had interdicted all air travel between cities, but fighting on the ground had slackened off considerably in the four days following the departure of Chancellor Berlino from the system. In the twenty-four hours before the launch of the MR, there had been only a few small skirmishes between the Elysian defense force and the invaders. The mercenaries on the ground had moved to cut off all major routes into University City, stopping the flow of fresh produce and meat from the outlying farming districts, but that could not be called a real siege because the residents were, of course, able to fall back on replicators. Even if the siege could be total, it would take years before inefficiencies in the replicator system could cause serious shortages of raw materials for the nanotech assemblers.

"It could mean that they were waiting for reinforcements," Lon had told his staff and battalion commanders during a working lunch. "That makes more sense than to think that they're just padding their contract, adding unnecessary days to the job. They certainly weren't hired just for minor harassment operations unless it's just another scheme to get the Elysians to submit to the CHW. Put the threat on the ground, then give them time to get frightened enough to accept whatever terms Union wants to grant."

"If it's that," Tefford Ives had said, "it could be a break for us. According to Chancellor Berlino, the CHW didn't have a representative on Elysium at the time of the attack. That would mean that the mercenaries would have instructions to wait long enough for an exchange of MRs, and we might almost be there by the time they quit waiting."

"What if the government of Elysium gives up before we get there?" Vel Osterman, now a lieutenant colonel and commanding the regiment's 2nd Battalion, asked. "Berlino is only the number two man. The president might have decided not to wait."

"I don't think that's likely," Lon said. He shrugged. "If something like that *does* happen, then we've got ourselves a month's cruise, paid for in advance . . . and then some. I don't think anyone will complain *too* loudly." *Certainly not me,* he had thought.

The Dirigent Mercenary Corps had developed a ritual—almost a spectacle—for sending troops off on contract. Although there was a more than adequate aerospaceport on base, used to transport equipment and baggage to the ships, departing troops were bused through Dirigent City to the civilian port across town. When they returned from contract, they would come back the same way, paraded through the city . . . unless they failed to fulfill their contract. *Then* they would come in through the port on base.

The dead always came home that way.

With two regiments going out, the bus drivers had a

hectic afternoon, taking one load to the port and then hurrying back for the next. Civilian traffic in the city remained snarled throughout. Two regiments also meant more noise than usual in the city because of the number of shuttles taking troops up to their ships. The civilian port was well away from the most heavily populated districts of Dirigent City, and the traffic patterns had been designed to minimize overflights, but there was still the noise of jets and rockets, especially when the shuttles went supersonic. It was no secret how many men were leaving, and the more soldiers who worked off-world contracts, the more money would be filtering back through the local economy.

Colonel Hayley and his headquarters staff were in the first shuttle that took off. Lon and his staff would be in the last. The troops of 15th Regiment started moving from base ninety minutes before 7th Regiment was mustered for the deployment. By the time Lon received the final manning reports in the regimental area, the buses had arrived to take 1st Battalion to the port, and the buses to handle the rest of the regiment arrived at less than ten-minute intervals.

"It amazes me that we can get this many people deployed all at once," Lieutenant Colonel Ives told Lon while they were waiting for the staff car that would take them to the port. "Two regiments strain the system almost to the breaking point. Three would be a logistical nightmare. They'd almost have to hold one back a few hours to get anything accomplished."

"This is all for show, Teff," Lon said. "It would have made a lot more sense to send one regiment up this morning and the other now, or afternoon and evening, space things out one way or the other. But this is all to make sure the civilians really *feel* the size of the deployment. Rub their faces in it. 'Look what we're doing for you.' Hell, if we had four regiments going out together they'd still try to do it all at once. Besides, two regiments going out on an open-ended contract *is* a big deal. You know how rare a job this size is. The Elysium contract damned near ensures a budget surplus for the year, even if we get the mission accomplished in only three months."

"As long as we come out on top," Ives said. "We've never gone head-to-head with New Sparta on a large contract."

The parade through Dirigent City had been going on so long that few people on the streets paid any attention to the final buses or the staff car that carried Lon and his executive officer. It might take a little time before the civilians realized that the show was over. The empty buses would return to base by a more circuitous route, avoiding the main boulevard connecting base and port.

Lon didn't give the passersby much attention either. He was thinking about Sara and Angie, and the baby who wouldn't be born for seven months. If this contract was extended, if 7th and 15th Regiments put in a full six months on Elysium, there was a chance that the baby would be born before Lon got home. A small chance, *assuming I get home at all,* Lon thought.

For the moment, Junior did not occupy much of his father's thoughts. Junior had come to the house the evening before, spent the night before deployment with the family. Junior had been somewhat more subdued than before his previous contracts, but not overtly nervous or apprehensive about the mission.

Sara had been quiet and supportive, as always—watching Lon to see how he was handling the situation—but restrained, both with her husband and their son. Angie had been visibly upset, though she had tried to hide her emotions. Lon's departures had long bothered her, and now she had to say good-bye to her brother as well, with no guarantee that either of them would return. Angie did not know that her father had heard her tell Sara, "I'll *never* marry a soldier. I couldn't stand it year after year, not knowing if he'd come home." *That's the smart way,* Lon had thought at the time, suspecting that she would change her mind, perhaps many times, before she married.

Lon's command shuttle was waiting near the military terminal building. The shuttles of his 4th Battalion were just taking off. The shuttles of the Heavy Weapons Battalion would follow in three minutes. That would leave only the three craft that would carry Lon, his staff, and the regimental headquarters and service company. There had been no traffic tie-up in the air. The port's controllers were efficient.

"We'd better get aboard," Lon told Ives. They were the only two who hadn't boarded; their shuttle was the only one that had not yet "buttoned up" for the ascent. The command shuttle's crew chief was standing in the one open hatch, waiting to seal it as soon as the last two officers got aboard. The two men walked toward the hatch, not obviously hurrying. "I'm going to ride up front with the pilots," Lon said as they moved up the ramp and past the crew chief into the shuttle.

The armada that had been gathered to take the two regiments to Elysium waited in a circular formation roughly two hundred miles above Dirigent, several hundred miles south and more than a thousand miles east of Dirigent City. Most of the ships would have been visible from the ground in daylight, but they were over deserted ocean and the desert that occupied much of the southeastern district of the world's primary continent.

There were ten of the new Raptor-class troop transports, each more than seven miles long and half a mile in diameter at the point of their greatest thickness. Each could carry a battalion of soldiers along with their equipment and supplies for more than four months, in more comfort than the older Dragon-class ships could manage. Three converted Dragons accompanied the fleet to carry additional supplies and munitions, including *Long Snake,* which had carried Lon on many contracts over the years. The heavy weapons of the two regiments were on *Patton* and *Rommel,* along with their mechanics and crews. *Ag-*

amemnon and *Odysseus* each carried a squadron of Shrike II aerospace fighters. *Sidon,* the smallest ship in the armada, would be used primarily as a courier vessel, alternating duty with *Tyre,* which would not be accompanying this task force, traveling between Dirigent and Elysium on a monthly schedule . . . or more frequently, as dictated by conditions on Elysium. The two smaller ships would carry messages, supplies, and—if needed—bring home casualties who needed extended regeneration and rehabilitation treatment, and take replacements to Elysium.

Lon sat in the cockpit of his shuttle, behind and slightly above the two pilots, and watched as they moved toward rendezvous with *Golden Eagle,* the ship he would be riding. The entire fleet was visible, even though night had arrived on the surface of Dirigent below it. Lights were visible on the ships—navigation markers and open shuttle hangars. Over Dirigent there was no need for the darkness of stealth conditions. In any case, the Raptor-class ships were so large that stealth was a relative concept. Within normal operating distances from a planet they could be seen from the ground during daylight hours and occulted a significant arc of space after dark.

"Quite a show, ain't it, Colonel?" Captain Art Felconi, Lon's pilot, said as he started to move the command shuttle into line for its rendezvous with *Golden Eagle.* "I know I've never seen anything like this in the ten years I've been flying these bugs for the Corps."

"Quite a show indeed. Nobody's seen a show like this in a long time, Art," Lon said. Felconi had been "his" pilot since Lon had assumed command of 2nd Battalion, and had moved along with him to regiment. There were still a few shuttles visible ahead of them, rendezvousing with their ships. Most were already secure in their hangars, their passengers moved out to shipboard quarters. "Been a dozen years since there was anything close to this. It may be another dozen years, or more, before it happens again." *Long after I hang up my pips,* Lon thought.

"I'm handing control over to *Golden Eagle* now, sir," Felconi said. "I show a lock on remote. The launchmaster has the con. All we have to do is sit back and let her drag us in."

"Just don't take a nap," Lon said, leaning forward against the straps of his safety harness to tap the pilot on the shoulder. "I feel a lot better with a good pair of hands at the controls here, just in case."

"You and me both, Colonel," Felconi said with a laugh. "I always stay ready." The pilot did not take his eyes from the monitors in front of him, and his hands always remained near the controls, ready to override *Golden Eagle*'s launchmaster if he thought it necessary. The odds were against that happening, but Art Felconi was an almost obsessively cautious man.

Lon leaned back. Almost unconsciously, he gripped the armrests of his seat more firmly, though it was not the death grip he had achieved the first few times he had ridden in a shuttle cockpit. This was a routine maneuver. Mishaps were vanishingly rare, fewer than one per hundred thousand dockings, and most of those produced no casualties. The shuttle decelerated, quickly at first, then more slowly, finally coming to a stop—relative to *Golden Eagle*—thirty feet from the hangar door. A boom telescoped out from the top of the hangar and grappled the command shuttle, then drew the craft inside, turning it so it would be facing out. Captain Felconi did not take his hands from the controls until the shuttle had come to rest and its passengers felt gravity from the ship's Nilssen generators. Felconi switched off the shuttle's engines and seemed to slowly slump back into his seat, finally relaxing.

The hangar bay's huge clamshell doors closed in silence. The hangar was pressurized, a process that took nearly three minutes. When it was complete, a series of green lights appeared on the hangar wall and on one of the monitors in front of Felconi. That was followed by an announcement from the launchmaster that it was safe to open the hatches of the shuttle.

Only then did Lon and the crew of the shuttle unbuckle their safety harnesses and stand. "Another uneventful hop," Felconi announced. "Just the way I like 'em."

By the time that Lon got back to the passenger compartment of the shuttle his staff was already moving onto the hangar floor, where a man from the ship's crew was standing to direct them. Although 7th Regiment's headquarters staff had never deployed together on contract since *Golden Eagle* had been commissioned, they had rehearsed this a half dozen times to make certain that everyone would be able to find their way around the ship. The Corps did not like to leave anything to chance.

Lon was met at the hangar exit by the launchmaster, a lieutenant commander from the ship's complement. "Sir, the captain's compliments," the launchmaster said, saluting. "He asked me to extend an invitation for you and your executive officer to dine in the wardroom with him and his department heads this evening at nineteen hundred hours."

"Thank you, Commander," Lon said, returning the salute. "Tell Captain Ewell that we will be delighted to dine with him." There was no surprise to the invitation. It was a tradition in the Corps.

By 1900 hours the armada was under way, heading out-system toward their first Q-space jump, five days away.

8

Accommodations aboard *Golden Eagle* were not as luxurious as those aboard the best passenger liners, but they were a marked step up from the Dragon-class ships, and worlds better than the extremely cramped quarters available on Port-class ships such as *Tyre* and *Sidon,* each of which could carry a single company of soldiers or function as a small freighter. The improvement that most passengers appreciated most, however, had nothing to do with living space. The Raptors escaped what had been the major inconvenience of interstellar travel. Older classes of ships required passengers to be strapped in during Q-space transits because that maneuver demanded the full power of all three Nilssen generators—which provided artificial gravity as well as propulsive energy. That meant that all activity had to be suspended three times during each interstellar journey. Raptor-class ships had a fourth Nilssen, allowing them to maintain artificial gravity even during Q-space transits.

A combination of factors had led to the inclusion of what had previously been decried as "useless luxury." The size and cost of the latest Nilssens had declined, making the addition of a fourth to each new ship more practical. But the rationale had little to do with the momentary comfort of soldiers. A fourth Nilssen gave a ship an element of redundancy, a "spare" in case one was damaged during a combat contract, allowing the ship to perhaps escape destruction without being forced to wait in hostile space until repairs could be effected.

Lon arranged to view *Golden Eagle*'s first Q-space transit of the voyage from the launchmaster's station, one of the few locations that offered the *illusion* of a direct window on space. The dome-shaped protrusion boasted floor-to-ceiling monitors giving a real-time view outside, allowing the launchmaster to handle incoming and outgoing shuttles as if he could actually see them. The resolution was so high that the illusion was nearly perfect. When he first stepped into the chamber, Lon felt an instant of vertigo, as if he had stepped out into open space.

"Whew! That's something," Lon said. There were only two other people in the room, an ensign and a petty officer. The only interior lighting was muted, coming from the complink monitors and various status lights on different pieces of equipment, all of which were arranged in the center of the room.

"Yes, sir," the ensign agreed. "It gets everyone the first time, and some people always have that kind of reaction. I've even seen people gasp for breath, as if they thought they stepped into a vacuum." The ensign chuckled. "By the way, sir, we've got about five minutes before Q-space insertion."

Lon glanced at his watch and nodded. He had started making his way toward the dome as soon as the thirty-minute warning sounded. *That* hadn't changed, even though the reason for it did not exist about Raptor-class ships. *Tell everyone what's coming so it doesn't catch anyone by surprise.*

"Don't expect to see much during the jump, Colonel," the ensign said. "It's really not much of a show."

"I've seen it on monitors—*small* monitors—before, Ensign," Lon said. "I just want to get the, ah, full effect."

"You will get *that* here, sir," the ensign said. "Best view on the ship, better than what the skipper has on the bridge."

Lon walked around the center island, looking outward, picking out stars he could identify, and the rockets of some of the other ships in the fleet, hot points of light.

One minute before Q-space insertion there was another warning broadcast throughout *Golden Eagle*. The entire armada would jump simultaneously and, if every ship's calculations were correct, emerge in the same formation at the far end of the transit in one of the major shipping lanes, forty light-years away.

Thirty seconds: another warning. At ten seconds, a countdown was broadcast on the loudspeakers: . . . *Three . . . two . . . one.* "Q-space insertion," the loudspeaker announced.

Under the last numbers of the count, Lon had felt the ship's normal vibrations increase markedly as the Nilssens cycled up to full power. There was no audible sound to accompany the vibration. The Nilssens were in separate pods outside the main hull of the ship, with the connections well insulated. The vacuum of space carried no sound. As the voice on the loudspeaker said "Q-space insertion," the view around Lon changed instantaneously. The familiar rich star field visible from Dirigent's system was replaced by a featureless, uniform light gray. There were no visual clues to tell the observer how far away the "horizon" was.

"A void without form," the ensign said, "like it says in the Bible. I know what the manuals say, sir, and I had to sweat my way through the transformational math in training—the basic, practical levels, not the deep theoretical stuff—but I can't really say I *understand* it. The Nilssens generate an ovoid bubble of quantum-space, a pocket universe, that is just barely larger than the ship. Theoretically, we are tangent to every point in the 'real' universe, but we're all alone, out of touch with that universe or the similar Q-space bubbles holding each of the other ships in the convoy. The Nilssens stress the bubble *just so* for *just so long* and then reverse polarity, dropping us back in normal space however many light-years we may have jumped. Our bubble universe will disappear, cease to exist, its Big Bang and Big Crunch happening just minutes apart—if time has any real meaning in it—the only evidence that the bubble ever existed a series of gentle gravity ripples that damp themselves out until they can't be detected. That's why we wait three days between transits, to make sure the, ah, residue from one jump doesn't affect the next."

I know the theory, Lon thought, but he just nodded, not paying much attention to the ensign's school text recitation. Lon was too busy staring at the blank gray surround, illuminated only by the few exterior lights *Golden Eagle* showed.

The transit did not last long; they rarely did. Two minutes after Q-space insertion there was an announcement that extraction would occur in thirty seconds. Lon waited. Again there was a countdown through the last ten seconds and then normal space blinked back into view, abruptly. The star field visible through the dome's monitors was considerably different. Other ships *were* visible, right where they were supposed to be—as far as Lon could tell.

"Thanks for the briefing, Ensign," Lon said. "An interesting show."

"Glad you're so easy to please, Colonel. Always nice to have company here. Don't get many repeat customers."

Lon kept busy during the voyage. He spent hours each day studying the database on Elysium, committing as much of the material to memory as he could—concentrating on the most likely area of operation, the region surrounding the capital, University City. He sketched out possible plans of attack, based on the information that Chancellor Berlino had brought to Dirigent, and the updates contained in the MR that had arrived just before the fleet left. Lon scanned large-scale maps, looking for whatever advantages of terrain might be found. *What would I do in this circumstance, or this?* Try to determine what the enemy might have done in the four weeks between the dispatch of that MR and the arrival of the Dirigenters. The final plan, based on what the Dirigenters learned when their ships emerged from the final Q-space transit of the journey, would be made by Bob Hayley, but he would seek the advice of Lon, the senior staff officers of the two regiments, and the battalion commanders, as well as the planners in the combat information centers of the fleet ships.

In addition to the routines of administration and his planning efforts, Lon had to reserve an hour each day for physical exercise in one of *Golden Eagle*'s four gymnasiums. An hour was spent with the SMO, Dan Norman. Eight hours for sleep, guaranteed by the patches that Major Norman had prescribed, another two hours for eating and other personal necessities.

"You're doing well," Norman told Lon the day after the second Q-space transit. "And the regiment is holding together nicely as well."

"I'm staying too busy to . . . brood," Lon said.

"That's part of the therapy. By the way, unless something goes terrifically haywire with your blood chemistry in the next twenty-four hours, I think we'll be able to forget that second session in the trauma tube."

"Best news I've had since we left home," Lon said. "We might have had trouble fitting it in, since Colonel Hayley wants a full staff meeting on *Peregrine* before we make the final transit. Senior regimental staff and all the battalion commanders and executive officers. That could take most of a day, with the commute there and back." *Peregrine* was the ship carrying Colonel Hayley and would serve as flagship for operations during the Elysium contract. Its combat information center would coordinate all activities of the ships and would handle communications between the fleet and the force on the ground.

The three senior Elysians—Chancellor Berlino, Minister for External Affairs Beoch, and Treasurer Chiou—were also present for the planning session aboard *Peregrine,* more as observers than as participants; primarily, they were there to answer questions. The conference was held in a room next to CIC, in the area of the ship between crew territory and the passenger section. There weren't enough complink stations around the U-shaped table for everyone to have a place. Staff officers and seconds-in-command had seats behind their principals.

In the center of the U a three-dimensional projection of Elysium and its system spun, mimicking in scale the motions of the real system. Elysium's sun was slightly hotter than Earth's sun. Elysium was slightly farther away, giving the planet conditions very similar to those on Earth, Dirigent, or hundreds of other worlds that humans had settled. So many hospitable worlds had been found that colonists rarely had to accept anything that was not "just right."

"Tomorrow morning, we transit Q-space into the Elysian system," Colonel Hayley said once everyone was seated and the initial small talk had ended. He gestured at the holographic chart. "The plans we make today must be seen as extremely preliminary and subject to almost certain change once we are in-system and learn what developments there have been since the Elysians sent that last MR. The information that contained will be twenty-nine days out of date when we hit Elysian space, so it is possible that the situation may have changed drastically." The Elysium contract was no different from any other in that regard, and the situation was often much worse. The available information might be two months or more old by the time the mercenaries reached their destination. Most commanders made a point of emphasizing the age of their data.

"As a precaution, the fleet will emerge from Q-space in three separate elements, widely spaced, too far apart for the enemy to easily intercept all of us even if they're sitting there just waiting for us to arrive." He cleared his throat and made a hand gesture. A chief petty officer from *Peregrine*'s crew, sitting at a console at the rear of the room, inserted red arrows in the holographic map, all well away from the system's ecliptic, two coming from "above" and the other from "below." Colonel Hayley detailed which ships would come in at each point. "The commanders of each ship already have their navigational data," Hayley said. "We will—subject to change once we see what the New Spartans have waiting for us—be able to rendezvous in attack orbit seventy-one hours after we emerge from Q-space." That elicited a few soft murmurs around the table. Standard doctrine called for ships to emerge seventy-two hours, or more, out from any significant planetary mass.

"An hour is the most we can afford to risk, even though the commanders of all the ships agreed that it leaves a considerable safety margin," Hayley said. "The problem is that we don't know *how* considerable. But being able to get into position even that much sooner might give us a slender advantage, even though we can expect that the New Spartans will calculate our course and speed in fairly short order once we emerge from Q-space." He smiled. "We should, at a minimum, throw a hint of uncertainty into their planning. If we're willing to chance doing one thing that the 'book' says we shouldn't, what else might we attempt that they won't be expecting? That is, at least, our hope.

"The basics of our attack plan are fairly simple, again, depending on what we find." Hayley gestured again, and the CPO at the controls adjusted the holographic view again, moving Elysium to the center, enlarging it, and showing only the surface of the planet and space directly around it. The amount of surface detail increased, and the district centered on the capital was highlighted in a bright yellow.

"*Agamemnon* and *Odysseus* will move to engage the enemy's capital ships with their own weapons and the Shrikes they carry, striving to keep them fully occupied while we put troops ashore. If the enemy's strength and disposition on the ground have not changed significantly, the initial landing assault will include seven line battalions, leaving 7th Regiment's 4th Battalion aboard ship as reserve. The heavy-weapons battalions of both regiments will also remain aboard ship until our people on the ground establish safe LZs to bring in their tanks and guns and we can use Shrikes to cover the landing of their equipment. If initial operations go well, the delay might be no more than an hour or two. If necessary, we can use a landing by 4th of the 7th as a diversion for the heavy weapons." Another gesture, and the projection of Elysium stopped rotating and the image of the highlighted area trebled in size.

"Once on the ground, ður initial objective will be to engage the enemy around University City and break the siege. Once we break the cordon the New Spartans have thrown around the capital, we can start working to roll up their line and—hopefully—convince them that their contract is one they cannot fulfill."

"Do you plan to use *all* the Shrikes against the enemy ships?" Tefford Ives asked. "Or will you reserve some to cover the initial landing?"

"That depends on how the New Spartans use their fighters. If they withdraw all of them to defend their ships or to attack our vessels, we'll use all the Shrikes in space. If they leave some fighters low to oppose the landing and continue interdicting local air travel, then we may divert some of our Shrikes to keep them occupied." Hayley cleared his throat again and let his gaze drift all the way around the table.

"Just remember, gentlemen, this is still extremely speculative. The New Spartans have had four weeks to redeploy, reinforce, or even withdraw their forces. Until we see what assets they have in place and how they are deployed, we can't make firm plans, and even those will be subject to change depending on how they react to our arrival. But this briefing will allow you to tell your men what our thinking is at present. Make sure everyone knows where we stand." Keeping everyone as informed as possible was standard procedure in the Corps. Bob

Hayley went perhaps a little farther than some command-ers.

"Right now," he continued, "I just want you to recall one important provision of our contract. If we arrive in-system and find that the New Spartans have massively reinforced their presence beyond what we can expect to handle readily, our instructions are to report that fact to Dirigent immediately and await our own reinforcements, even withdrawing from the system, if necessary, to avoid useless losses before those reinforcements reach us. We don't spend our men carelessly."

9

Lon spent fifteen minutes with his battalion commanders before they all returned to their respective ships. He asked how things were going, repeated Hayley's admonition to make certain the men were told everything, then wished them luck. "The next time we meet, we should be on the ground on Elysium." Lon and his senior staff officers waited until all of the battalion commanders and executive officers had left before they boarded their shuttle to return to *Golden Eagle*.

"I don't know if it's progress or not," Lon said after his shuttle had been launched from one of *Peregrine*'s hangars, "but we've come a long way in how quickly a major operation can be planned and executed. Back on Earth, as late as the end of the twentieth century and into the early twenty-first, an operation this size would have taken weeks—more likely months—to plan and launch, and there would have been none of the improvisation we'll have to do in less than three days to actually decide how to use our assets. The planners would have had virtually constant surveillance information available to them throughout the planning period. Half a century earlier, a major operation might have taken a year or more to plan and mount."

"I seem to recall that there were exceptions," Ives said, "operations on the scale of what the Corps gets involved in that were planned and executed in short order. And operations where one of the major powers of the time couldn't defeat an enemy whose total population was less than the size of the military force that could have been brought to bear against them."

Lon nodded. Torrey Berger, now a major and regimental operations officer, spoke. "There was a lot more to consider in the last half of the twentieth century. That was the era of massive nuclear weapons establishments. The two major powers had enough nuclear warheads to totally waste a hundred planets, and no way to get those warheads anywhere but their own world."

"That's one concern we don't have today, thankfully," Lon said. "It's been more than seven hundred years since a nuclear weapon was used, almost as long since the last stocks on Earth were destroyed."

"Assuming, of course, that no one has started making them again, Union or Buckingham, for example—or even Earth," Ives said. "The information is available. The technology hasn't disappeared. Constructing one would be much simpler today than it was then. You'd just have to program molecular assemblers and make certain they had the necessary raw materials."

"I can't see anyone risking that," Lon said. "The repercussions if the secret got out would be too overwhelming."

Twelve hours remained until the fleet would make its final Q-space transit, emerging in Elysium's solar system. Lon had talked with nearly every man in his headquarters and service complement. It gave him a chance to judge the morale of his people firsthand, though surveying the H&S ranks was certainly not the same as talking with the frontline troops. *One more remove from the heart,* he thought as he ate supper with his staff, *one more stage of isolation.* There was the expected level of tension, but nothing so great as to give him cause for alarm. *Some* tension was needed; it wouldn't do to have the men as relaxed as if they were going to a picnic in one of the parks around Dirigent City. The talk among his senior officers at supper was generally casual. There was curiosity about what they would find when the fleet emerged in Elysian space, speculation about what the New Spartans might have been doing the past month.

Lon did more listening than talking, observing the faces of his officers. And he attempted to take stock of his own mental condition. *I'm doing pretty well, maybe better than I've felt just before hitting hostile country since . . . before Junior was born.* Lon's worries had not evaporated, but they were no longer paralyzing him. Junior. Angie. The unborn baby not due until after Lon was scheduled to get back home, even if he spent six months on Elysium. Sara. *Sometimes I wonder how she's put up with me all these years,* Lon thought with a smile. *Between the brooding before a contract and the long absences, it's a miracle.*

After supper, Lon spent a couple of minutes chatting with Tefford Ives, mostly about minor administrative details, then retired to his stateroom—actually a two-room suite—leaving instructions that he was not to be disturbed until three hours before the scheduled Q-space transit except in case of emergency.

Lon sat on the edge of his bunk and took off his boots and socks. Only one of Doc Norman's special eight-hour sleep patches remained, one more certain night of undisturbed sleep. *Once we ground, sleep takes a backseat again,* Lon thought. He glanced at his watch. He still had a half hour before he needed to put the patch on his neck and go to bed—to give him his eight hours of sleep and allow him to wake three hours before the fleet made its final Q-space transit.

He spent five minutes recording a letter to Sara and Angie, adding on to portions he had recorded almost every day since leaving Dirigent. When he was away from home, his letters were almost a diary, added to when he had a chance, sent when a message rocket was being dispatched. Return mail from Sara and Angie was similar. *They'll see that I'm calm, not agitated or overly worried,* he thought when he switched off the complink's recorder. *Give them less reason to worry.*

Then Lon finished undressing and did the things he needed to do before going to bed. After he turned out the cabin lights, he lay down and put the sleep patch on his neck. In less than two minutes, he was asleep.

There was no foggy area of transition. Lon went from the oblivion of drug-enhanced sleep to total alertness in a heartbeat. The special patches Dan Norman had provided always brought Lon out of sleep quickly at the end of their allotted time, but this time it was abrupt, almost disconcerting. He blinked several times and sucked in a deep, convulsive breath. Briefly, his heart rate increased dramatically, then settled to a normal resting rhythm. He turned his head to look at the timeline on the complink near his bed.

Right on schedule, he thought. *This is the day we find out what we're going to face.* Any landing was three days away at a minimum, but that did not mean that there could be no danger for those three days. *How fast will the New Spartans react?* Lon wondered. If they responded promptly to the arrival of the fleet, combat might come in little more than thirty-six hours—combat in space, between ships and aerospace fighters, combat that the soldiers in the transports could not affect. *If they come after us,* Lon thought as he sat up and swung his legs off the berth. There was even a slight chance that combat could come sooner, *if* the New Spartans had ships posted farther out from Elysium, waiting for the arrival of the Dirigenters.

It would take one hell of a stroke of bad luck for them to be someplace where they could get to us quickly, Lon told himself as he stood and stretched. That was one situation he had never experienced in all his years in the Corps—having his ship come under attack. *The odds must be longer than having two royal flushes honestly dealt in the same hand of poker.* The enemy would have to be in the right place, at the right distance, on alert, ready to strike.

"Not too damned likely," Lon mumbled. He crossed to the complink and checked for messages, scrolling through the only two entries in his communications log before going to the bathroom to get ready for the day. After showering, he stood and looked at himself in the mirror. There were no scars to remind him of the many wounds he had suffered in the Corps. The body's HMS was far too efficient to leave visible scar tissue. But Lon could recall each injury. He touched several of the spots, as if trying to evoke some memory of the pain he had felt. Nothing.

"Like the dreams," he whispered, focusing on his eyes in the mirror. "Nothing visible."

When he emerged from the bathroom, he looked at the complink again. It was three in the morning. Ship's time had been adjusted to match local time in Elysium's University City. The fleet would emerge while it was still night over the capital, and they would reach attack orbit in the night . . . in three days, if nothing happened to disrupt their schedule. *If.*

Reveille sounded for the troops aboard *Golden Eagle*. "There shouldn't be any sluggards today," Lon said, almost managing a chuckle. Everyone knew the fleet would be jumping into Elysium's system within hours and that shortly after that they should know the size of their opposition. Unless the government of Elysium had fallen, there would be direct updates as quickly as the ships could establish contact. The ships' own sensing gear would quickly seek the enemy's ships and start trying to determine the situation on the ground—though this gear would be only minimally helpful until the final day of the approach. Later, once the planners *knew* more, the troops would be put on a relaxed schedule, their main instructions to get as much rest and eating in as possible for the landings. Once they were on the ground, sleep and meals might be scarce.

Lon took his time dressing, even taking a moment to buff his boots before going to the galley to eat breakfast.

Look smart, project confidence: Those were important for an officer. Don't give the rank and file any reason to suspect that their commander might be less than supremely confident about the outcome of the pending operation. *Put on an act if you have to, but sell it,* Matt Orlis had told him many years before. Recalling Matt took the smile from Lon's face. Matt had retired from the Corps after his only son had been killed in action. It was a reminder Lon would rather have missed.

Lon and Tefford Ives waited for the final Q-space transit in the small office attached to Lon's cabin, drinking coffee and doing a poor job of trying to make small talk. This was a time for minor jitters, which made it an excellent time to be away from the rest of the men aboard the ship.

"I wonder if the New Spartans even suspect that the Elysians might have help on the way," Ives said when the waiting got to be too much for him.

"If they notified Union by MR immediately when Berlino's ship left, they could have word back that he didn't get there," Lon said. "They might have had a couple of days' notice. That wouldn't give them time to get additional forces here, unless they were already on the way. I think what we face will depend on just one thing. Were the New Spartans sent to conquer Elysium, or just to scare them into accepting the Confederation?"

"A toss of the coin," Ives said, "and I've been tossing it mentally since we first learned of the contract." He glanced at the time. "We should have a pretty good idea soon."

He had scarcely finished saying that when the announcement was broadcast that one minute remained until Q-space insertion. Both men looked at the timeline on the complink then.

"Don't hold your breath," Lon said, grinning.

"I quit doing that years ago. I think." Ives shook his head. "At least we're not strapped down in our bunks for transits anymore. I always hated that. Made me feel like

I was a prisoner and someone was going to do unspeakable things to me."

The final seconds of the countdown dragged past, concluding with the standard announcement "Q-space insertion." Lon closed his eyes, feeling the vibration of the ship as the Nilssen generators ran at their maximums, stretching the bubble universe around *Golden Eagle*, stressing it according to some arcane mathematical formula containing more variables than a six-month weather forecast. Lon opened his eyes and stared at the elapsed-time indicator on the complink. This would be the longest transit of the journey, almost three minutes. It felt like a *long* three minutes, and the final ten seconds of the countdown to extraction seemed to occupy ten minutes. When the speaker announced "Q-space extraction," Lon let his breath out, slightly embarrassed to realize that he had been holding it in.

"I figure it will be an hour, minimum, before we get anything from Elysium," Lon said, hoping that Ives had not noticed the breath-holding. "But we should have our first view of the New Spartans' ships in minutes." Out of date by the number of light-minutes away the planet was: If a ship were ten light-minutes away, the view would be of where that ship had been ten minutes earlier, not where it was *now*. Every ship would be scanning, and the information would be collated in CIC aboard *Peregrine*, then relayed to each ship in the Dirigenter flotilla.

"What will it be, about twelve minutes before the New Spartans get their first view of us?" Ives asked.

Lon shrugged. "Something like that. If they're looking in the right direction."

"They will be," Ives replied. "We would. Scanning the entire system even if we had no reason to suspect that trouble might be coming. They're professionals, too." He paused. "I have to keep reminding myself of that. This time we're not going up against amateurs."

I know, Lon thought but did not say. He just nodded.

The complink started to show an image of Elysium, still

little more than a dot moving against the star field until the computers magnified and enhanced the raw feed. The system needed another five minutes before it could highlight the even smaller points that indicated ships in orbit around the world—seven blips, seven ships.

"Enough to account for a single regiment," Lon said. "They haven't brought in reinforcements."

"Yet," Tefford Ives said, but that was not enough to stem the relief Lon felt.

The news that started to arrive from Elysium was not nearly as bad as it might have been. There had been no large-scale fighting in the past month, just skirmishes between small units of the defense force and the invaders. In the farming districts surrounding University City, the invaders had dispossessed people, sent them in toward the capital with no more than they could carry, but the New Spartans had been careful not to harm anyone who did not actively resist. Buildings and farm equipment had been destroyed methodically. Crops in the fields had been burned if they could not be easily harvested by the invaders. Livestock had been commandeered to feed the New Spartans.

There was no orbital video of the deployment of the New Spartans on the ground. They had destroyed every Elysian satellite on the first day following their arrival, and had thwarted the few attempts the Elysians had made to replace those losses. That also meant that there was virtually no communications between population centers. Travel between cities was impossible. New Spartan aircraft kept local shuttles out of the air, and there were occasional raids against ground vehicles attempting to move from one city or town to another.

Within four hours following the arrival in-system of the Dirigenter fleet, the New Spartans had recalled all of their aerospace fighters, bringing them back aboard their carriers. Shortly after that, the two fighting ships of the New Spartan task force started moving to a higher orbit, a thousand miles above their transports. But they did not attempt to intercept the Dirigenter fleet away from Elysium.

The three separate elements of the Dirigenter force continued toward Elysium and rendezvous. *Agamemnon* and *Odysseus* slowly pulled ahead of the other ships. The plan was still for them to engage the New Spartan battlecruisers, the ships that carried their fighters and heavy armaments.

"The idea is to tie up their firepower, especially their fighters, so they can't oppose our landing," Lon said on a linkup that included all of his battalion and company commanders. "If that works, it will make our landing much easier. All we'll have to worry about is the enemy on the ground."

"Colonel, do you know yet if we're going to have any Shrikes to cover our landing?" Captain Harley Stossberg, now commanding A Company, 2nd Battalion—Lon's old company—asked.

"No, and we probably won't know until we're in the boats ready to go in," Lon said. "That depends on what the New Spartans do. If they hold all their fighters to defend their ships or to attack *Agamemnon* and *Odysseus,* then we'll most likely have to use all our Shrikes in space. We're going to try to ground far enough from any New Spartans to stay out of reach of any surface-to-air missiles. We haven't decided on the details of deployment yet, but the preliminary plan calls for 15th Regiment to land outside the cordon around University City and for our first three battalions to land inside. We move at the New Spartans from both sides then, put them in a pincer, break the line, and do our best to roll them up in a hurry. Our initial operations will probably all be on the north bank of the Styx River, where the majority of the enemy troops are."

"There isn't a lot of current data on the New Spartan mercenaries in our data banks, not *specific* data," Parker Watson of 4th Battalion said. "Do we have anything at all on how they're armed?"

"We don't have much," Lon conceded. "They're as

tight about security as we are. I couldn't find any reliable information on the armament and capabilities of their aerospace fighters. As for the men on the ground, we assume they'll be equipped about as we are, with one possible exception. One of the reports we have from the people on Elysium says that some of the New Spartans are armed with needle rifles, capable of firing huge quantities of tiny slivers of metal, possibly depleted uranium, at extremely high muzzle velocities. We don't have reliable confirmation, but it is possible. Our R&D people are working on similar weapons, though it will be a year or more before they're ready for issue, if the Council of Regiments decides to go into full production."

More raw data flowed into CIC. Thousands of scenarios were created and critiqued, tweaked, and run through every conceivable variation. As the fleet continued to move toward Elysium, obsolete scenarios were discarded, the remainder graded, the rankings changed with each new influx of data. Lon and Colonel Hayley spent hours linked together with the staff of *Peregrine*'s CIC. Thirty-six hours after the final Q-space transit, they had narrowed the possible assault scenarios to a manageable dozen, depending on what the New Spartans did in the last hours before the DMC soldiers entered their attack shuttles. Beyond the moment of landing, battle plans had to remain generalized, limited to primary objectives and very elastic timetables. The number of variables quickly became too extreme for precision.

Aboard the troop transports, men recorded letters home. Those were merged on large message chips, ready to be dispatched via MR before the attack began. For some, it might be the last word their families ever would have from them.

10

The day before the landings, Lon spoke to his men. Company by company, he addressed the officers and sergeants through ship-to-ship links, and he recorded messages to the rank and file, individualized for each battalion. The sessions with officers and sergeants were two-way, allowing them to ask questions and receive answers. It also gave Lon a few seconds to speak with his son, though they could do little more than wish each other good luck. The conversation was not private. Aboard *Golden Eagle,* Lon spoke to officers and men face-to-face in small groups. Those sessions ran longer than the complink hookups. Altogether, Lon spent more than six hours giving his pep talks and laying out the latest version of the plan of attack.

"This may be the hardest day's work I've ever put in," Lon told Phip Steesen after the last session. "I'd hate to be a politician and have to talk this much every day. Parker Watson is still upset at having his battalion held in reserve. Wouldn't matter who drew that, the commander would still bitch."

Phip laughed. "Goes with the territory, I'd say." The two men were alone in Lon's office.

"This contract *is* going to be different from any we've been on," Lon said after a short silence.

Phip snorted. "Sure is. I bet the brass in the Contracts Division are already licking their chops. If we best the New Spartans head-to-head, it gives us a big boost in marketing. Proof we're the best. More contracts, higher rates."

For a moment, Lon stared at his lead sergeant and best friend, almost stunned by the comment. Then he burst out laughing. "I knew you were cynical," he said, "but I never realized just *how* cynical."

"Cynical, hell, just looking at it honestly. Tell the truth, Lon, didn't that get mentioned when you were talking about the contract?"

Lon hesitated before he said, "Not in so many words, but, yes, I guess the implication was there . . . and the concern that if we were to lose it might cost us future business, send some potential customers to New Sparta. But every contract has that element of risk. Anytime we fail to fulfill a contract we risk losing business to competitors. Anytime we succeed, it gives us a better record to show customers."

"This is orders of magnitude beyond that, Lon. Dirigent and New Sparta are the two major mercenary worlds, and we're going head-to-head, in strength. What happens here could affect the economies of both worlds for decades. We can't afford to let them win; they can't afford to let us win. Can you imagine what conditions would be like at home if the Corps had to lay off three or four regiments because there wasn't enough work? What that would do to the economy? Take jobs from fifteen or twenty thousand soldiers and it would mean a lot of lost civilian jobs as well, in Camo Town, in factories, everywhere. More people would be forced to live on basic maintenance in neighborhoods like the Drafts. More crime. On and on."

"I guess I never thought it that far through," Lon said after considering what Phip had said. "I've just thought about it in terms of a hard job that has to be done . . . mostly because it *is* our job, and if we're not the best, then too many men don't make it home."

"I might not have thought of it either," Phip admitted. "Jenny pointed it out to me, at some length, the night before we left." Jenny was his wife. She and her brother Kalko had grown up in the Drafts, the closest Dirigent City had to a slum district. "A discussion of the economic necessity of victory wasn't exactly what I was expecting the night before I shipped out on contract."

" 'Come home with your shield or on it'?" Lon quoted softly.

"What's that?"

Lon shook his head. "Ancient history. What the women of the original Sparta, on Earth, supposedly told their men before they went into battle. War was their business, too, in a way."

"Sparta, a city-state in classical Greece, noted for its military prowess," Phip recited, showing that he had learned something along the way. "I looked it up once, wondering where the 'New' in New Sparta came from."

"You get to where three hundred Spartans held off an army of a hundred thousand until they were outflanked and slaughtered?"

"Thermo-something?"

Lon laughed. "Thermopylae."

"All in all, I've never been fond of last stands," Phip said. "No curtain calls, no rematches."

A short while later, Lon was getting ready to head to the galley for supper when he received a call from Colonel Hayley on *Peregrine*. "Are you alone there?" was the first thing Hayley said when he saw Lon's face on his complink screen.

"I'm alone, Bob. Something wrong?" Lon asked. He sat at his desk to get his face on the same level as Hayley's.

"Not wrong, just something I can't remember if I mentioned to you before." Hayley hesitated. Lon thought that he looked troubled. "From right now until this contract is concluded, one way or the other, you and I stay as far apart physically as we can. No face-to-face meetings, nothing that might let the enemy get lucky and take us both out at once. I know we've both got capable execs who can take over, but . . . just the same. Keeping the top commanders separated is sound practice."

"Sure, Bob. I've got no argument with that," Lon said, thinking, *No, you didn't mention it before, and why do you think it has to be brought up now?* Keeping top commanders, or a commander and his second-in-command apart whenever possible on a combat contract was a standard precaution, something that shouldn't have needed this sort of special mention.

"We stay in contact by complink or radio. My staff and CIC will route everything to your staff. That way, if something happens to me, you can take over at the double, not waste time getting up to speed." Hayley glanced away, then back.

"No need to borrow trouble, Bob," Lon said. "Sure, we're up against professionals, but we've got the numbers on them—two to one or thereabouts, not counting the Elysian Defense Force, and if the Elysians have been able to stand up against New Spartans for a month, they've got something on the ball, even if the Spartans weren't given orders to conquer Elysium outright."

"Just covering all the possibilities, Lon," Hayley said, attempting to pass it off lightly. But his face didn't agree with the words. "If our intelligence is right, a New Spartan regiment is about twenty percent larger than one of ours, but you're probably right. No reason not to think that the landings and initial deployment will go smoothly. I just don't want to forget anything that might prove important later."

"Yeah, I know how it goes. We worry about it every contract," Lon said, going along with Hayley's rationalization. "Worry so much we don't get enough sleep. My SMO nags me about it all the time." *I do understand,* Lon thought. *It could be me. It* has *been me, many times.* He blinked. *Have I ever looked that nervous to the people around me?* He was afraid that the answer was yes, many times.

"So does mine. One other thing. You get any brilliant ideas, don't wait to be asked. Hit me with them right away."

"The only brilliant idea I've had lately is for us to keep our heads and butts down so they don't get shot off," Lon said.

Bob Hayley managed a weak laugh. It was a good note to end the talk on.

Supper the last night aboard ship was shared with Lon's staff officers. Although Lon kept trying to direct the conversation elsewhere, the talk kept coming back to the contract, and the combat landings scheduled to take place before dawn. There were traces of jitters, but no more than usual, Lon thought, and everyone was trying to cover their nervousness—with more or less success. That was normal, something Lon saw every time he was leading men into a combat contract.

Men ate past what they were comfortable with, until they couldn't force another bite. That, too, was standard. *Eat when you can; you never know where the next meal is coming from once you're in combat.* Each time, each contract, Lon recalled the way everyone had seemed preoccupied with making him stuff himself, as if he might have been in danger of starvation, even in garrison. Even those who finished eating early did not leave the table. They waited. Lon knew what was expected.

"As long as everyone keeps on their toes and does their job, we should make out all right on Elysium," he said when it was clear that the few who were still eating were just waiting for him to speak. "We've got the manpower advantage, even if the New Spartans are as good as we are, man for man, and we don't know that they are." That elicited a few nervous laughs.

"They've been on the ground more than a month, doing pretty much what they want, terrorizing civilians and swatting at the Elysian Defense Force. Until we popped out of Q-space they probably had no idea they might have to face the hardest opposition they've ever seen. Now they've had two and a half days to worry about that, to wonder just what they've gotten themselves into." *Two and a half days to plan what they're going to hit us with when we get in reach,* Lon thought. "Their commander is probably looking hard at his contract, trying to find an honorable loophole to let him get his people out relatively intact."

"They want to run for home, we let them?" Torrey Berger asked, drawing a bigger laugh than Lon had received.

"In a second," Lon said. "But don't count on that. They might not have been cautious enough getting escape clauses in their contract."

"Man's gotta have a few dreams, Colonel," Berger said.

"You give up dreaming about women, Torrey?" someone asked from farther down the table.

"Even asleep they slap his face," someone else contributed. "He can't stand the rejection anymore."

Lon smiled and nodded. He couldn't answer for the line battalions, but his headquarters people were as ready as they were ever going to get.

Lon sat on the edge of his bed. The only light in the cabin came from his complink screen, and that was blank, a dark blue, except for the red numerals of the timeline. Eight hours remained until the scheduled call to board the attack shuttles. Reveille would be in five hours, to give everyone time for one final meal aboard ship. Lon knew he should already be asleep—long since. He had undressed two hours ago. He had a four-hour sleep patch handy. He suspected that he would be forced to use it if he were to get any sleep. Soon . . . but not quite yet.

They—the New Spartans—*could have run as soon as they could make out how many of us there are,* he thought. *They could have been on their way out-system quickly enough that we couldn't have caught them. They chose to stay, even though they must realize that they're outnumbered. Why?* That question, rather than personal worries or obsessions, was the one that had kept him awake. This time. He had made his preparations for sleep in plenty of time to allow him eight hours. He had laid out his gear for the morning, recorded additions to his latest letter to Sara and Angie. He had gone back through the main points of the assault plan a couple of times. It was that process that had brought the question to the fore, forcefully. It had come up, in passing, a couple of times during the planning conferences. Staff members had proffered a dozen possible reasons for the New Spartans to remain in place, ready to face a superior force. The simplest and least satisfactory was, "They're too damned cocky. They think they're twice as good as we are." The more likely, and more disturbing, were variations on two related themes. "They know they have heavy reinforcement coming in, soon, and figure they can hold out long enough." "They have a hole card, some weapon or system we're not allowing for, something they figure either evens the odds or tilts them in their favor."

They must hope to be able to knock out a lot of our shuttles before we get on the ground, Lon thought. He did not rule·out other possibilities, but that seemed to be the most likely. *Knock off as many of us as possible before we can get out of the box.* That was the way Lon and his men thought about a combat landing in a shuttle. While they were in the box, the shuttle, they could not defend themselves. A rocket or heavy cannon fire could knock out a shuttle . . . and everyone inside.

We plan to land far enough from their men on the ground to eliminate—as far as we can—the danger from shoulder-fired SAMs, Lon reminded himself. The plan of attack called for the shuttles to follow routes that kept them away from the lines New Sparta had established around the Elysian capital, coming in well away from the ships in orbit, getting low and following the terrain in, grounding miles from known enemy positions. That would also, theoretically, minimize· the danger from enemy aerospace fighters, if they were sent after the landing craft instead of being held to defend the New Spartan ships.

What else is there? What are we missing? Lon asked himself. *If anything.* He blinked as the timeline on his complink ticked over from one minute to the next. *We know how many ships they have, how many men they could possibly have on the ground, how many fighters their weapons platforms can carry.* All of the enemy ships would have some armament—missiles and heavy-duty energy weapons, beamers—but those were more defensive than offensive, especially on the transports.

"At least the way *we* use them," Lon whispered. The New Spartans had not moved their transports out of harm's way. They were still in orbit over Elysium, not quite directly above University City. "That may be it." Lon turned to the complink and typed in a short message to CIC aboard *Peregrine,* with a copy to Bob Hayley.

"Suggest watching enemy transports closely in case they use their energy and projectile weapons to target our shuttles."

"It might be a long shot," Lon whispered as the message was acknowledged by CIC, "but it might be the answer, at least *part* of it." *This landing could be hairier than any of us wants,* he thought as he blanked the complink screen again. *We may have to use Shrikes to cover the shuttles regardless of how the enemy uses his fighters.*

Lon lay down, finally, but he stared at the overhead for several minutes, hardly blinking, trying to think of any additional steps they might be able to take to protect the troops on their way in. Eventually he shook his head. It was too late, and reveille would come too early. He applied the sleep patch to his neck and barely had time for a prayer before he fell asleep.

Please don't let me fail my men.

Reveille sounded before the nightmares had time to build after the patch wore off. Lon had just started to sweat in his sleep.

11

There was no indication of chaos in the morning—actually, the middle of the night—as ten thousand men woke and prepared for the landing. Breakfast was served. The men who were to take part in the initial landing ate as heartily as they could, then returned to the troop bays aboard their transports to give helmets and field gear one final check before putting them on. Helmet electronics were put through diagnostic routines; radio channels were checked. By squad, platoon, and company, the men went to armories to draw weapons and ammunition. Squad leaders inspected their men. Platoon sergeants inspected squad leaders. Company lead sergeants inspected platoon sergeants and officers. Lead sergeants were checked by their commanders. No one would board a shuttle until he had thoroughly inspected his own gear and weapons, and had his judgment confirmed by someone else.

On nine ships, men were ordered to their shuttles. Roll was taken at the hangar door and again once everyone was in their shuttles. The men found their seats and fastened their safety harnesses, each man's rifle clipped securely to the front of the seat between his legs.

Lon found the routine comforting. The normal demands of launching a combat assault kept him too busy for mental roving. He thought about his family only in passing, instants marked by a quick stab of longing. There was no time for more. Of his men on *Golden Eagle,* only a few would not be going down in the first wave. Tefford Ives and one platoon from headquarters company would remain behind, with half a dozen technicians who would not be needed at once, to be deployed with the Heavy-Weapons Battalion or 4th Battalion, whichever came first.

He also kept a radio channel open to CIC once he had his battle helmet on. The battlecruisers *Agamemnon* and *Odysseus* had each launched half of their Shrike II fighters to engage the enemy's capital ships and aerospace fighters, holding the rest until the enemy's reaction could be gauged. They also had started direct fire on the enemy ships with missiles and heavy beamers. The New Spartans were returning fire. They launched two dozen fighters to intercept the Shrike IIs. Both sides had their antimissile defenses ready.

Lon was the last man to board his command shuttle, the last man in 7th Regiment—of those going down in the first wave—to board a shuttle. He did not choose to ride in the cockpit this time. That was not exclusively because he didn't want to have the most vertiginous view possible as the shuttle accelerated toward the surface of Elysium, then skimmed the ground reaching for its landing zone. When the shuttle landed, Lon and his men would need to exit the craft as quickly as possible—get out of "the box" before it came under enemy fire. And a speedy exit was far more difficult from the cockpit.

Two shuttles were required for each full line company. That meant eight landers for a battalion, plus a command shuttle. There were seven battalions in the first wave—sixty-three shuttles—plus four shuttles from *Golden Eagle* and four from *Peregrine*. The shuttles from each ship were launched and rendezvoused several miles from the ship. The various groups moved toward their landing vectors, courses spread to make it extremely difficult for the enemy to intercept all of them, or to target them effectively at long range. Each battalion's shuttles started their descent to time the landing so that all of the troops would hit the ground at the same time.

The landing zones had been chosen and assigned. Each pilot knew exactly where he was supposed to touch down.

Especially near the end of the flight, many of the shuttles would be in close proximity, landing only a few dozen yards apart, close enough to let the troops emerge and set up an initial defensive perimeter the way they practiced every month in training on Dirigent. Throughout the flight, each battalion's shuttles would remain as close together as practical, allowing them to mass their firepower—rockets and multibarrel cannons—if they were attacked by aerospace fighters.

Please don't let me fail my men. Lon repeated his prayer as he felt the first acceleration of his command shuttle as it dove toward the atmosphere of Elysium. Shuttles had no artificial gravity, but the acceleration pushed Lon back into his seat with more than the equivalent of one g, and the push grew stronger. The shuttle appeared to be diving directly toward the center of the planet, intent on self-destruction. Monitors spaced around the passenger compartment ensured that everyone could see where they were going. Many of the men around Lon closed their eyes, or did everything they could to avoid seeing the images. This was the point where those who were subject to motion sickness were most likely to vomit.

"We're being tracked by hostile radar," the shuttle pilot told Lon. "Looks as if they're trying to target all the boats, from their transports as well as the big ships."

"What about their fighters?" Lon asked on the same channel.

"They don't seem to be moving to pursuit vectors," Felconi reported. "Still worried about our Shrikes, I guess, defending their ships. But the roundabout way we're going in, they'll be able to come after us even if they don't start for another nine minutes. It'll be almost as long before we can be sure we're out of reach of rockets launched from their transports."

"Keep your eyes open for anything, Art. I've got a hunch they have something extra to hit us with, and I don't know what."

Most of the shuttles were still more than forty miles

high when the New Spartans started to hit. A few enemy fighters had been diverted to the chase, but most of the counterstrike came from the transports—rockets and guns. Shuttle pilots maneuvered and used electronic counter-measures against the missiles. Crew chiefs rotated the high-speed cannons as a last line of defense against missiles.

Lon had started to sweat almost as soon as he heard that the enemy had targeted the landing force. He listened to the conversations among the shuttle pilots and the Di-rigenter ships, heard the first reports of hits. At times the talk was hard to follow because there were so many men talking at once, but it was clear that the Dirigenters were taking casualties . . . losing men by the hundreds. Each at-tack shuttle carried about one hundred men, soldiers and crew.

The surviving shuttles hit atmosphere at more than three times the speed of sound, braking at the last possible minute—reversing thrust, at full throttle—as the pilots ad-justed their angle of approach. By that time, Lon was certain that at least three shuttles had been lost, the chance of anyone aboard those landers surviving infinitesimal. The stress on the men aboard the shuttle was greater than it was on the craft. Lon and the rest were thrown against their safety harnesses. Lon felt blood rushing to his face, as if looking for any available exit. If there were no ex-plosion aboard, a Dirigenter shuttle might be salvageable after plunging headfirst into ground at a thousand miles per hour . . . after the remains of its unlucky passengers were hosed out.

When the shuttles leveled out, three hundred feet above ground level, they were traveling a thousand miles per hour, braking more gradually now, relying more on air brakes deployed from the fuselages than on reverse thrust from the engines, reducing the pressures on passengers and crew. Breathing became simpler. The few men who had suffered nosebleeds were able to tend to them. Up and down had a more normal feel.

"Lock and load," Lon ordered. He slipped a full magazine into his rifle, then ran the bolt to insert the first cartridge into the firing chamber. He took the rifle from its clips on the front of his seat and moved the safety to the "off" position, the selector switch to "automatic."

Art Felconi warned his passengers that thirty seconds remained until landing. They passed quickly. The shuttle's engines reached maximum again, reverse thrust, as it braked and slid into the final glide toward the LZ.

The shuttles of 7th Regiment had the safer landing zones, outside the ring of New Spartan mercenaries around Elysium's capital—a change in assignment Bob Hayley had ordered, to put his full regiment between the New Spartans and the Elysian capital. Only one of 7th's shuttles had been hit coming in. Fifteenth Regiment had lost two shuttles, and it lost three more as they crossed enemy lines to land inside the ring. The rockets the New Spartans launched were not the shoulder-fired variety, but longer and heavier, fired from at least six different locations on the ground—mobile rocket artillery.

Lon did not have time to realize that those rocket launchers were one item that the planning had not allowed for. By the time he heard a pilot comment on them, Lon's shuttle was skidding to a stop in an open field, in the middle of the shuttles of his 2nd Battalion. As soon as it came to rest, Lon shouted "Up and out!" on the radio channel that connected him to all his people in the command shuttle. At the same time, he slapped the quick release on his safety harness and lurched to his feet. By that time the two exits were swinging open. It took less than thirty seconds to get everyone out of the shuttle.

In less than another minute, all but two of the shuttles were back in the air, burning for orbit. Lon had intended to keep his command shuttle on the ground, but the crew remained aboard, ready to use its weapons or try to escape if enemy fighters targeted it. One shuttle from 1st Battalion's Delta Company had experienced trouble landing, being flipped on its side when it skidded and hit a rock. No one aboard was seriously injured, but they were slow getting out of the box. By that time, 2nd Battalion and regimental headquarters had moved into their initial defensive posture, ready for any enemy attack on the ground or from the air. Lon was receiving reports from his three battalion commanders. All had hit their designated LZs north of University City. The lost shuttle had carried half of 3rd Battalion's Bravo Company, including the company commander and one of its two lieutenants.

Reports from CIC indicated that the enemy fighters that had come after the Dirigenter shuttles had broken off the pursuit. Instead of going after the empty landers heading back toward their ships, the New Spartan fighters were racing to protect their own ships. One of the New Spartan transports had been severely damaged by rockets fired from Shrike II fighters. The attacking pilots reported that one of the transport's Nilssen generator pods had been blown off the ship, meaning that it would be unable to jump to Q-space.

Three minutes after he had left his shuttle, Lon contacted Colonel Hayley. "We're on the ground, in position exactly where we're supposed to be, Bob. I lost one shuttle and the men it was carrying, one other shuttle damaged on the ground, no one lost from it. We've set up our initial perimeter and are not, repeat *not,* under attack. My 3rd Battalion reports that they can hear gunfire at a distance, closer to University City, but they're not part of it."

"I expect they're hearing the Elysian Defense Force. The EDF was to mount diversionary attacks to cover our landing," Hayley replied. "You were lucky, losing only one shuttle. Five of mine didn't make it in. That's more than half a battalion. Between us we've lost three companies before the fight even started. I've lost two company commanders and Tony Falworth." Falworth, the newest lieutenant colonel in 15th Regiment, had commanded its 2nd Battalion. "But we're on the ground, also in position, and not under attack. I'm going to need fifteen or twenty minutes to get the holes in our deployment covered, then we'll proceed as planned, start moving against them while we bring in the heavy-weapons people." Hayley hesitated. "And your 4th Battalion to make up for some of the losses."

The plan was for the two regiments to move in concert, toward each other, attempting to pincer the New Spartans, fragment their line, cutting as many holes as possible through the center. Seven battalions were to move toward the line of New Spartans, meshing like the teeth of a zipper.

"If this goes as planned," Lon told Phip Steesen, "the New Spartans won't have many options, and none of them good. If they try to withdraw one way or the other, we've still got them cut in two and can take our time rolling up their lines. If they bring men in from the sections we're not attacking, they still don't have the people to even the odds, and they leave themselves open to an easy flanking movement."

"I don't think they're going to fall in with our script," Phip replied. "They've made it clear they're not going to just roll over for us. That rocket artillery, they might start aiming it at us anytime if it's dual-purpose stuff, and I'd bet a month's pay it is."

"They can't keep it hidden while it's firing," Lon said. CIC had located the batteries that had fired at the incoming shuttles, but those batteries had gone silent, cutting all electronic emissions, as soon as they had launched. Undoubtedly they had started moving as well. Fire and move, or fire while moving, then cut emissions to make tracking more difficult—standard maneuvers. "And once we get our heavy weapons on the ground, we'll negate their advantage."

"If we get our guns and rockets in soon enough," Phip said.

They didn't. Two minutes later, CIC broadcast a warning that enemy rocket launchers were active. Lon warned his people to stay down, but none of the rocket fire came toward 7th Regiment. A heavy bombardment was directed entirely at 15th, located between the New Spartans and University City.

"At least six launchers involved," Lon told his battalion commanders, relaying word from CIC on *Peregrine*. "Looks like four-rack self-propelled carriages, and they're popping missiles out as fast as they can. So far 15th is catching all the hell, but don't let anyone get careless. The enemy might switch targets any minute. Be ready for anything. We might have to go looking for them."

Heavy artillery fire, either rockets or shells, was something that Lon had never been on the wrong end of. The closest he had come was mortar fire, so long ago that he had nearly forgotten that the incident had ever happened. *Was it on Calypso or Aldrin?* he asked himself. It was inconsequential at the moment, but he could not avoid thinking about it. *Aldrin, I think. In between two colonies fighting to dominate the world.*

Men were scraping out shallow trenches and piling the dirt around the edges. They worked quickly, knowing that every inch down they could go improved their chances of survival if their turn did come at the receiving end of enemy artillery fire.

Lon kept glancing at the timeline on his helmet's head-up display, waiting to hear that the order had been given to launch the shuttles carrying the HW battalions and 4th Battalion of 7th Regiment. *I thought Bob was going to order them in right away,* he thought, but he waited, not wanting to interrupt Hayley while his people were under bombardment. *He won't forget.* But as the minutes ticked past, Lon grew more concerned. *The faster we get our guns on the ground, the faster we can go after those rocket launchers.*

"Colonel Nolan?" The voice was a shout in Lon's ears, someone almost screaming into his radio transmitter. "Colonel Nolan, are you there?"

"I'm here. Who is this?"

"Fal Jensen, XO of 15th. Our regimental headquarters took a direct hit from one of those rockets, maybe two.

We're still trying to get to the casualties. Colonel Hayley is down. I'm not getting any signal from his helmet, not even vital signs. I don't know if he's dead or alive, but it looks like you're in command now, at least until . . . whenever." Jensen's report came out in one long burst, ending when he had to gasp for air.

"Okay, Fal. Take it easy," Lon said. "I'll link to CIC and get things going again. You take care of 15th. Let your battalion commanders know what's going on. Find out what shape Bob Hayley and his people are in and get back to me when you know something definite. I'll keep you in the loop, fast as I get things sorted out."

Lon heard the sound of someone gulping air before Lieutenant Colonel Jensen replied. "Yes, sir. I've got my sergeant talking to the battalion commanders now. The regimental lead sergeant is down, too, with Bob Hayley. I don't know how many others. I think two rockets must have hit pretty close together. Knocked out a lot of helmet electronics. That's why I can't be sure who's dead and who's alive. We've been hit hard, Colonel."

"Listen, Fal, I'm going to postpone the start of our offensive, give you more time to get set, but we can't wait too long. Twenty minutes from now, we move as planned. Give the enemy something to think about besides plinking us where we sit."

"Yes, sir, twenty minutes," Jensen said. Lon squeezed his eyes shut. Jensen still did not sound as if he were totally in control of himself. That could be a major problem.

12

A deep breath, let out slowly. Lon opened his eyes and looked around, a quick scan. *I wasn't ready for this* could not be an excuse, only a confession. He had to deal with the situation he had inherited, whether he was ready or not. Lon passed along the new timetable to his battalion commanders, then linked through to CIC aboard *Peregrine*. Four Shrike II fighters had already been vectored in to try to knock out the enemy's rocket artillery. Lon gave the order for the rest of the troops—and the weapons of the two heavy-weapons battalions—to be launched as quickly as escorts could be assembled. The tanks and self-propelled artillery were already loaded aboard their shuttles on *Patton* and *Rommel*. Their crews, and the men of 7th Regiment's remaining battalion, were moving toward the shuttles. It would be fifty minutes before they were all on the ground, and the heavy-weapons people would need five minutes to get their vehicles out of the shuttles and ready for action.

Call it an hour before everyone's on the ground and ready, Lon thought. The heavy-weapons battalions would be landed west of University City, thirty miles from the nearest enemy units. At that distance, only the rocket batteries—ten vehicles in each battalion—would be able to take the enemy under fire immediately. The self-propelled howitzers needed to get within twenty miles, and the tanks' 125mm cannons had a maximum range of nine miles. Each heavy-weapons battalion had six 225mm howitzers and eight tanks mounting 125mm cannons.

Fourth Battalion of Lon's regiment would be put on the ground to link up with the regiment's right flank, not quite directly in front of the heavy weapons but close enough to be able to move south to keep the New Spartans from attempting to intercept the big guns on the ground.

By the time we get the rest of our people down, the fight should be fully involved, he thought. *The New Spartans should be too damned busy to be able to do anything about our heavy weapons.* That was the hope, anyway. The shuttles carrying the big guns were slower and less maneuverable—more vulnerable than the attack shuttles that brought in the infantry.

For ten minutes Lon was continuously on the radio, going from one channel to another, receiving reports and giving orders, occasionally involved in two conversations simultaneously. Then Lieutenant Colonel Jensen came back on line.

"Colonel Hayley is alive," Jensen reported, sounding only marginally more in control than he had ten minutes earlier. "But the medtechs aren't sure he's going to make it, even though they're putting him in a trauma tube right now. If he *does* survive, he'll be out of action for weeks, maybe months. On top of everything else, he has massive head trauma that's going to need extensive time for regeneration of brain tissue."

"Get him and the rest of your most seriously wounded men ready for evacuation to *Peregrine,*" Lon said. "Use whatever shuttle you can get them aboard, fast. We've got Shrikes coming in to target the enemy rocket artillery, and our best bet is to get the shuttle off while you've got that cover. Understand?"

"Yes," Jensen said. "We'll move the colonel as soon as he's in the portable trauma tube. As many of the others as we can manage, too. How long do we have until the Shrikes get here?"

"Three minutes."

"We can't be ready that fast."

"I know, Fal, but the Shrikes will stay on station as

long as they can, until they run short on munitions. Get that shuttle loaded and ready for takeoff as quickly as you can. Try to have them ready before we launch our attack." Lon glanced at his timeline. "That leaves just over eight minutes."

"We'll manage somehow," Fal said.

"I know you will, Fal. Keep this channel open for me. Once we start hitting the enemy, we'll need to stay in touch. One more thing. Who's your second-in-command?"

Jensen hesitated several seconds before he replied. "I guess that would be Cooper McBride of our 1st Battalion. He's the senior battalion commander."

"Make sure he knows he's your backup, and have him contact Tefford Ives directly to make sure we've got two liaison channels operating. You'll have to patch together a staff as best you can, once you know who you have left."

After ending the conversation with Jensen, Lon had a few seconds of silence on his radio, a chance to take another look around to double-check the deployment of his headquarters detachment. Men who were clerks or drivers in garrison manned their rifles with every bit of competence that the men in the line companies possessed. In the Corps, everyone was a rifleman *first*. A secondary perimeter had been established around Lon. Seventh Regiment had moved out of the open field where they had landed, under the cover of trees and wild shrubbery, improving their positions as the terrain permitted.

What an unholy mess, Lon thought. *More than six percent casualties before we get our first licks in.* Six shuttles meant three companies, six hundred men, plus the casualties on the ground from the enemy bombardment. *There'll be hard questions to answer when we get home, even if we don't lose another man in the campaign.* And *that* was an unlikely possibility.

"It's not working out the way we thought it would," Phip Steesen said on a private channel to Lon. They were forty yards apart, in a standard dispersal pattern. There wasn't anyone above the rank of corporal within ten yards of Lon except for his aide and driver, Sergeants Howell and Dorcetti.

"You've been reading my mind again," Lon replied, no trace of humor in his voice. "We thought we'd come in, show them we had them outnumbered, outgunned, and outclassed, and they'd be ready to cut their losses and run. I haven't heard an offer to surrender and leave coming from the New Spartans yet."

"I think we're in for the fight of our lives," Phip said. "All that stuff Jenny told me about the economics of this, why neither side can afford to lose."

"Yeah, I remember. We ready to move out?"

"I've talked with all the battalion lead sergeants. We're ready. The consensus is that it's time to start getting a little payback. Can't say that I have any argument with that."

"Don't let it get anyone careless. Times like this are when it's most necessary to remember that we're professionals. Four minutes, Phip. Get back to the lead sergeants. Make sure they keep a lid on their people."

"I warned 'em all before, Lon. I'll do it again, too," Phip added before Lon could tell him to.

There were last-minute reports from CIC, Lieutenant Colonel Jensen, and the battalion commanders in 7th Regiment. Lon set up a command conference channel with the battalion commanders in both regiments. The order to begin the offensive would go directly to each unit. Seven battalions would attack simultaneously. There would be little air cover. The Shrikes that had come in to hunt the rocket artillery might be able to make quick strafing passes on enemy infantry positions, but they would have to burn for orbit again very soon, to replace the Shrike IIs that would be escorting the remainder of the Dirigenter force in. The ships could not be left without protection, not even briefly, as long as the New Spartans still had capital ships and aerospace fighters to threaten them.

Two minutes. Lon glanced to his left, in the general direction of 1st Battalion's positions, though it was too far away for him to see anyone there. That was where Junior was, with the two platoons he led—on the left flank, with no friendly troops to guard it. The units of the EDF weren't all that close. Their job was to harass the sections of the New Spartan line that were not directly confronted by Dirigenters, to keep them from reinforcing the units caught in the middle. Any serious coordination with the local forces would have to wait until after this first battle was fought. Chancellor Berlino and his companions were still aboard *Peregrine*. They weren't scheduled to land until the Dirigenters could make that safe.

Will we both make it through the day? Lon wondered, still thinking about Junior. Hidden deeper in his mind, Lon was almost unaware of *What would I tell his mother?* nagging at his subconscious defenses. He squeezed his eyes shut, trying to force his thoughts away from that unpleasant prospect. *I can't allow myself to be distracted, not now.*

One minute. Time for a last hurried call to CIC for the latest updates. One of the enemy artillery units had—apparently—been hit by the Shrike IIs and put out of commission. The shuttles carrying the three remaining battalions of the strike force were on their way in and would soon be out of reach of the weapons aboard the New Spartan transports.

Time. . . .

Lon watched the last seconds tick off, then gave the command. "Move out." Only right in front of his own position was he able to see any movement directly. The men of 2nd Battalion got up and started moving forward. For the first half mile—barring any surprises—they would move forward in three staggered skirmish lines, closing in as quickly as they could. Then, once they were in range of rifle fire from the New Spartans, the troops would switch to fire and maneuver tactics. That would be slower.

How much slower would depend on the level of enemy resistance. With seasoned mercenaries on the other side, it might be very slow indeed. The corridors of advance for the battalions of the regiments on either side had been carefully calculated to minimize the chances for friendly-fire casualties.

Watch out for mines and booby traps, Lon thought, as if he were instructing his men. *Watch for enemy electronics, not just helmets but also snoops. Remember that they're good, damned good. We've got no room for mistakes.*

"Phip, we'll let the advance move three hundred yards, then move my command post to just this side of that creek out there, behind that patch of heavy undergrowth. We'll set up there, close enough to see some of what goes on, far enough back that we shouldn't have to scramble to get out of the way."

"Right," Phip replied. "I had already marked that spot. There's a rock outcropping to give us a little protection from stray shots, too well concealed by the trees for there to be much chance the enemy registered it for their artillery."

Both of them could hear gunfire, just starting. At first there were just scattered shots from three or four points, quickly answered by Dirigenters, but within thirty seconds the firing became general. "They didn't wait for us to come to them," Lon noted, still with a channel open to Phip. "We sure didn't move a half mile before the action started."

"Suits me," Phip said. "The sooner we start, the sooner we can make a finish of it."

That's easy to say when we're this far away from it, Lon thought. He *knew* he was where he belonged, out of immediate danger, in position to direct the entire fight, but he couldn't banish a nagging guilt at being relatively safe while sending thousands of men into imminent peril, knowing that some of them would not live through the engagement. It wasn't *just* that his only son was one of the men in danger. He had felt this way before, long before Junior joined the Corps.

Lon scanned the various command frequencies, eavesdropping on reports from company commanders to their battalion commanders, even from platoon leaders to their captains. The New Spartans had used the time well, forming lines facing in both directions, closing the gap on either side, preparing what defensive protection they could. The shuttle carrying Colonel Hayley and two dozen other wounded men from 15th Regiment got off the ground, trailed by the Shrike IIs that had attacked the New Spartan rocket artillery.

"Been a long time since we fought a pitched battle this soon after grounding," Phip commented in one of the rare silences on the radio. "Offhand, I can't remember ever fighting this soon."

Once or twice, Lon thought, but he remained silent, switching channels again and again, stopping just long enough to catch what he could. Offhand, *he* couldn't remember where or when those instances might have been either. There had been too many fights on too many worlds . . . and far too many deaths.

"I make it three hundred yards 2nd Battalion has moved," Phip said a moment later. "A long way short of the half mile we hoped. They've dropped, using fire and maneuver now." The advance slowed dramatically, one platoon of each company moving forward a few yards while the rest laid down covering fire. The next platoon would leapfrog them, and the next, and. . . .

"Right, Phip. Let's get our people moving," Lon said. He waited until the order had been passed, then got up and starting moving toward the location he and Phip had chosen for their next sanctum. The distance was only about two hundred yards, but before Lon had run half that distance, he felt as if he had run a mile. Lon paused for no more than twenty seconds, sucking in a couple of deep breaths. His chest was heaving as he gasped for air. He was a little light-headed. For an instant his vision blurred, then cleared after he blinked several times, quickly, and shook his head.

This is ridiculous, he thought. *I know damn well I'm not this far out of shape.* He shook his head again and trotted the rest of the distance, moving more slowly now. At least there was no incoming fire to worry about. Yet.

The rock outcropping that he had spotted was nowhere more than eight feet higher than the ground just north of it, rising abruptly on the left and dwindling away gradually on the right. On the far side, the south, the rock fell sharply into the edge of a shallow, narrow creek—five feet wide and two feet deep—that meandered across the entire 2nd Battalion front. Much of the stone was covered with a mosslike growth. Vines climbed up over the top from the creek on the far side. A number of bushes hemmed the rock in on either side.

Lon did not simply collapse against the rock and slide to the ground, though the notion tempted him until his breathing got back to something approaching normal. He remained on his feet, protected by the rock, looking around to see that all of the men who were with his headquarters detachment made it to their new positions. Without instruction, they formed their new perimeter and started scooping out slit trenches, working quickly in moist soil, taking advantage of the terrain to give themselves what protection was available.

Before Lon had a chance to say anything, he heard two explosions, separated by five seconds or less, well separated, almost blanketing other explosions farther away.

"They've got that rocket artillery working again," Phip said on their private channel. "Most of it's still going against 15th, but that's two aimed toward our people, near both ends of the line, in 1st and 3rd Battalions."

Junior? screamed in Lon's head like the stab of a severe headache, but what he said was, "Get reports on casualties when you can, Phip." His voice sounded almost calm.

What do we do next? Lon asked himself. He wasn't too

disconcerted by the fact that the preliminary plan of attack had proven inadequate, obsolete almost before it could be begun. *Once we get on the ground, we start with a blank page.* It was all too frequently like that. Few enemies were considerate enough to do exactly what the Dirigenters hoped they would do.

Lon's musings were interrupted by a call from Fal Jensen. "We've got to do something about those rockets," Jensen said. "They've got us zeroed in. We're taking casualties from those and from the enemy on the ground in front of us." There was no hint of panic in Jensen's voice now, but there was tension.

"Keep pushing forward, Fal. Get close to the New Spartans on the ground and they'll have to quit firing rockets at you. It's going to be at least twenty minutes before the next flight of Shrikes can get in, longer than that before we get our heavy weapons on the ground and out of the box. We've still got to deal with the enemy on the ground between us."

"Are we getting any help from the Elysians?" Jensen asked.

"Very little so far, but they weren't supposed to be doing much more than harass the enemy away from our positions."

"If we've got any liaison, the more they can do right now, the better off we're going to be, Lon."

You know what liaison we've got, Lon thought. Jensen should know better than anyone. He had been aboard *Peregrine,* privy to the discussions between Bob Hayley and Chancellor Berlino.

"Just as soon as I get a chance, I'll put a call through to Berlino," Lon said. "But don't expect much, not soon. Even if they have forces available, it's going to take time to get them in position to act. We've got to sort out this mess on our own."

"I was afraid you were going to say that," Jensen said before signing off.

If he doesn't pull himself together, he's going to be no

help at all, Lon thought, frowning in the privacy of his helmet. *Maybe he's spent too many years in staff jobs, not enough on the line.* Lon had known Jensen, casually, for years, as he knew all the senior officers in the Corps. But he did not know him well, and what he had heard so far did not give him great confidence. *I'm going to have to find out who else is left over there, just in case,* he thought. But, like so much else, that would have to wait until the immediate situation was in hand.

"Lon." Phip waited for Lon to acknowledge the call before he continued. "I've been checking with the noncoms up front. I think we underestimated the number of New Spartans here, maybe by fifty percent. They must not have left all their transports in orbit. Maybe some of them had to make two trips to get everyone here. There could be as many as eight thousand of them on the ground between us and 15th Regiment. We sure as hell don't have them outnumbered two to one. Even when we get the rest of our people down here, the numbers won't be much better than even."

"The way they've hit us so far, I can't say that surprises me," Lon said. "How good are the estimates you're getting?"

"I wouldn't bet against them no matter what odds you offered," Phip said. "I've sorted through the usual exaggeration, cross-checked, everything. One other thing. One of Junior's platoon sergeants says the New Spartans do have those needle guns we heard about, at least a few. Says they can turn a tree to mulch in ten seconds, but the effective range doesn't seem to be much past a hundred yards."

"We get the chance, I'd like a look at one of them, and a little ammo—something to take home and let the R&D people play with," Lon said. "But I don't want anyone taking foolish chances to get it."

"I already passed the word, Lon," Phip said.

• • •

Lon sat with his back against the rock outcropping and took out his mapboard, a specialized complink that unfolded for use in the field. He put as much of the area around University City on the screen as he could to get a feel for the battle that was developing. The New Spartans were not being shy about using active electronics. There were so many blips that they blended into smudged lines—red for the enemy, blue for the Dirigenters, yellow for the few members of the Elysian Defense Force who were involved in the fight.

I hope someone on Peregrine *is going through this, trying to get a solid estimate of enemy numbers,* Lon thought. By increasing the magnification and going through the area one small grid at a time it would be possible to tell exactly how many enemy soldiers were using helmet electronics at any given time. *Something we can report back to Dirigent on with reasonable assurance.* As soon as possible, he was going to have to send an MR out, report to the Council of Regiments on what they had found and what had happened—including the fact that Bob Hayley was out of action for at least the next several weeks . . . if he survived. *I might not even know that for another hour or more,* Lon thought, glancing at the timeline on his visor display. *I guess I need to wait until I get something from the medtechs about Bob, if he's going to survive.*

He looked up from the mapboard. *And I'm going to have to make a recommendation on whether or not we need another regiment to reinforce us.* His immediate impulse was to say, *Yes, we need help,* but it was too soon to make that call, and—in any case—it would be at least a month before help could arrive.

By then it might be far too late.

13

"**We're at a** stalemate here, Lon," Lieutenant Colonel Vel Osterman, CO of 2nd Battalion of the 7th, reported. "The New Spartans are dug in. We can't break through their lines without taking unacceptable levels of casualties, and I'm not sure we could do it even if we weren't worried about losses."

"Have your men dig in as best they can until we get the situation sorted out, Vel," Lon said. Less than an hour and a half had passed since the Dirigenters had landed. So much had happened so quickly that it seemed impossible. "I'm getting the same kind of reports from other units. For the moment, I'm more concerned with holding what we've got and keeping the New Spartans contained until we can bring our full force to bear.

"Our 4th Battalion and all the heavy weapons will be down in a few minutes. I'll put the rocket batteries to work as soon as they're out of the box, the long guns should join in about fifteen minutes later, and the tanks will head full tilt toward the enemy, along with our 4th Battalion. I just got off a link to Chancellor Berlino. He's going to see if more of the Elysian Defense Force can move against the New Spartans, but that's going to take time, probably several hours."

"I hope we can shake something loose sooner than that," Osterman said. "Anyway, so far the New Spartans haven't shown any inclination to try to push us back. They're in improved positions, dug in well. They've had three days to get ready for us. That's part of the problem."

"We get all our people down, it'll be more *their* problem than ours," Lon said. "They're geared toward mobile operations, the same as we are. Static defensive positions rob them of a good part of their strength. As long as we're on the outside with freedom of movement, the advantage is still ours."

"We'll hold on," Osterman said.

Well, I've got him convinced, Lon thought. *Now, if I can just convince myself. The trouble is, we can't use our mobility yet, not without unpinning the New Spartans in the process.*

The heavy-weapons battalions would come in first. Lon's final battalion would land a few minutes later. There would be four Shrike IIs in for those few minutes as well, to protect the shuttles and make a few passes at the New Spartan defenses. With a little luck they might knock out one or two more of the enemy's rocket artillery launchers.

We've had one break. The New Spartans haven't been able to bring any fighters down to hassle us, Lon thought, glancing skyward. He had received several updates on the continuing struggle in orbit. Both sides were moving ships, trying to stay out of each other's way, taking stabs at the other as best they could. The one New Spartan transport that had been damaged was moving farther from Elysium, under only partial power. Since it would be unable to jump to Q-space, it could only hope to escape further damage—or destruction—by putting as much normal space between it and danger as possible.

Don't let this settle into a long-term static front, Lon reminded himself. *The first side to get truly mobile should have the advantage.* He had already decided how he wanted to use his 4th Battalion and the heavy-weapons units. The artillery—howitzer and rocket—would take the enemy under fire as quickly as possible. Lon would aim the tanks and his 4th Battalion at the enemy line, just south of where the units already in place faced each other.

Punch a hole in the line and turn up the middle, like closing a zipper. It sounded *good.*

The last three Dirigenter battalions made it safely to the ground. No shuttles or men were lost. The New Spartans launched rockets toward the LZs, but by the time those rockets arrived, the men and vehicles were out and the shuttles were back in the air, burning for orbit. Separately, one shuttle was coming in with equipment to get the lander that had tipped over upright. Those shuttles could then both be used to evacuate wounded.

That was the good news. The bad news was that the opposing fleets had moved far enough apart that the New Spartans had aerospace fighters heading in to provide close air support for their troops. And they would arrive a couple of minutes ahead of the Shrike II fighters that *Agamemnon* and *Odysseus* were dispatching to counter them. Lon's rocket artillery and the shoulder-launched surface-to-air missiles would have to hold the enemy fighters off until help arrived.

"Well, Colonel, we've got holes to flop in at least," Jeremy Howell said, lifting his helmet visor partway so he wouldn't need to use his radio to talk with Lon. Howell and two privates from Lon's security squad had been "fixing up" the area behind the rock outcropping for Lon's command post—mostly digging slit trenches, piling the dirt up around them.

"Thanks, Jerry," Lon said, looking around and nodding. "Let's hope we don't need it for long." Everyone was on the ground. The Dirigenter rocket artillery had joined the fray. In another three or four minutes the howitzers would be in range. It would take nearly an hour before the tanks could join in, and after that it would only be a few minutes before the tanks and 7th Regiment's 4th Battalion would hit the enemy line.

"I don't know about you, Colonel, but I'd feel better if we could get *under* this rock," Howell said. "Those rockets are more'n I bargained for. This is beginning to look like one of those old wars from Earth, whole armies on both sides."

"It's not that big, Jerry, but I know what you mean. This is the biggest fracas I've seen." *Too big,* he thought. *A battle this size isn't always decided by which side has the better leader. It's the men up front, junior officers, noncoms, and men in the ranks who can make the difference.* But it was the commander who would take the blame for any defeat, or for losing too many men in a victory. *Too many ways to lose, not nearly enough ways to win,* Lon thought, shaking his head.

"We lost too many men coming in, Jerry," Lon said. "Nothing can make up for that." There had been *years* in which the entire Corps had not suffered as many contract deaths as 7th and 15th Regiments had taken during the initial landings. Even a resounding victory would not balance the books. Almost as bad—the addition of insult to injury—it would probably be impossible to return the bodies of most of those dead to Dirigent. The shuttles that were blown apart in space would leave few remains to recover.

"This is Jensen." Lon held a hand up to keep Howell from replying so he could concentrate on the radio call.

"Go ahead, Fal," Lon said.

"The New Spartans are attempting to break through my lines on the left, toward University City. I guess they've been told about our new landings. I'm not sure we're going to be able to hold them. If I move more men in front of this thrust, it'll just open the way for a breakthrough somewhere else."

"Do what you can, Fal," Lon said, relieved that Jensen's voice sounded firmer now, more under control. Lon scrolled the view on his mapboard to show the center of this newest fighting. "We don't want to let them into the city. That'll make it a lot harder to take care of them, and we risk friendly civilian casualties. Don't forget, they're going to have fighter cover. Those aircraft will be on station in less than two minutes now."

"We're doing what we can, Lon. Can you redirect some of our heavy-weapons fire into the van of this thrust?"

"You've got it. I'll switch over and give the order now. The self-propelled howitzers should be just coming in range. We'll give you as much help as we can."

Even at a distance, the rumble of the artillery shells as they exploded was unmistakable, the sound of thunder but far too regular for nature. For a few minutes Lon kept his mapboard open, watching the pattern of explosions on a visual overlay. The targeting, using data fed from CIC and directly from 15th Regiment, was deadly accurate, hitting the point of the wedge that the New Spartans were trying to push through 15th Regiment's line. At first the New Spartans kept pushing forward, but soon the advance stalled and, finally, they pulled back into the positions they had held before.

"We'll keep an eye on them, Fal," Lon said when he called Jensen back. "For now, I'm going to redirect our fire to support our attempt to roll them up. Our heavy weapons have to do some fancy moving, staying out of the way of the enemy's air cover."

The New Spartans had sent in six aerospace fighters, Javelins. One was brought down by 15th Regiment's rocket artillery on its initial approach, before it had a chance to fire any of its own munitions. A second Javelin was blown out of the sky by a shoulder-fired rocket launched from 7th Regiment's 4th Battalion. After that, the enemy fighters tried to stay above ten thousand feet, to give them a chance to outrun anything else fired at them from the ground, which limited their effectiveness. And then the Shrike IIs were on them, and the aerial fight moved away from the ground forces, drifting quickly to the east.

I feel so damned useless, Lon thought as the last aircraft moved beyond University City. *I'm not contributing anything.* He had spent too many years fighting on the front lines, in direct contact with the enemy of the moment.

This doesn't feel as real as the arcade games Junior used to spend hours playing.

Reports and requests kept coming in. Questions and replies went out. Lon switched among more than a dozen radio channels, talking with others and trying to plot what he learned against what his mapboard showed him. CIC tried to coordinate as much of the raw data as it could for him. His own staff put together individual pieces of it.

He tried to monitor his 4th Battalion's attack on the New Spartan line most closely. As soon as they managed a breakthrough, *if* they did, things would heat up all along the lines. Lon had everyone alerted to put as much pressure on the enemy as possible. "Don't let them reinforce their people in front of 4th Battalion," Lon told all of the other line battalion commanders. "As soon as the tanks and 4th turn the corner, we're going to hit them with everything we've got, all along the line, try to end this quickly."

Even while planning for that, Lon kept asking himself, *What will the enemy do to stop us? They must have some plan, some ace still up their sleeve. It can't be this easy, not against pros.*

The answer came just as Lieutenant Colonel Parker Watson was reporting that 4th Battalion had cracked the enemy line and was starting to feed men to the left, while leaving one company in place to keep the New Spartans from hitting their flank from the south. Lon's mapboard showed the sudden appearance of more enemy electronics, well to the north of 7th Regiment—*behind* them. Twenty seconds later, CIC reported that a considerable number of rockets had been launched from the newly revealed enemy position.

"Everyone down!" Lon said on the channel that connected him to all his battalion and company commanders. "Incoming!" He took what cover he could himself, scanning the headquarters area on his way down to make certain that everyone else also was taking cover.

The distance was not extreme. The first enemy rockets

started to fall within seconds after the warning. The New Spartans had obviously pinpointed the location of virtually all the Dirigenter infantry units. Rockets were fired as quickly as launchers could be reloaded. The New Spartan batteries that had been identified earlier also joined in. As many as a dozen enemy rockets at a time might be in the air.

For three minutes, the rocket fire was primarily New Spartan. The Dirigenter units had to move before they could start firing back—counterbattery fire, targeting the enemy launchers while trying to avoid being targeted themselves. As the artillery units dueled, the New Spartan infantry gained a breather, and Parker Watson's battalion had to dig in where they were instead of starting to roll up the enemy line.

At the same time, the New Spartans did move. Those trapped between 7th and 15th Regiments slid clockwise around the semicircle, running the gauntlet. The New Spartans in the southwestern portion of the line surrounding University City moved toward the Elysian capital, pushing aside two companies of the local defense force that were rushing to block them.

As soon as Lon received those reports, he called Watson. "Parker, you're going to have to turn your battalion the other way. I want you to overtake the New Spartans before they get into the city, if you can; at least don't give them a chance to set up solid defensive positions. Forget about trying to close the zipper. The New Spartans there are moving away from you. As soon as I can get a few Shrikes in, I'll set them against the enemy van in front of you, to slow them down. Keep 7th Regiment's tanks with you. I'm going to direct 15th Regiment's tanks across the arc to try to hit the New Spartans' main force."

Watson's acknowledgment was lost in the blast of an enemy rocket that impacted eighty yards from Lon. Lon felt the ground shake violently. Rock, dirt, and other debris rained down on him for nearly a minute following the blast. The ringing in his ears was even slower to fade.

When he was able to lift his head past the ridge of dirt surrounding his trench, he saw that many of the trees that had sheltered regimental headquarters had been broken or knocked over.

It looks like a war zone at last, seemed to echo through Lon's head. Then casualty reports started to come in.

From both ends of the semicircle the New Spartans moved toward University City. Parker Watson's men weren't able to stop the units moving from the western flank of their initial line, and those on the eastern flank had no opposition at all. But the New Spartans who had been on the northern arc of the perimeter had to move east, away from the city; that meant about 60 percent of their strength *. . . their known strength,* Lon reminded himself—*known strength north of the River Styx.* CIC was no longer certain how many men the New Spartans might have south of the river. The bridges across it had been blown, cutting them off from the main fight. CIC was also no longer certain what the total number of New Spartans on the world might be. The exposure of more rocket artillery units had been a complete surprise. There might be significantly more infantrymen as well.

"There's a good chance they're going to be short on rockets," Lon said on a conference call that included Colonel Jensen and battalion commanders from both regiments. "They've used one hell of a lot, and their supplies can't be infinite. If we can keep them from resupplying the rocket batteries, we'll save ourselves a lot of grief later on. *Agamemnon* and *Odysseus* are on alert for that, to intercept any enemy shuttles. I don't know if the New Spartans have any resupply setup like ours, but even if they do, I doubt that it's set up to handle anything as large as rockets for those launchers." The resupply rockets the Dirigenters used were not identical to those Lon's company had tested more than twenty years before, but they were direct descendants. These rockets could be launched by shuttle, Shrike, or directly from a ship in orbit, with the final stage of their descent guided by a man on the ground. A trained operator could soft-land a rocket within ten feet of a mark, close enough to retrieve its cargo—up to five thousand rounds of rifle ammunition or two cases of rocket-propelled grenades—controlling the landing through his helmet radio. Everyone received some training in the operation, and at least two men in every line squad drilled enough to be considered experts.

"We don't know how many they stockpiled before we got here," Tefford Ives pointed out. "They might have more rockets for their artillery than we do, on the ground."

"Possible, but unless they knew we were coming it wouldn't have made much sense, and they didn't put a lot of shuttles on the ground after we appeared in-system," Vel Osterman said.

"We can't underestimate the possibility," Fal Jensen said. "They had the launchers on the ground. They had to plan for enough firepower to handle the armor and artillery the Elysians have. If the New Spartans are anywhere near as thorough as we are, they would have included enough and to spare for that."

"Whatever," Lon said. "CIC says they've used a hundred rockets this morning, and the two launchers we're sure we've destroyed might each have had eight to ten left onboard. The estimate is that each of their launchers can carry two dozen, plus whatever their attendant supply trucks carry."

"Either way, it could be difficult for either of us to resupply our heavy weapons," Ives said. "They're sure to go after our shuttles, and I assume we'll go after any they launch."

"Both of us have to use our fighters to defend our ships, ahead of anything else," Lon said. "That gives both sides room to maneuver, to get things in and out. Maybe we have a slight advantage, since our shuttles are armed and theirs aren't. Whatever the situation, we'll deal with it.

"Right now, there's one other thing. I'm going to send

an MR to Dirigent within the next hour or so. Link your reports through to CIC on *Peregrine,* anything that needs to go out, casualties and operational status, and any personal mail that might have collected." Lon shrugged. "There shouldn't be much of that, since we sent mail back just ahead of the landing.

"Fal, I'll give them the news on Colonel Hayley, that he's going to need extensive time for regeneration and rehabilitation, that I've taken over command of the contract, and that you have assumed command of 15th Regiment. As soon as I finish my report, the MR will be launched, so don't dally. Get your men reorganized—fed if there's time. Figure we'll be moving in an hour or so. I'll give you detailed deployments shortly, but we're going to have to operate in two main sections again now that the New Spartans have split up. We have to deal with the units moving into University City and those we forced out into the wild."

An hour, Lon thought after he had acknowledgments from all the others. *I have to finish my report on what's happened so far. And I have to decide whether or not to ask for another regiment. The* easy *decision would be to opt for requesting help. But reinforcement will require a month. We'd still have to hold out that long.* Lon shook his head. He worried over the question until that was the only item left to add to his report, taking every minute he could before he dictated the last sentences. Asking for reinforcement if it wasn't absolutely necessary would be almost as bad as not asking for it if it was. *Almost.*

"It is a close call. We have really not been able to fully assess the situation yet, or to determine exactly how many men the New Spartans have deployed on Elysium. Reinforcement might be necessary, it is perhaps even extremely likely, but I think I should take more time before making that decision. I would suggest alerting the troops for possible deployment, subject to my next report. I will try to get that out within the next forty-eight to seventy-two hours."

Not very satisfactory, Lon thought, *putting off the decision that way. Wishy-washy.* But he didn't change it. *Peregrine* launched the message rocket two minutes later.

14

The senior medical officer of 15th Regiment had been killed by the rocket that had wounded Colonel Hayley. Six other men had been killed by the same explosion. The only thing that had saved Hayley was that a portable trauma tube had been close and had—somehow—avoided serious damage. The medtech who had treated the colonel told Lon that it had been a miracle that Hayley had survived. "I don't think I'm exaggerating when I say that if we'd been five seconds slower getting him into the tube he wouldn't have made it. I didn't think he was going to make it as it was." Listening to the detailed listing of Hayley's injuries had been almost enough to make Lon physically ill.

The back of Bob Hayley's head had been literally blown off, along with a significant percentage of his brain. That was the injury that mattered. The fractures and shrapnel penetrations were minor by comparison. Hayley would require three weeks for the physical regeneration of lost brain tissue and the missing section of his skull, most of that time sealed in a trauma tube. After that there would be months of rehabilitation. The SMO on the flagship said that Hayley would have to learn how to walk and talk again, and the odds were strong that he would never regain much memory of his life before the injury. "I don't think there's one chance in a million he'll be able to continue in the Corps," the ship's SMO said. "But he will survive."

It was some hours later before Lon thought, *There goes*

the odds-on favorite for election to General . . . not that we were likely to make it home in time for him to get it this year. He shook his head. *Even if we were going to make it home in time, the Council wouldn't give it to him this year, not after we lost so many men making our landing here. There'd have to be a board of inquiry first.* Even if a board cleared him of misjudgment, losing so many men would remain a mark against Hayley and might keep him from ever becoming General.

By noon, the fighting had decreased to almost nothing. Parker Watson's battalion, 4th of the 7th, was skirmishing with the enemy on the outskirts of University City. Vel Osterman's battalion, 2nd of the 7th, was moving toward the enemy rocket artillery north of the city. Fal Jensen was moving 15th Regiment east to stay between the bulk of the New Spartan forces and the Elysian capital. His 4th Battalion was angling toward the southeast, looking to engage the enemy troops who had moved toward the capital on that end of the perimeter.

Lon was moving with his remaining two line battalions—closer to University City, staying on the north, ready to move whichever way necessary, depending on how the situation developed through the next hours . . . or days. He wanted to be able to move into the capital to prevent the two elements of the New Spartan force from linking up inside the metropolitan area. The rocket and howitzer batteries of both heavy-weapons battalions were moving closer to Lon's 1st and 3rd Battalions. The tanks were moving to reinforce both regiments' 4th Battalions on the edges of University City.

Chancellor Berlino and his companions had just landed, without incident, near Lon's position. Overhead, the two fleets were moving farther apart, and higher, away from Elysium. But not *too* much higher. Both wanted to stay close enough to use their fighters to support operations on the ground.

Berlino and the two other Elysian cabinet ministers were escorted to Lon's command post by two platoons from 7th's 3rd Battalion. The chancellor appeared quite shaken, his eyes wide, constantly moving, looking around as if he feared attack at every step. Thomas Beoch, the minister for external affairs, and Flora Chiou, the treasurer, simply looked exhausted.

"I can't offer you much hospitality," Lon said. "Sorry. We thought it safer to bring you in well outside the city. Too much chance that the New Spartans would shoot the shuttle down. They have at least a battalion of troops near your main spaceport. They might control it. They're certainly close enough to shoot down any shuttle trying to land there. Make yourselves as comfortable as you can. Sitting on the ground might not look dignified, but that's all we have."

"I'm not too proud to sit on the grass," Chiou said. Beoch simply dropped to the ground next to her. Berlino was slower to sit, but that seemed to be just because of his nervousness.

"I've been following the reports from your CIC," Berlino said when he finally did sit. "Up until we got off the shuttle. Any significant change, Colonel?"

Lon shook his head. "I wish I could say that there is, Chancellor, but there isn't. As soon as we can do so safely, we'll get you into the city, back to your colleagues and families. It appears that, so far, the New Spartans aren't trying to fully occupy the capital. There aren't enough of them on that side to manage, not with most of your defense force still active and nearby. Right now we're not sure if they're just trying to get as far from us as they can or if they hope to fortify sections of the city to try to hold against us."

Berlino nodded slowly. "I was able to follow that much. How do you intend to proceed?"

"We have three immediate goals on the ground," Lon said. "We want to neutralize—destroy—their artillery. We need to isolate the troops they have inside University City. And we want to keep those troops and their main force from reuniting, mostly by keeping the main force away from the capital. The artillery and the enemy force inside the city will be our priorities. After that we can worry about their main force. As long as they're away from the urban areas, they're the minor threat, unable to cause major difficulties for your people. We can take our time with them."

"I agree," Berlino said. "Our first concern has to be the enemy force inside University City. Is it possible that they will try to use our civilian populace as . . . hostages?"

"Possible but not probable," Lon said. "I doubt that the New Spartans are much more likely to do that than we would be, and Dirigenters would absolutely not use unarmed civilians as hostages or shields. But you can assume that the New Spartans will deal harshly, and summarily, with anyone they catch or strongly suspect of actively operating against them. Combatant civilians forfeit any special consideration."

"Our people will resist, strongly," Chiou said, lifting her head for the first time. She had been staring at the ground in front of her. "We cherish our independence, and there was intense anger over the invasion from the start. Many of our people will seize any opportunity to strike at the invaders."

"I agree," Berlino said. "There will certainly be acts of resistance, which means that the sooner we can . . . evict the invaders from the city, the fewer of our people are likely to pay the . . . ultimate price."

"We're doing our best to keep the enemy too busy to worry much about civilians, Chancellor," Lon said. "But we're limited, too, if we want to avoid civilian casualties and excessive damage to buildings and so forth. And we do want to avoid those."

"We can repair or replace buildings, Colonel," Berlino said.

"People aren't so easy to replace," Lon said. "We hate to see lives wasted—civilians, our own, even those of our enemies. We'll do what we have to do, Chancellor, but as economically as possible."

"Speaking of economics, Colonel," Berlino said, "I will authorize bringing in a third regiment if you think it's needed. And another fighting ship with its aircraft."

"I haven't decided yet, Chancellor," Lon said. "I warned Dirigent that it is possible, but . . ." He shook his head.

"But what, Colonel?"

"You know the limits of interstellar travel, Chancellor. It will take a month to get reinforcements in. And if we don't have enough people here now to do the job, there might not be enough of us left in a month to be an effective fighting force. One regiment might not be enough to do more than cover an evacuation of survivors, and that wouldn't do your people any good. I know we made provisions in the contract for reinforcement, but the scenario involved was if we arrived and knew right away that the New Spartans had brought in more men, we would have waited in space for our reinforcements, not landed the way we did. The only way I could be . . . fairly certain of maintaining an effective force for a month would be to simply pull out into the wilds, away from the enemy, to wait for reinforcements. That would give the New Spartans a month to do . . . whatever they want to your cities and people. We don't even have a realistic option of returning to our ships to wait. A withdrawal like that might cost another six hundred men, the way the landing did, or more."

"Besides, if you pulled away from the enemy, disengaged," Chiou said, "I doubt that the New Spartans would simply sit around and wait for the next act. We can't count on their continued willingness to simply lay siege to University City."

"There is that," Lon conceded. "We've joined the fight. There's no way to back off." *No honorable way,* he thought. *No way that does not concede victory to the New Spartans and relegate us to second-best status.*

· · ·

In the next hour, Lon moved his command post again, this time to the ruins of a farmhouse. Only the plascrete shell of the house remained intact. The interior had been burned out; the roof had collapsed. Lon's men cleared out enough of the rubble to let him set up an "office" inside, for what minimal protection it would provide. They checked for mines, booby traps, and electronic snoops, then set up their sentry posts outside.

"We're not going to stay here long," Lon told Phip. "Twenty minutes, tops. Too much chance the New Spartans will have this location registered for their artillery."

"I was afraid you might have overlooked that possibility," Phip said. "They drop a high-angle shot inside these walls, the medtechs would have to scrape our remains off the plascrete." He gestured around. Some of the stains on the walls might have been from the previous occupants.

"We'll set up outposts just inside the ring the New Spartans set up, past where they burned everything, but I don't want to move all our people into the city if we can avoid it. That might tempt the other side to start lobbing rockets in among civilians. We'll wait for dark to move against the first batch of the enemy in the city, get the ones around the spaceport. While that's going on, we'll send the chancellor and his people in under heavy escort. I'll feel better once they're off our hands."

"You really think we're going to be able to pull this one off, Lon?" Phip asked, moving closer to Lon, simply whispering with the faceplate of his helmet up halfway.

Lon glanced around the ruins of the farmhouse. The only other person inside was Jeremy Howell, and he was over near what had been the front door. "We don't have any choice. We *have* to pull it off. Somehow. Probably with just what we have here now. Even if I call in another regiment, we're going to have to do it ourselves." He shook his head. "Now let me be for a few minutes. I've got to see where everyone's at."

Pieces of a puzzle. *I don't have all the pieces, and there's no cozy holo to tell me what the finished puzzle is supposed to look like,* Lon thought as he scrolled across his mapboard, seeing where each of his battalions were and where the enemy units were located. The enemy's main force was still moving east, doing what they could to stall the pursuit—leaving booby traps and small rear-guard units to harass the Dirigenters—apparently looking for sound defensive positions, rather than simply looking for a little space to regroup, or actively trying to consolidate their forces, bring the smaller units back to them.

That doesn't make a hell of a lot of sense unless they know they've got reinforcements coming, Lon thought, shaking his head idly. *The farther they go, the more likely it is that they've got more assets coming in . . . and soon.* He stared at the chart for a moment, then touched the screen softly. *If they go past this point, they must know they have help on the way.* It was an arbitrary decision, with no guarantee that it would have any relationship to reality, but he needed some reference mark to help focus his thinking. Then he turned his attention to the smaller New Spartan elements.

The New Spartan rocket artillery was still trying to get lost in the wild country to the north, staying under cover of the forests, maintaining electronic silence as far as possible. For the most part they were successful at evading detection. They were moving too fast, and too erratically, for the Dirigenter artillery to knock them out on the rare occasions when they were located. And the infantry of Lon's 2nd Battalion had not been able to close with the enemy yet.

The enemy troops who had manned the southwestern arc of the New Spartan line around University City were in the industrial district neighboring the capital's primary aerospaceport. Parker Watson had his battalion close, moving to keep the New Spartans in place. Vel Osterman was with Watson, taking tactical command of 4th of the 7th and the heavy-weapons units supporting it. Several companies of the EDF were moving into position behind those New Spartans. They were in direct contact with Osterman.

Fifteenth Regiment had not yet closed with the New Spartans they were chasing—the units that had been on the southeastern end of the perimeter—or scare them into static defensive positions. Fal Jensen had one battalion moving to get between those New Spartans and the most heavily inhabited districts of University City. He was leading the rest of his regiment out on the other flank, hoping to keep the enemy units he was after from turning northeast to rendezvous with their main force.

And here I sit with two battalions, as far from the fighting as I could get without actually running from it, Lon thought, making a face of disgust. *Half a regiment that can't contribute to any of the battles for at least three hours.* That did not feel proper, though he kept telling himself it was. He had three members of the Elysian cabinet with him, and a dozen of their staff people. All had to be turned over safely to their own people, moved inside University City and the defensive lines of the Elysian Defense Force.

Lon glanced skyward. The dance going on involving the ships and fighters of both sides was another element of the puzzle, one he felt far from qualified to judge, let alone direct. The skipper of *Peregrine* remained in tactical command of that part of the Dirigenter force. Even when it came to using the Shrike IIs for ground support or attacks on enemy ground forces, Captain Kurt Thorsen—*Peregrine's* captain—had to be consulted, not commanded. That was part of the interservice diplomacy between the Corps' line officers and the officers of its ancillary services. The defense of the ships was Thorsen's responsibility, and the Shrike II fighters were his first line of defense.

Lon got to his feet, folded his mapboard, and stuck it in the specially designed pocket on the right leg of his battledress trousers. *I can't see anything better than keeping on the way we've been going,* he thought, gesturing to Phip Steesen, who had drifted off to the other side of the room. "Let's get the men up and moving, Phip," Lon said over their radio link. "We're not doing any good here chewing our tongues." Lon alerted the two battalion commanders, then went out of the shell of a house to where the Elysians were sitting together.

"We've got to get moving again. Sorry the rest couldn't have been longer," he told them. "With a little luck, we'll get you back to your people tonight. If nothing else goes wrong."

"Don't worry about us," Berlino said, the first of the Elysians to get to his feet. "We'll manage." He seemed less nervous than before, as if all he had needed to collect his wits were a few minutes to rest. He gestured to hurry his compatriots to their feet. "We can all do with the exercise, in any case."

Moving half a regiment was not as simple as moving a platoon or a company. It was not just scale, but growing complexity as the number of levels increased, communications and making sure that each subordinate commander knew his unit's responsibilities and which other units were responsible for other necessities. The two battalions with Lon were spread out over more than half a square mile. Even for a short break they had moved into a defensive perimeter, no one completely relaxing, no one forgetting that there were hostile soldiers about—and the possibility of rocket attack with very little warning. Now, flankers were put out on both sides. Platoons were put out in front to scout the line of march and warn of any ambush. One company waited to follow the rest as rear guard. This time the rotation of duties put Junior's company from 1st Battalion behind the rest, split in two elements, covering both lines of march.

Lon was very near the geographical center of the strung-out formation, with his headquarters detachment, the men forming a loose shield around him. Phip Steesen was near the front of this inner formation. Torrey Berger was near the rear. In the middle, only Jeremy Howell was especially close to the regimental commander. He always stayed close to Lon. Two squads of troops flanked them. The Elysians were not far behind, with their own squads of bodyguards.

Several times in the next hour, the entire formation came to a halt when the point squads spotted possible mines or booby traps. Those had to be checked out carefully and the real explosives detonated or inactivated before the march could start again. Electronic snoops—left to report on troop movements—were also deactivated, destroyed, when they were found.

On the march, Lon moved just like any private under his command—rifle at the ready, finger resting over the trigger guard, his eyes sweeping from side to side, looking for any possible threat. That there was little chance of any enemy getting close to him mattered little. He felt no lessening of the tension he had always felt in a potential combat situation, though he handled it far better than he had as a young man. There was always a *chance* of trouble—a sniper, a booby trap that had somehow been missed by everyone else, *anything*.

At the same time, he was kept busy with the demands of command, keeping track of his far-flung units, receiving updates from Jensen and his own battalion commanders and from CIC. The one good thing about the sheer volume of communications was that it gave him no time to worry about his own physical well-being . . . or that of his only son, now about five hundred yards north of him, in the rear guard.

That was where the trouble came.

15

Lon heard a crackling sound like wood burning in a fireplace, distant and faint, but he recognized the sound for what it was: automatic gunfire. He had heard it often enough over the years. Seconds later, he took a call from Captain Jaz Taiters, commander of D Company, 1st Battalion, 7th Regiment—D-1-7 in military shorthand. Taiters was a nephew of Arlan Taiters, the lieutenant who had mentored Lon through his stint as an officer cadet . . . and who had been killed on Lon's first combat contract. Jaz also was Junior's company commander.

"We're being hit on the left, Colonel," Taiters reported, his voice well under control. "Sounds like maybe two platoons. They were already firing before they switched on electronics, so we didn't have any warning. I guess they infiltrated after everyone else went by. Doesn't seem possible they could have been sitting there for long and not been spotted."

"Can you handle them alone, or do you need help?" Lon asked, fumbling his mapboard out of its pocket.

"If we've got anyone close, I wouldn't turn down help," Taiters said, "but I think we can handle them alone if we have to. I do have four men down already, and they're gonna need medical help in pretty short order."

Lon bit off the question he wanted to ask, about Junior. "Have your men keep their heads down. I'll order an artillery strike. I have the positions of your opposition on the mapboard. Can you tell if any of your wounded are in critical condition?"

"Two of them are going to need trauma tubes as fast as we can get them. Hang on while I tell everyone to get down. Your son is leading a platoon to try to flank the ambushers."

Lon used the delay to order one battery of self-propelled 225mm howitzers to drop a load on the New Spartan positions. "Take care with the coordinates," he told the battery commander. "We've got men within fifty yards of them." *Junior's okay. So far,* he thought with relief—almost with too much relief, considering how many other men were also in harm's way.

"Fire mission on its way," Lon told Taiters when the captain came back on line. "I'll get the medtechs and trauma tubes started your way while you finish off any of the enemy the artillery misses."

"Will do, Colonel, and thanks."

It was only marginally appropriate, but after he had sent the medtechs on their way, Lon dialed up his son's platoon channel to listen in. He could hear gunfire more clearly over this channel—Junior apparently was much closer to the New Spartans than Captain Taiters—but there was no unnecessary chatter. The order to take cover had already been given. He heard the whistle of incoming artillery rounds and then the explosions. The first blast was isolated, but the rest overlapped each other so thoroughly that it was impossible to guess how many rounds had been fired.

When the barrage ended, there was only an instant of silence before the rifle fire resumed. Lon heard Junior say, "Come on. Let's finish this before they pull their heads outta their asses." Stifling a laugh was almost painful for Lon. He shook his head. *Colorful,* he thought, *but at least he communicates effectively.* For many young officers, that was the hardest skill to acquire.

Lon blinked several times and looked around. The march had not stopped, but Lon had allowed his vigilance to flag ever so slightly while he concentrated on the problems of his son's company. He continued to listen as Junior's platoon closed with the remnants of the New Spartan ambush, but he forced himself to pay more attention to his own surroundings. Briefly, he switched channels to tell all of his commanders about the ambush on the rear guard, and to urge greater vigilance in case there were other attacks along the flanks or against the point. Then he returned to monitoring his son's channel.

"We've got them all, Captain," Junior reported to Jaz Taiters. "Two of them still alive, but in extremely bad shape. I don't know if either will last long enough to reach a tube."

A few seconds later, Taiters called Lon to give the same report. "One of the company's medtechs is already with them," Taiters said. "He said there doesn't seem to be much purpose in hurrying trauma tubes, that they're not likely to make it."

"I'm sending them anyway, Jaz," Lon said. "We make the effort whenever possible."

"Yes, sir, that's what I told the medtech."

"We're setting up a temporary hospital near where I am now," Lon said. The SMO, Major Norman, was handling the details, and positioning the two platoons of line soldiers who would provide security for the medical personnel and wounded—and move the temporary facility to new locations as that became necessary. It would not be left too far from the bulk of 7th Regiment. "Bring the casualties here. We'll treat those we can and make arrangements to evacuate anyone hurt too badly to return to duty after a few hours in a tube. When we can."

When we can might not be anytime soon. After Taiters acknowledged the message, Lon dropped out of the line of march and went to where Major Norman was setting up the field hospital.

"You've got four men coming in from Delta of the 1st, two in tubes," Lon told him. "Maybe one or two New Spartans in tubes as well, if they survive until we get tubes to them."

"I know about them," Norman said, nodding. "You

have any idea when we'll be able to evacuate casualties?"

"Not a clue. The situation up top is . . . uncertain just now. The two fleets are dancing around trying to stay out of each other's way. That keeps the New Spartans out of our way, but it limits what we can do. My hope right now is that we won't have anyone hurt badly enough to need evacuation in a hurry, until . . . well, until things are a little clearer."

"From the reports I've had from the medtechs on the scene, Delta's wounded are all going to be able to return to duty after they do a few hours in the tubes. If the two New Spartans make it, they might both need additional treatment. If we get that far, stable and out of danger, perhaps we can arrange to transfer them back to their own people." Norman hesitated just a beat before he added, "Since we're dealing with professionals."

"One step at a time," Lon said. "The situation might not arise, from what I heard. The medtech on the scene doesn't think they'll last until we get trauma tubes to them."

Norman shrugged. "If the fighting picks up, there might be others. I'd rather stabilize enemy casualties and get them off my hands than tie down resources we need for our own people."

"Transfer any who are hurt too badly to be able to pick up a rifle and rejoin the fight after four hours in a trauma tube," Lon said. "We don't want to have to put the same people down twice." He turned and walked away before the SMO could reply to that.

Sunset. It had been nearly fifteen hours since the initial landings. Lon had stopped the two battalions with him an hour before, after making contact with two companies of the Elysian defense force on the outskirts of University City. The nearest residential district started half a mile from the point of contact, past a thickly wooded strip of ground that sloped gently toward the Styx. The men had dug in, defending an oval area a mile long and about a third of a mile wide at the broadest section. On the south and southeast, there was a creek in front of the Dirigenter line. Electronic snoops and mines had been planted out beyond the perimeter, around the entire oval. Patrols, generally single-squad in strength, would start scouting around farther out once dusk gave way to dark.

Inside the perimeter, everyone had eaten. Once the defensive positions were prepared, Lon gave the word for each unit to go on half-and-half watches—50 percent on watch, the other 50 percent sleeping, or trying to. Lon was sitting in a trench that was covered by a camouflage tarp that also served as a thermal insulator—another layer of camouflage in the dark to defeat enemy infrared night-vision systems. He had loosened the closures on his boots but had not taken them off. He had eaten, mechanically, more because of training to eat whenever possible in the field than because he had been hungry.

The afternoon had ended up relatively calm. Neither side had been able to bring in fighters for effective missions against the enemy, because when one side launched fighters, so did the other, and they either fought plane-to-plane or had to take up defensive positions around their ships.

On the ground, most of the New Spartan forces continued trying to put distance between themselves and the Dirigenters. The rocket artillery that had been north of the landings, now estimated at half a battalion in strength, was moving farther north. They were very nearly out of range of any Dirigenters except the ones who were pursuing them on the ground. The other New Spartan rocket artillery, what remained of the batteries that had first taken 15th Regiment under fire—perhaps only a single battery of four or five launchers—had moved east with the New Spartan main force, which was now nearly fifteen miles away from Lon's headquarters, still pursued by 15th Regiment.

The New Spartan infantry units that had been on the southeastern section of their initial encirclement of University City had moved almost to the River Styx before turning east, also withdrawing as rapidly as they could. The only enemy force that had not been able to pull away from the Elysian capital was now trapped in and around the aerospaceport. That was where Lon expected the only heavy fighting in the next few hours. Parker Watson's battalion and two companies of Elysians, supported by 7th Regiment's tanks and artillery, were going to attack at 2200 hours—ten o'clock that night—little more than an hour away.

Lon took his helmet off for the first time since before boarding his shuttle on *Golden Eagle* more than sixteen hours earlier. His scalp itched; he scratched it, vigorously, with both hands. He rubbed at his face and eyes. *I've got to find a little time for sleep myself,* he thought. He was tired, physically and mentally, which seemed to aggravate the minor aches that being on the move all day had brought. *Sleep before my mind gets too fogged up to function.* Stim patches would help, but there was a limit, and sometimes there were side effects.

I'll wait until I know that we've got Berlino and the others back to their people, Lon decided, nodding to himself. As soon as the attack on the aerospaceport started, two companies from 1st Battalion would escort the Elysians who had traveled to Dirigent into the capital to hand them over to their own military for escort home. *By that time we might even have a decision at the port.* He did not doubt that the New Spartans there would be defeated, forced to surrender. The main question in his mind was how expensive it would be. How many of his own people would be killed? *Combat economics* was how the Corps referred to the subject, and it came complete with budgets and balance sheets—a macabre species of bookkeeping that disturbed many field commanders when they could put names and faces to the numbers on the spreadsheets.

Lon yawned, almost out of control. His eyes started to water. *Maybe I'd better not wait,* he told himself. He took a deep breath and let it out slowly. *I need sleep.*

"Teff," Lon said, putting on his helmet to talk to his second-in-command. He waited for Ives to acknowledge, then said, "I'm going to try to get a nap in before you hit the port. I'll have everything fed through to you until then. Give me a call when Parker is ready to move."

A nap. Sleep. *Get it while you can.* That was one of the first tricks most soldiers learned about combat contracts. Lon lay back in his slit trench, using the webbing of his helmet as a pillow. *Fifty minutes, even forty, and I can get through the night,* he thought as he shifted around to get as comfortable as possible. The temperature was acceptable, and it wasn't raining. There wasn't much more an infantryman could ask for in the field. Lon closed his eyes and concentrated on his breathing—long, slow breaths—while he tried to shut out everything else.

This time it even worked. He drifted into sleep—light and easily disturbed—within two minutes and didn't come all the way out of it until forty minutes later when Tefford Ives called to tell him that 4th Battalion was staged to begin its assault on the aerospaceport and the New Spartans around it. "Two minutes," Ives concluded.

Lon had come completely awake at the mention of his name on the radio. "Keep me posted, Teff. As soon as you get things going there, I'll start our Elysians home. We'll get them in before the New Spartans can even think about getting in the way."

Next, Lon called Jaz Taiters, who was leading the two-company element of 1st Battalion that would escort the New Spartans on the last part of their journey home.

"We're ready to move whenever you give the word, Colonel," Taiters said. "We got everyone up forty-five minutes ago. Our guests seem anxious to get this over with."

"Just make sure your point men keep their eyes open for mines or other booby traps, and snipers," Lon said. "Other than that, you should have fairly clear sailing. Get our VIPs home safe, then check in with me. I don't know yet if I'm going to bring you back here or not. We may want to use you to help seal the enemy in near the port."

The first distant sounds of cannon fire rumbled in then. The tanks and howitzers had opened up on the New Spartan positions. In less than a minute the infantry would start moving forward as well, if the schedule held.

"Five minutes, Jaz," Lon said. "I'll get back to you."

Lon spent those minutes listening to reports from Ives, Parker Watson, and CIC. Watchers on *Peregrine* had the best view of the barrage launched against the New Spartan positions. A number of buildings were either destroyed or severely damaged, including the port's main terminal. It was suspected that the New Spartans had been using those buildings. *Better to waste buildings than our people,* Lon thought, shaking his head. *Even if they are our hosts' buildings.*

"We're on the move," Parker Watson reported, right on schedule. "Only light enemy small-arms fire so far, except in one location on my left. The tanks are going to help there." There was a pause, during which Lon heard what sounded like several rounds of tank fire hitting almost as one. "There, that should do it," Watson said. "I'll get back to you as soon as I can."

Lon watched the timeline on his helmet display, then called Captain Taiters. "Get moving, Jaz. The fight is joined at the port. Good luck."

16

The sun can be your enemy. It lets unfriendly eyes see you, target you. Night is your friend. Embrace it as a vampire might. Revel in the darkness; use it. No matter how good the night-vision system your opponent uses, it won't give him as good vision as daylight. That gives you an edge, a slight extra margin of safety in almost any operation on almost any world. The memory came from Lon's days in recruit training just after he had arrived on Dirigent, before he had qualified as an officer cadet and been assigned to A-2-7. One of the drill instructors had shouted that message at his troops, virtually every day. Even now, Lon could almost hear the man's voice, even though that DI had died twenty years before and a hundred light years away.

I never seem to think about the ones who retired or resigned, just the ones who died in battle, Lon thought. He tilted his helmet's visor up to look around, sticking his head out beyond the cover of the camouflage tarp. The darkness was not quite complete. It was *never* total . . . aboveground. Here, heavy tree cover and a low cloud deck had combined to minimize unaided visibility, but the clouds were just moving in. To the east, just above the horizon, the sky was partially clear. A few stars and Elysium's moon—which was almost as large as Earth's—gave texture to the darkness, a backdrop against which trees moved in the breeze. Silhouettes danced against the blackness.

It's going to rain before long, Lon told himself. He

fancied he could feel the approach of precipitation on the breeze, confirming the forecast he had received from CIC earlier. A front was moving in from the northwest, with rain showers and occasional thunderstorms. CIC thought that the heaviest storms would most likely stay farther north, away from the main zone of operations. Only 2nd Battalion might experience any of those and, according to CIC, even that was not especially likely.

Lon pulled his visor back into place. Vision improved to about 80 percent what it would have been in broad daylight, the faintly greenish tint of objects too familiar to even be noticed; his brain trained to integrate the view from infrared sensors and available-light multipliers in the duplexed night-vision system. The fighting around University City's main port had been going on for a bit more than an hour. The New Spartans were being forced into a smaller perimeter, compressed and pressed. *They're running out of places to hide,* Lon thought, trying to reassure himself. *They'll have to surrender before much longer. None of their other forces are close enough to come to their aid . . . not in time.*

Chancellor Berlino and his compatriots were only minutes from being reunited with their people. Then the two companies from 1st Battalion would be available. *I'll have to decide if I'm going to use them to reinforce 4th Battalion pretty soon. Turn them west to force the issue there or . . .* Lon had several options. He could send those two companies east to help block the fragment of the enemy force that had gone south to the river before turning, try to keep them from rejoining the main New Spartan force. He could bring them back to rejoin their battalion. Or he could send them northeast, set up another line between the main New Spartan force and the Elysian capital.

The fewer pieces we split into, the better off we are, Lon reminded himself. *Make sure we have tactical numerical superiority over any enemy force we engage. There's no need to fragment ourselves. So I bring those companies to one or another of the segments we've got out now.* Back under the cover of his tarp, Lon pulled out his mapboard and opened it.

I need to start moving 7th east, east-northeast, he thought, adjusting the view until it included all known enemy positions as well as those of the Dirigenter troops. *As soon as we know we've got this one batch of the enemy taken care of. Work at enveloping their main force with 15th on the right and us on the left, keep them from turning off in either direction. Maybe reinforce 2nd Battalion to put down the enemy rocket artillery running around north of here.* There were two segments of 15th Regiment operating apart from each other. One shorthanded battalion was keeping pressure on the New Spartans moving east along the Styx. The rest of the regiment was following the main enemy force east, drifting gradually more to the north.

He looked up from the mapboard, trying to picture the movements in his head. *If we can get rid of those rocket launchers, the rest should be just a matter of running the enemy down and forcing them to fight or surrender.* He squeezed his eyes shut. The planning always seemed so simple—crisp, clean, uncomplicated. But no enemy could be counted on to fall in with those plans, no matter how elegant they seemed.

How far can they run? How far will *they run?* Lon shook his head, then opened his eyes to stare at the mapboard. He still had no hard count on the number of New Spartans on Elysium, but CIC's best estimate was that Lon had them slightly outnumbered, maybe six-to-five, overall. *Which will improve if we neutralize the one batch around the port,* he reminded himself.

He didn't think that the firefight around the port would continue very much longer. Soon, very soon, the New Spartans would have to realize that they were hemmed in, outnumbered too heavily—locally—to win that engagement. Then . . .

"Twenty enemy rockets vectoring toward our troops near the port!" There were no preliminaries to the report from CIC. The speaker followed by saying that the warning also had been broadcast directly to the Dirigenter units around the port and that coordinates for counterbattery fire had been fed to the rocket launchers and howitzers of 7th and 15th Regiments.

Seventh Regiment's 4th Battalion had less than a minute's warning before the New Spartan missiles started exploding among them. The Elysian troops behind the port had virtually no warning at all. There were no direct communications channels between *Peregrine* and the EDF units. More than half the rockets targeted that section of the encirclement.

"Lon, they're making a breakout!" Tefford Ives shouted over the noise of a pair of secondary explosions—somewhere near him. "Right through whatever's left of the Elysians on the far side, moving a little south of east. There's not one chance in hell that we can head them off on the ground."

"Easy, Teff," Lon said. "Get me a report on our casualties as quickly as you can. Leave enough people to take care of the wounded, then pursue the New Spartans. I'll move the two companies from 1st Battalion to intercept." While he talked, Lon scrolled the view on his mapboard and increased the magnification to give him a better view of the area between Captain Taiters and the fleeing New Spartans. It looked as if it might be a tight race. Lon switched radio channels and gave Jaz Taiters his new orders, then switched back to talk with Ives again.

"It's going to take an hour to get those two companies moved, and I'm not sure that'll be fast enough. I'll have the rest of the regiment moving in fifteen minutes, sliding in on the side. If the enemy looks as if they're going to try to move deeper into University City, you'll have to try to get around on their south, force them to keep going east, or even northeast."

"Should we just start angling that way now? Keep them from even trying?" Ives asked.

"No." Lon shook his head, even though there was no

way Ives could see the gesture. "You do that and they're liable to double back to the west and get out of range of interception. We'll have to wait until I get the troops here close enough to make it impossible for those New Spartans to move in that direction. Get on with Parker and get his battalion moving as quickly as you can. Coordinate with the Elysian units you've been working with. I've got to get things started here."

Lon spent five minutes giving orders to company and battalion commanders, and setting up missions for his artillery—as much to slow down the escaping New Spartans as to cause casualties. There might be as much as a battalion and a half of New Spartans trying to get out of the pocket, twelve hundred men. Half of Lon's 1st Battalion and all of 3rd were ready to move in less than ten minutes. The advance scouts had already started along the routes that the six companies would follow. Lon's headquarters detachment formed and moved onto the line of march.

"They sure don't seem to know how to give up," Phip Steesen said on his private link to Lon.

"Maybe they've decided that they don't have to defeat us completely to fulfill their contract," Lon said. "Maybe the commander of the New Spartans has convinced himself that all he has to do is demonstrate to the Elysians that they're vulnerable even with outside help—unless it's the Confederation's help. Make the Elysians too frightened to say no, which must have been their original mission in any case."

"You mean, even if we beat the New Spartans it might not be enough?" Phip asked.

"That might be what the New Spartans think. I don't think that's the case myself. I think our employers are too set on maintaining their independence, no matter the price." *I hope,* Lon thought. *Otherwise this whole exercise is a waste.*

The lights went out in University City. There had been no blackout during the weeks that the Elysians had waited for the Dirigenters to appear out of Q-space. The locals had tried to keep everything as normal as possible. Now, though, the lights went out—not all at once, as if all power had been cut, but gradually, over ten or fifteen minutes, as the message circulated from one neighborhood to the next. Lon saw the lights go out a floor at a time, top to bottom, on one of the three tallest buildings in the Elysian capital. He wasn't certain what the structure was, but thought it was the main building on the university campus. The urban glow faded quickly.

The point squads on the two columns set a fast pace, and Lon did nothing to slow them. *Use the night. It doesn't last forever.* He felt a prickling sensation at the back of his neck, the anticipation of action, the almost subconscious thought that he himself might get close to the front in the next firefight. Anticipation, almost a perverse eagerness for battle—something he had not felt since he was an officer cadet out to prove himself and win his lieutenant's pips. When he realized that, his pace faltered for a second. He almost stumbled.

That's crazy, he told himself. *This is just another job that has to be done, not the spring dance back at The Springs.* The Springs was the unofficial name of the military academy of the North American Union, back on Earth, where he had almost become an officer. He would have, too, and perhaps never left the planet of his birth, except for a political decision to commandeer the top graduates of his class for duty in the federal police, suppressing the dissident poor in their urban circuses—ghettos—putting down riots with maximum violence and hunting out those who might foment future difficulties. *Might.* As an idealistic young cadet, Lon had considered that career revolting—as had others, including the commandant of The Springs, who had helped Lon and a few others escape the onerous duty.

Maybe some of those others are in the New Spartan force, Lon thought, and the notion was startling. None of the other cadets who had used the commandant's disciplinary scam to escape duty in the NAU's federal police had come to Dirigent with him, though at the time Lon had understood that Dirigent was to be the destination for all of them.

Not too likely, I guess, not after all these years, he told himself. He took a deep breath and looked around. *It's been too long. Even if some of them did go to New Sparta, the odds are against any of them still being on active duty, more so against even one of them being here, across the lines from me. That would be too much of a coincidence.*

His momentary distraction was ended by a call from CIC. The latest estimate was that two-thirds of the New Spartan rocket launchers had been destroyed by counter-battery fire following the barrage that had let the enemy that had been hemmed in around the port break out. Two-thirds of the launchers that had taken part in that attack, CIC qualified. More hopeful than certain, the duty officer in CIC added, "They can't have many more rockets available for the launchers they still have, not with all they've expended since we've been here."

"Don't let that hope blind you to what they *might* have," Lon cautioned. "They haven't started waving white flags yet." He didn't hesitate long enough to get a reply. "Sorry, that was uncalled for. I know you won't quit watching."

Lon kept his men on the march for an hour and a half—covering nearly five miles—before he permitted a five-minute rest. He sat with his back against a tree trunk and pulled out his mapboard. He had been receiving frequent updates from his subordinate commanders as well as from CIC. Now he needed to look at the chart to help him fix all of the changes in his head.

The main enemy force had stopped moving and appeared to be setting up and reinforcing defensive positions—even if they only intended to remain in them for a few hours, long enough to give their men a chance for a little sleep. The smaller force to the southeast was still moving, trying to angle north, hoping to rendezvous with the main force . . . but unable to because of the battalion from 15th Regiment between them. The force that had broken out of the trap around the port was also moving east, but leaving skirmishers and booby traps to slow pursuit. That was where the only real fighting had been going on. To the north, Lon's 2nd Battalion had come across the remains of four rocket launchers and several dozen dead soldiers. There was evidence that some of the enemy had survived and were continuing to move away, north and east, but not obviously on a route designed to rendezvous with the main New Spartan force.

Phip Steesen sat next to Lon. Phip laid his rifle across his legs after checking to make certain that the safety was on, then lifted the faceplate of his visor. "They get off into the wilds, we might chase them for months and never be able to force the issue," he said when Lon also raised his faceplate. "Time for them to get reinforcements in or force the issue up top. Whatever." Phip shook his head.

"That's okay," Lon said. "If we can get them all away from the city, past the main farming belt, and far enough in the wild to let the Elysians get back to business as usual, we've got the time. Three months, six, even longer. Keep the New Spartans occupied until the General can send another regiment and a fighting ship or two. If it comes down to it, Dirigent has more resources to call on than New Sparta does—men, ships, and everything else."

"Yeah, but even Elysium doesn't have bottomless pockets," Phip said. "And I doubt their patience will be endless either. You think we're going to be able to bottle up that one batch of the enemy yet? The ones who broke out from the port."

Lon tilted his mapboard so Phip would be able to see it clearly. "I'm not sure. Right now I'll be happy if we can make them keep moving on their current route. If they take a right turn and head into the city, then we could have more serious problems. They're only two miles from the main campus of the university. If they get in there, the Elysians will really get their tail feathers ruffled."

"*Can* we stop them?"

"It's close, too damned close. The EDF is on that side, about six hundred men, doing what they can. Parker can get maybe two companies in the way, and we're still using our artillery to harass the New Spartans, but they're zig-zagging enough that we can't be too . . . profligate with the artillery. Too much chance of destroying Elysian buildings now that they're right on the edge of the urban district, and I'm not sure that all of the civilians are out of that area."

"The way we're moving here, we might force the New Spartans farther into the city," Phip said. His finger moved across Lon's mapboard, tracing the route. "If I were commanding that unit of New Spartans, I'd sure as hell want to get out of our way."

"That boxes them in, sooner or later," Lon said. "They've already shown they don't like boxes. They're like us, Phip. They want to be where they can maneuver, where they have freedom of movement." Lon tilted his visor down just enough to view the timeline on its display. "Speaking of movement, it's time for us to get on our feet again."

"Yeah, I'd better get back where I belong." Phip got to his feet and pulled his faceplate into place, then jogged toward his position fifty yards away.

Lon was slower to get to his feet, using his rifle to help him. *We can't go forever without taking more time for rest,* he thought, shaking his head. That forty-minute nap he had taken seemed weeks ago, and he doubted that many of his men had managed much more sleep than he had. Some of them had probably had much less, and a few—especially among his junior officers and noncoms—likely wouldn't have had any. *Not yet,* he told himself after giving the order to start moving again. *We can't afford the time until we either catch this batch of the enemy or drive them away from the city.*

• • •

It was 0300 hours. The left-hand column was stopped
again. The platoon on the point had run into an ambush
set by a squad or two of New Spartans. Jaz Taiters was
moving the rest of his company up to finish the firefight
as quickly as possible. It gave the other companies in the
two columns a couple of minutes to rest—though everyone remained alert in case there were more of the enemy
nearby hiding, ready to pounce.

Lon did not sit this time, but rested on one knee, using
his rifle to help keep his balance while he waited for Taiters' company to finish the firefight. *Rotate them off the
point when it's done,* he told himself. *Give them a break.
Rotate the point on the other side, too.* He tried to focus
on the few reports he could hear on the radio, eavesdropping on the platoon frequency to get some sense of what
was going on. *Hear* the sounds of fighting, the rifle fire
that occasionally sounded like strings of small firecrackers
going off in quick succession. Mostly he tried not to think
about Junior. It had been one of his two platoons on point,
though he had been farther back with the other platoon—
which had quickly moved to support the first—when the
ambush was sprung.

"*Captain! The lieutenant's been hit. He's down!*"

The words hit Lon like a hard blow to the gut. The first
coherent thought that came after that was, *Not Junior; the
other lieutenant,* but it was a vain hope. At the moment,
Lon couldn't recall the name of the other lieutenant in
Junior's company. He held his breath, waiting for something else . . . and dreading what it *might* be.

"How badly is he hurt?" Lon recognized Jaz Taiters'
voice.

"I don't know. The medtech just got to him." That was
one of Junior's platoon sergeants. There seemed to be an
impossibly loud rushing noise in Lon's ears. "I've got two
other men down, too; one of them dead."

"Hang on, we're in position."

Over the radio, Lon could hear a sudden massive increase in the amount of gunfire. That lasted for nearly a

minute, and when it ended, there was . . . something approaching total silence.

What's going on?! Lon's mind screamed at him. It took total concentration to keep from yelling over the radio for news about his son. He didn't even notice that he had gotten to his feet and taken a couple of steps in the direction of the firefight—half a mile away. It must have been another two minutes before Lon received a call from Jaz Taiters.

"Junior's been hurt, Colonel," the captain reported. "The medtech says he *should* be okay. They're moving him to a trauma tube now."

Lon did not acknowledge the message. His knees buckled under him and he fell, the weight of his combat pack pulling him over backward. He hit the ground hard, butt first, stunned, but did not *quite* lose consciousness.

17

The flush of embarrassment was worse than anything else. His fall had knocked the air out of him, but as soon as he recovered from that—twenty seconds or less—he started to get back to his feet. It was not quickly enough for him to escape notice. Frank Dorcetti and Jeremy Howell were both at his side before he could stand, and Lon saw Phip hurrying toward them as well.

"I'm okay," Lon said as Dorcetti and Howell moved to support him. "I just lost my balance and fell. Nothing's hurt." *Nothing but pride.*

"Maybe you'd better let a medtech check you out anyway," Howell said. "I knew a guy got a concussion falling that way."

Lon took a deep breath and closed his eyes for an instant. "The medtechs have enough to do with real casualties. I'm okay."

By that time Phip had arrived, and Lon had to tell him the same thing. "I'm okay. Come on. We've got work to do. First Battalion has squashed that ambush. Get the companies moving again. Everyone back in place."

Howell and Dorcetti moved away from the colonel, but Phip didn't. "I heard about Junior," Phip said softly, with his visor up so his words weren't transmitted. One of Junior's platoon sergeants had called Phip directly. He had also received an update from the medtech. "His wounds aren't life-threatening. They've got him stabilized and on his way to a trauma tube."

Lon nodded abruptly. "I know, Phip. He'll be okay, and

so will I. We can't let this interfere with what we've got to do." His voice sounded harsh, but Phip just nodded and headed back toward his own position in the line of march.

We can't let this interfere, Lon told himself as he watched Phip move away. He felt anger, but it was directly entirely at himself. It had been difficult not to snap at his aide and driver—even at Phip, his best friend—but that would have just been to cover how foolish Lon felt, and he would have felt even worse if he had. He was certain his face had flushed bright red, but that was something the others couldn't have seen through the tinted faceplate of his helmet. *Get a grip on yourself.* The anger had not faded. If anything, it had grown stronger, and the more rational part of Lon's mind noted that as well. *Take a deep breath. It's done and over. Concentrate on what you've got to do now. You're responsible for more than eight thousand men. You can't let worry about one of them paralyze you.*

One deep breath, let out slowly. A second. Lon started walking, his head moving from side to side, his eyes scanning. *Get back in the rhythm. Junior will be okay. Make sure you don't do something stupid and get yourself hurt, or show everyone that you're falling apart.* Years of worry about Junior joining the Corps and then about his safety once he did had all hit him at once, knocked him for the proverbial loop. *I'm still not thoroughly Dirigenter,* he thought. *I can't take something like this in stride.*

Jaz Taiters called to say that the enemy ambush had been wiped out—twenty New Spartans dead, or wounded and captured; no more than two or three had escaped. If Taiters hadn't added his assurance that Junior would recover, the routine message would have helped Lon bring his mind fully back to the necessities of the moment. As it was, the comment made it that more difficult, reminded him how vulnerable he had become through worrying about his son.

Lon forced himself through another series of breathing exercises, designed to help him relax. He called each battalion commander in turn, to ask about position and progress, and added an unnecessary reminder to be especially watchful for ambushes. Then he called Fal Jensen to check on 15th Regiment. Finally, he made a routine check with the duty officer in CIC aboard *Peregrine*. Concentrating—*fiercely*—on the minutiae of routine helped. Lon could feel his body adjusting, coming back down to the "normal" level of tension for a field situation with combat possible but not probable at any minute.

He glanced at the timeline on his head-up display. Less than thirty minutes had passed since he heard that Junior had been wounded. *We've only been on the surface twenty-four hours.* That realization was startling. It seemed as if the Elysian campaign had lasted half an eternity. Lon squeezed his eyes shut for an instant. His head throbbed dully with the tension. He forced another deep breath, opening his eyes so he wouldn't stumble and have everyone on top of him asking after his health again. Though he tried to ignore it, the thought *You'll be reminded about falling on your butt as long as you're in the Corps* would not be denied. Lon growled, almost under his breath.

The terrain the Dirigenters were crossing was tame, farm fields and orchards, country lanes, with occasional stands of "wild" trees. What fencing there had been had all been knocked down by the New Spartans during the weeks in which they had surrounded University City and raised havoc in the farming districts. There were no civilians around, and no intact houses or barns. *No livestock, and not even much wildlife,* Lon thought as his headquarters group crossed what had been a farmyard. The ruins of house and barn had already been checked to make certain they harbored neither enemy nor booby traps.

The last of the night's stars had been occulted by the encroaching clouds. Lon heard talk over the radio that the men in the rear guard had already started to see rain, moving faster than the column, so he was not surprised when the first drops spattered against his faceplate. At first the drops were large but few. It was another ten minutes before the tempo increased significantly. Lon tightened the collar of his battledress blouse to ensure that no water would run off his helmet and down his back. The camouflage battledress was water-resistant. It would take a lot of heavy rain to soak through the fabric. Helmet and faceplate shed water so efficiently that there was scarcely any beading to obscure vision, rarely a need to wipe water away. And Corps boots were almost totally waterproof, so the rain should not prove too much of an inconvenience.

Another distraction, Lon thought, but at the moment minor distractions were welcome. Lon stopped, stepping out of the line of march to watch men move past. Each glanced his way in passing, but no one said anything. Jeremy Howell dropped out of line as well, to stay near his boss. There was nothing unusual about that. Lon sometimes thought of Howell as *"my shadow."* Nothing was said just then, and after a few minutes Lon moved back into the line of march and Jeremy followed him.

"Almost wouldn't know we were on contract if it didn't rain," Howell said once they were walking again. He had a private channel connecting him with Lon, one that was shared only by members of the headquarters staff. "The eternal foot soldier, rain above and mud below. I think there's something in the manual says that's the way it's supposed to be."

Lon smiled. "Don't give up your day job just yet, Jerry. You're not ready to take the stage as a comic. But get used to the rain. The forecast says it will probably continue through most of the morning. When we stop for a long break, we'll be sleeping under the faucet."

"That won't bother me, Colonel," Howell replied, "but one of these times Frank Dorcetti is liable to drown in his sleep. He sleeps with his mouth open, and his snoring through a mouthful of water is purely god-awful, if you know what I mean."

This time Lon did chuckle. "I know what you mean.

Lead Sergeant Steesen used to be the same way." He took in a deep breath and let it out slowly. He did feel better. It would be easier now to resist the urge to call the med-techs to ask about Junior. *They'll let me know when there's something to say.*

It was just past 0430 hours when both Jaz Taiters and Parker Watson called to report hearing a series of explosions. In each case the blasts were some distance away and not directed at their men. By comparing the direction given by the two men, Lon was able to pinpoint an area on his mapboard. A minute later, CIC confirmed the location of the explosions.

"They're using surface-to-air missiles against civilian targets," Lon reported to his battalion commanders and Fal Jensen. "Buildings not being used by the Elysian Defense Force. I don't know if it's random or not. Yet. I don't even know if there were any civilians in any of those buildings."

"You think they're trying to divert our attention?" Jensen asked. "Make us siphon off resources to firefighting and rescue work?"

"If that's their intent, it won't work," Lon said. "The Elysians will have to attend to that. We'll have a better idea what the New Spartans are up to once we find out if they're hitting random targets to cover their withdrawal or specific factories, maybe munitions facilities or something similar." He scarcely hesitated before he said, "I know we all need a chance to get a few hours' sleep, but that has to wait. We have to keep pushing to get that one detachment of enemy soldiers away from other civilian targets first. That doesn't apply to the men you've got near the enemy main force, Fal. Let your men get what rest they can. You're going to have to be ready if those New Spartans try something."

"I've already got those men on half-and-half watches," Jensen said. "When the main force settled in, I figured we'd have to be able to match them in the morning, whatever they decide to do next. Any good estimates on what *that* might be?"

"I'm beginning to think they must expect massive reinforcement from New Sparta," Lon said. "How soon that might be, I can't even guess, but the longer they go without trying to go on the offensive, the more likely it is. What I'm looking for now is, mainly, what the enemy main force does this morning. If they start moving farther away from University City and not directly toward one of the other urban centers, we should have a pretty good indication."

"If that's what they do, will you advise Dirigent to send out our reinforcements?" Jensen asked, almost hesitantly.

"I'm not going to make a decision on that yet, Fal," Lon said. "I'm leaning that way, but I want more information before I blow the panic horn. Assuming, for the sake of argument, that the New Spartans *do* have reinforcements on the way, we'll be a lot better off if we can force the issue on the ground before more players join the cast. By the way, *Peregrine* says Colonel Hayley is definitely out of danger now. He will recover."

"That's good to know," Jensen said. "He's a good man."

A good man who'll never be the same, Lon thought. *A man who'll never be able to remember just how good he was. There are still some things a trauma tube can't fix.*

"We'll talk again later, Fal. You'd better try to get some sleep. I'll let you know if anything comes up, and we'll talk before I decide whether to ask for another regiment."

Elements of 1st Battalion managed to close with the New Spartans moving east across the northern edge of University City just before sunrise. The firefight lasted twenty minutes before the New Spartans were able to disengage, still moving east. This time they had no assistance from their rocket artillery. *Either we got all of them, or they just don't have the missiles to spare,* Lon thought. He would gladly accept either option.

Second Battalion had settled in for a few hours' sleep earlier. Lon had decided to stop the pursuit of the small New Spartan force to the north, leaving just a few patrols to make certain he would not lose contact with them. Ten minutes after the end of the latest clash on the outskirts of the Elysian capital, Lon gave the order for the rest of 7th Regiment to find good defensive positions and settle in. "I hope to make it for at least four hours," he told the battalion commanders, "but no guarantees."

Set up a perimeter. Dig minimal slit trenches. Put out patrols, electronic snoops, and a few land mines—just to keep the enemy on his toes. In each squad, one fire team would try to sleep while the other remained on watch against possible enemy activity. Make routine communications checks. Lon spoke with each battalion commander and with CIC. There was nothing urgent. Finally Lon yawned and lay back in the slit trench Howell and Dorcetti had fixed for him, with the camouflage tarp propped over it, arranged to catch the slight breeze from the northwest while keeping most of the continuing rain off.

The rain had been almost constant since it had started, never heavy, sometimes little more than a mist. For the most part, Lon had been able to ignore it. The ground he had been walking over drained well. There had been few patches of mud, even after several hundred men had crossed. It was only when he lay down that Lon really thought about the rain, watching it. He was careful where he lay his rifle, keeping it close to his body, the muzzle propped up close to the tarp.

Sleep, Lon told himself. He was exhausted enough that sleep would come without a patch. He had allowed himself thirty seconds to call the medtechs to check on his son. Junior was out of the trauma tube and back with his unit, so Lon had given himself another thirty seconds to talk directly to him. *He sounded a little unsteady,* Lon thought, *but that's to be expected. It was his first time hurt.* "Don't dwell on it," Lon had advised. "I know that's not easy, but it's the best way."

Sleep came, the deep void that permitted no dreams, no nightmares. Sleep that consuming was rare on a combat contract, almost unprecedented, a dangerous luxury. The only problem was that it did not—could not—last long enough. Lon had left instructions. After three hours, Jeremy Howell woke him.

"I really hated to do it, Colonel," Howell said. "Seems like nothing's happening. Another couple of hours would do you a world of good, sir. Lead Sergeant Steesen has reports from every battalion and company in the regiment, and he talked with 15th's lead sergeant, too. Things are quiet everywhere."

"Another couple of hours *would* be nice," Lon agreed after a long and satisfying yawn, "but it will have to wait." He tilted his faceplate up and rubbed at his face and eyes with both hands for a moment. "I need to talk to CIC, Colonel Jensen, and our battalion commanders first. We have any coffee packs handy by any chance? I could use a good caffeine jolt."

"Ten seconds, Colonel," Howell said. "I got the water poured. Just need to put the coffee crystals in." He started doing that while he talked. He ripped open the plastic packet and dumped the coffee in, then shook the field cup gently to help mix it up. The ten seconds were what the heating catalyst in the pack would need to bring the water up to drinking temperature.

As soon as the coffee was hot, Lon started to drink, taking down half the beverage before he took the cup away from his lips the first time. He watched Howell pull the heating strip on a meal pack—which also opened the container. Lon took one more sip of coffee, then set the cup down carefully and took the meal that his aide offered him. "You eaten yet, Jerry?" Lon asked before he took his first bite of the ham, eggs, and hard biscuit.

Howell nodded. "Two packs. I was hungry. You gonna want a second pack, sir?"

Lon smiled. "Probably, but not right away. I'll get this down, then make the calls I need to make." He concen-

trated on his eating, taking no more than three minutes to
finish the battle rations—two thousand calories enriched
with vitamins, minerals, high in protein and carbohy-
drates. One meal pack—breakfast or lunch/supper—was
supposed to include all the necessary nutrition to get a
man through twenty-four hours. "They put in everything
but good taste," was the usual reaction of men forced to
live on them for any length of time.

As soon as he finished his breakfast and coffee, Lon
started making his calls. CIC informed him that the remaining New Spartan transports had continued to withdraw. They were now eight hours out from Elysium,
moving in an elliptical orbit with a period of slightly more
than three days. The capital ships were much closer, staying near enough to use their fighters to support their
troops on the ground in a crisis.

On the ground, the New Spartans were continuing a
general move toward the east-northeast, away from University City, and apparently not toward any of the other
major concentrations of inhabitants. "It looks as if you
were right," Fal Jensen said when Lon talked with him.
"They're going to stooge around in the wild so they must
expect help, but probably not too soon or they wouldn't
go far."

"Unless we're overlooking something we shouldn't,"
Lon said. "I need your honest opinion on something, Fal.
Do you think I should ask for another regiment now or
hold off until we know something more definite?"

Jensen did not hesitate. "I think we should ask for it
while we can. We don't know if we'll be able to finish
operations against the enemy we have on the ground now,
how long we'll have before the New Spartans bring in
more people, how long we might have to hold out against
their reinforcements before ours can arrive. The time lag
could be a killer, since we have to figure thirty days before
our people can get here."

"I agree," Lon said. "If it comes down to a chance of
us looking foolishly overcautious or unnecessarily risking

our men, we have to opt for the former. In our first MR I said that I'd try to get my recommendations off within forty-eight hours, but I don't see any point in waiting that long. Get your reports ready for transmission as quickly as you can and we'll get the MR off within the hour. Will that give you enough time?"

"I'll get everything transmitted to CIC in thirty minutes," Jensen promised. "The sooner we get that MR off, the better I'm going to feel. This thing is giving me an itch I can't scratch."

Lon decided to move his 1st and 3rd Battalions another mile and a half east, to cut down on the distance to the main New Spartan force and to have better defensive positions in case the enemy doubled back to attack. The move and getting settled into the new perimeter took nearly two hours, and Lon told his commanders that—if possible—they would stay put at least until nightfall, perhaps longer. The last New Spartans were away from University City by then, with all of them moving east and northeast, apparently intent on a rendezvous. Lon held back the units chasing the enemy. "Let them rendezvous," he told the concerned battalion commanders. "If they're all in one place it'll be easier for us to keep track of them."

Lon took forty minutes to tour the new perimeter himself, at least the eastern half of it, where trouble was most likely to come. The line on that side was established at the top of the slope leading down to a creek and its now-dry floodplain. The creek was no more than four feet deep now, in midsummer, but from the extent of the floodplain on the eastern side, in the spring it might be extensive. There was another creek near the far side of the plain— a mile away—but it hadn't slowed the New Spartans at all, so it couldn't be very deep either.

Before noon, *Peregrine* reported that the MR was far enough out that the New Spartans could not intercept it. A New Spartan MR had been launched by one of their transports forty minutes before *Peregrine* launched its message rocket. Because of the position of the transport, there had been no chance for the Dirigenter ships to intercept or destroy that courier packet.

At least we know we're going to have help coming, Lon thought. *Or someone to pick up the pieces if we've got the short end of the stick.*

18

Melvin Rogers had been president of Elysium for six years. Throughout his term of office, he had continued to teach at the university, primarily graduate physics courses in Quantum-Space Dynamics. Nearly eighty years of age, he wore his curly strawberry blond hair shoulder-length, and tended to wear simple jumpsuits in primary colors. He came to Lon's headquarters by floater just before sunset, accompanied by Chancellor Berlino and four bodyguards from the Elysian Defense Force.

"Sorry I can't offer anything appropriate in the way of amenities, Mr. President," Lon said after the introductions were completed, "but, as you can see, our resources are rather meager at present." Lon's command post was in a grove of pear trees. The little fruit that had been left by the New Spartans was on the ground, rotting. Several of the trees had been banded, the bark cut completely around the trunk to kill them.

"That's of no concern, I assure you, Colonel," President Rogers said. "I tend to teach my seminar course out on the lawn when the weather is amenable. I wanted to speak with you, face-to-face, at the earliest possible moment, and this seemed appropriate." He sat on a tarp that several of Lon's men had spread after kicking away a few of the rotten pears. Rogers gestured, and Lon sat across from him, not too far away. Berlino also sat, forming the third point of an equilateral triangle with the other two men.

"It is a tremendous relief to have you and your men here, Colonel," Rogers said. "I understand that you lost quite a few men making your landings. I give you my personal regrets and condolences, as well as those of the government and people of Elysium. I wish there had been some way that we could have made your arrival less painful, less costly in human terms, but, unfortunately, that was beyond our power."

"Thank you, Mr. President," Lon said, nodding.

"Thankfully, your arrival has already had some salutary effect on the situation. The siege of University City has ended. The New Spartans have suffered heavy losses as well and have withdrawn most of their forces into the hinterland."

"I doubt that your troubles with them are over, Mr. President," Lon said. "I don't know what your analysts have forecast, but my senior advisers and I are convinced that the New Spartans expect significant reinforcements, that they have withdrawn to preserve their current forces on-planet until those reinforcements arrive. Although that might happen at any time, we suspect that we have at least several days, perhaps a week or even two, before they are likely to arrive in-system. But we have no hard intelligence, so all we can say for certain is that those reinforcements have not arrived in-system yet, so we know we'll have at least three days to try to degrade the New Spartan assets already here before help arrives for them."

"My military advisers have suggested that we have to prepare for possible New Spartan reinforcements," Rogers said. "They have given it a seventy percent probability rating. The invaders did not fully exercise their potential in the weeks they had on Elysium before you and your men arrived. They could have overrun our defense forces with little difficulty, though it pains me to say that. Instead, they toyed with us, put their siege around our capital, destroyed homes and crops, and the rest. In some ways that was more . . . humiliating than had they defeated our full army in battle. But they never gave us the opportunity for that, and merely flicked off such raids as

we were able to mount the way a man might wave at a
fly buzzing his head." Rogers' face clearly showed the
humiliation he felt. "They toyed with us, Colonel Nolan,
as if we were of no account at all."

"Had their contract called for them to conquer Elysium,
no doubt they would have acted differently," Lon said.
"If their contract was, as we suspect, merely to force you
to submit to the overlordship of the Confederation of Human Worlds, then their actions are perfectly understand-
able. Their job was to frighten you, or embarrass you into
accepting the CHW, and the Confederation would have
less use for an Elysium devastated by extreme rules of
engagement."

"We will *never* accept the Confederation," Rogers said.
"We were not so inclined before and, after what we have
been through in the last weeks, we would not submit as
long as one Elysian remained alive to contest the issue.
We sincerely hope that your people will be enough to
convince the Confederation to forget about Elysium. If
not, though, we will still not accept them. Should all else
fail, we will seek membership in the Second Commonwealth, though we would prefer not to."

"There is one matter that we need to bring to your
attention now, Colonel," Chancellor Berlino said after a
glance at the president indicated that Rogers was done
speaking. "It's something that may have slipped the attention of your staff. The New Spartans do still have approximately six hundred men south of the Styx. Since
both bridges across the river were destroyed early, those
men have been of less concern, but we have reports that
they are moving upstream, most likely looking for a place
they can cross to the north shore."

"We haven't forgotten them," Lon said. "Our ships
have been keeping track as best they can. Those companies have been minimizing electronic emissions, but every
time they use active electronics, we update our fix on their
positions, and we occasionally get a visual sighting as
well. As I understand it, there are no other bridges across

the Styx, and they will have to go forty miles east of University City before they can find a place where the river can be forded, correct?"

"Correct," Berlino said, and Rogers nodded. "Just slightly less than forty miles right now, because of the season. That is about twenty-six miles from their current position . . . as of fifty minutes ago."

"Are there boats on the south shore they could commandeer to make the crossing before that point? Or a place where they could use ground effect vehicles?" Lon asked.

"Not in sufficient numbers," Berlino said. "They might find half a dozen small rowboats and possibly twice that number of floaters. There are several places where the banks slope gently enough on both sides for floaters to get in and out of the water, but even if they used all of the floaters and rowboats they might find, they could hardly move sixty men at a time. But there are plenty of trees. I would think that they could assemble enough rafts to cross in short order. Or simply fell trees and let their men paddle across using them."

Lon's smile was minimal and quickly gone. "It's always good to see all of the possibilities, but I suspect that paddling rafts or logs across rates rather low on the scale. The crossing would take too long, and there would be far too great a chance that their preparations would be observed and we would be waiting to pounce as soon as they got in the water. An infantry commander would prefer to keep his men dry as long as possible, then make the most rapid crossing possible. If there aren't enough boats or floaters, they'll almost certainly wait until they get far enough upstream to ford the river." Lon shrugged. "If it were a matter of getting a patrol across to strike a specific target, it might be different."

"You do think they will attempt to cross at some point, though, don't you, Colonel?" Berlino asked.

"It seems likely. They appear to be drawing all their forces together. We'll be watching, though, and once those six hundred men get in the water, we'll use our rocket artillery to make the crossing expensive for them. In the meantime, we leave them strictly alone. If they think we've forgotten about them, so much the better. It might make them careless when they do make their crossing."

"And their main force?" President Rogers asked. "You do plan to move against them soon?"

Lon smiled. "*Very* soon, Mr. President."

The Elysians left, under strong escort. Lon's command post was relocated, half a mile farther east, and much of 7th Regiment shifted position as well, more to the north and east. Shortly after dark, elements of 15th Regiment started a series of harassing attacks against the perimeter of the New Spartan main force, never in more than company strength—with the men in each raiding patrol maintaining electronic silence as long as possible—in what Lon hoped would appear to be a totally random fashion. Similarly, the Dirigenter rocket artillery launched an occasional missile at the New Spartan positions. Lon knew he had to be sparing with his use of the artillery. There might not be a chance to land more rockets or howitzer shells, and Lon did not want to run out at a critical point. *Keep them off guard and guessing. Make it impossible for them to get any sleep. Frazzle their nerves.*

There was nothing radical to the plan Lon had laid out, but harassing tactics could never settle the main issue. All he wanted was to degrade enemy capabilities—psychologically and physically—while he moved his forces into position for what he hoped would be the final engagement of the contract. At the earliest, that would not begin for another twenty-four hours . . . unless the New Spartans forced the issue sooner. And that seemed particularly unlikely.

"They may turn and fight at some point," Lon had told Phip Steesen a little earlier, "but only when their commander decides it's the only viable option left. I expect the first thing he'll try, once he decides they can't just sit and absorb the punishment, is a further withdrawal, maybe more to the north, where the land gets rougher, try to find ground to his liking for the next fight, or just try to postpone the battle until he gets reinforcements."

"And we don't want to give him that much time because that will reverse our relative positions and put us on the short end of the stick," Phip had noted.

"Exactly."

The New Spartans had brought together all of their forces north of the River Styx . . . save, perhaps, for patrols that might have been left out for reconnaissance purposes, or to stage ambushes as the Dirigenters moved after the main force. South of the Styx, the approximately six hundred New Spartans there—the equivalent of three companies, a short battalion—were still moving east. It appeared as though they might reach the first ford slightly before first light—if they pressed—but it seemed more likely that they would not try to cross before dark the next night.

Lon spent twenty minutes conferring with Fal Jensen and the battalion commanders from both regiments. "It's too soon to start claiming victory," Lon told them, "but the situation looks fairly favorable. They can't have much rocket artillery left, maybe four or five launchers, but probably few or no rockets left for them to fire. Our own supply of artillery munitions is limited, but not near exhaustion. If we can't get new supplies of those in, we can at least keep the enemy from getting resupply. We definitely have at least a slight numeric advantage in troops, six-to-five, maybe even seven-to-five, even including the short battalion they have on the other side of the river."

"We are set up to get resupply of small-arms ammunition, aren't we?" Fal Jensen asked.

"We are," Lon confirmed. "I hope to bring in fresh supplies during daylight tomorrow, before we force battle with the New Spartans, at least for those companies that have had the greatest expenditure of ammunition so far."

The distribution had been uneven; some units had scarcely fired a single shot, while others had been through several intense firefights. "Assume that will mean using resupply rockets to bring it in, since it's not likely we'll be able to use shuttles safely."

At ten-thirty—2230 hours—7th Regiment started moving east, angling a little north. As they got close to the enemy, 15th Regiment would slide around the perimeter to the south, so that the Dirigenters would have the New Spartans pincered. The heavy-weapons battalions were also moving, on both sides, staying far enough away to be out of the reach of the New Spartans, but close enough to take part in the fight . . . when it came.

The day's rest had been welcome and needed, but Lon felt relieved to be on the move again. He walked with his headquarters detachment, near the middle of the two battalions with him. Second Battalion was to the north, moving toward a rendezvous with 1st and 3rd Battalions before dawn. Fourth Battalion was still to the south, and farther east than the rest of 7th Regiment. Closer to the enemy, 15th Regiment continued harassing the New Spartan perimeter, giving them no rest. The two heavy-weapons battalions were also on the move—almost a constant for them in the field; standing still was an invitation to disaster. The rocket launchers could cover the main New Spartan force and the short battalion on the south side of the river.

Lon felt as relaxed as he ever had during a combat contract when battle was in the offing, even though it did not seem imminent. It was almost a peaceful feeling, ironic though that might be. Junior had come by for a short talk during the afternoon. Father and son had spent thirty minutes together. Junior showed no obvious aftereffects of his wounds. In fact, Junior had seemed more concerned with his father's reaction than with what had happened to him. They had parted, their final words to each other the same: "Be careful." Junior had grinned and flipped his father a casual salute. Lon had returned it, his face serious, almost somber. *Be careful.*

Ten minutes past eleven was when the first report came in from Fal Jensen. "The New Spartans are heading northeast, as we expected. Their rear guard and flankers are keeping us occupied at the moment, resistance in strength. The time they've had, I think we can count on a few nasty surprises if we try to go through where they were camped, so I'm going to start angling my men around their flank, on the south."

"You have any people in front of them to slow them down?" Lon asked.

"Not enough, just a one-platoon patrol, and they're not directly in front."

"Have them do what they can. I don't want to call in an artillery strike yet. We may need the rockets and shells later. I'll turn my people to the north a little, and push the pace as much as I can. We're a bit farther from them than you are."

It's a good thing we had a day to rest, Lon thought after he gave the orders to his battalion and company commanders. *We're going to have to race to get anywhere near the enemy.* And if the New Spartans pressed their own move, it might be impossible to close with them before they reached ground they might choose to defend . . . or before their reinforcements reached Elysium.

It was impossible to just wheel the entire formation around to march on the new heading the way it could be done on a parade field in garrison. Advance scouts had to move onto the new route first to look for any surprises left by the enemy and to mark a trail. Flankers had to be moved as well. Then, company by company, the rest made the thirty-degree turn. After fifteen minutes everyone was moving in the right direction, and Lon gave the order to the point platoons to pick up the pace. Lon passed orders to keep active electronics use to a minimum, as close to electronic silence as possible, to make it that much more difficult for the New Spartans to track their progress. Not *total* electronic silence: An occasional blip on their tracking systems would not tell the New Spartans if the target was a squad or a battalion, and it might lull them, while total electronic silence would simply make them more wary.

How hard can we push the march? Lon asked himself. If they went too slowly, the New Spartans would keep their distance, even increase it, postponing battle until . . . whenever. If they went too quickly, the men would get exhausted, be unready for the fight when it came. There was also the danger of losing men to land mines or booby traps if the pace was too rapid to allow the men on point enough time to spot concealed devices.

Take a little more time between breaks, and keep the rest stops as short as practical. Don't push the pace too much to be dangerous. Lon shook his head. He really had little choice, at least during the hours of darkness. At night, the trip wire for a mine or a booby trap would be nearly invisible. Once morning came, there would be a chance to reassess, depending on how far the New Spartans had traveled, how fast they were moving.

If we have to, I can order a few rockets fired at their van then, Lon decided. In the morning. *Slow them down at least a little, or goad them into changing direction to something more favorable for us.* He hoped that would not be necessary. He still wanted to husband the finite supply or artillery munitions as long as possible, save them for the battle he hoped to force before the New Spartans could be reinforced from out-system.

It was not until just before one o'clock in the morning that Lon signaled for the first rest stop, and he held that to only five minutes. He sat down in place, stretching his legs out in front of him. After taking a quick sip of water, he massaged his calf and thigh muscles through the rest of the break, easing the aches that had started, and hoping to prevent cramps later. Lon was ready to get back to his feet when Phip came over and squatted next to him and raised the faceplate of his helmet.

"You know, we can't go on forever like this, two and a half hours hiking, five minutes resting," Phip whispered. "We'll end up going slower rather than faster."

Lon lifted his faceplate. "I know, Phip," he said just as softly. "There aren't many legs here older than mine, and they're talking loud and clear. I just wanted the fast start. If we can travel just a little bit faster than the New Spartans think we can, it gives us a little extra edge, maybe. We've got a lot of distance to cover and we can't expect them to sit still and wait for us to catch up. We'll go for maybe an hour and a quarter this time, then take ten minutes. After that . . . well, after that depends on what the situation is later."

Phip grunted. "Give it our all now, then fifteen percent more later. I know how that works." He got back to his feet. "Just remember, it won't do us any good to catch those buzzards if we're too tired to fight when we do."

"How could I forget when I've got you for a conscience and memory bank?" Lon laughed as he stood and adjusted the straps of his backpack. "Between you, my legs, and my feet, I'm not likely to forget. Come on. It's time to start hobbling forward again."

The next break came twenty minutes sooner than Lon had planned. The point men on the left came across a series of explosive devices that had to be deactivated before the march could resume.

"They weren't concealed very well," the sergeant leading the point squad reported. "It's almost as if they wanted us to find these. Makes me think maybe they've got a second set hidden better, to get us when we think we're in the clear."

"Take whatever time you need to make sure," Lon said. "If you can do it safely, just deactivate everything instead of detonating it. That way we avoid giving the enemy an easy marker for our progress."

"No problem, Colonel. That's what we had already started doing."

The delay gave most of the men time to eat a meal pack and get off their feet for a little longer. Once the mines had been cleared, Lon ordered a slight change in the direction of the advance, hoping to avoid any further traps that the New Spartans might have left.

On through the night the Dirigenters hiked, nearly silent, advancing toward the retreating New Spartans, moving to flank them on both sides. Men from 15th Regiment ran into two enemy patrols, occasioning brief and indecisive firefights; the New Spartans broke contact as quickly as they could. Second Battalion of the 7th encountered slightly heavier resistance, an ambush manned by perhaps half a company of New Spartans. That fight lasted nearly forty minutes and ended with most of the ambushers withdrawing safely. An hour before dawn, the point squad for 4th Battalion of the 7th tripped an enemy mine. Two men were killed. Another man was seriously wounded and had to be transferred to a trauma tube.

Overall, 7th Regiment averaged nearly 2 ½ miles per hour through the night. *Not bad*, Lon thought, though he would have been happier had they managed better. By dawn they were near where the New Spartans had been camped before this pursuit had started. The enemy was nine miles east-northeast of most of 7th Regiment, and continuing to move away from them. Fal Jensen's regiment was two miles closer. A battalion of Elysians was also on the move, on the right flank of 15th Regiment, almost even with them, pushing themselves to try to get in front of the New Spartans.

As the sun peeked over the eastern horizon, Lon called a halt for his regiment. "Thirty minutes," he said on the channel that connected him to his battalion and company commanders. "Make sure everyone eats."

Lon was halfway through his own breakfast when he received a call from *Peregrine* that completely killed his appetite. "Five New Spartan ships have just emerged from Q-space, four transports and one fighting ship, one of their heavy cruisers with room for maybe another twenty fighters. We estimate that they're seventy-four hours out from assault orbit."

19

"**Okay, gentlemen, we've** got our deadline," Lon told Fal Jensen and all of the battalion commanders. He had just passed the news from *Peregrine* about the New Spartan ships that had arrived in-system. "We need to get the issue settled on the ground before this new fleet can land its troops, and we'll be a hell of a lot better off if we finish with the enemy we're chasing soon enough to let us get some rest and get any wounded back to duty before we have to face the reinforcements. Four transports means a full regiment, or close to it. We don't dare let them land before we take care of what we're already facing." That much was obvious. No one on the channel questioned it.

"Fal, you've got troops closest to the New Spartans. That means you'll be the first to face them unless the Elysians set some kind of record moving around in front of them. I'm going to use thirty percent of our remaining rocket artillery rounds and half the howitzer munitions to try to slow them down enough to let you catch up with them by dark tonight and launch your attack. We'll pull the tanks from both heavy-weapons battalions forward to coordinate with your assault. My 4th Battalion shouldn't be more than half an hour behind you, and they'll join the fight as soon as they arrive. The rest of 7th will close as quickly as it can, but we're probably looking at two hours or more after you begin the action before we're all committed."

"Are you going to hold any troops as reserve?" Jensen asked.

"No line units," Lon said. "The rocket and gun artillery will stand by for possible fire missions. If things get too rough, we might end up using their crews as infantry." In the DMC, every man was a rifleman first. "The only other reserve will be the headquarters detachments, and they might get into the fight as well. We have to put everything we can into this."

"No argument on that," Jensen said. "Since this is an all-out offensive, will you try to bring in Shrikes to help?"

Lon hesitated. "Probably not. Realistically, the most we might manage is four to six, with the rest trying to keep the New Spartans occupied defending their ships. Captain Thorsen will undoubtedly argue against using even four fighters for close air support, especially with more enemy ships approaching. On balance, the good that four Shrikes might do isn't worth the risk, except *in extremis*."

"So we're on our own." Jensen did not bother to give that the inflection of a question.

"We're on our own," Lon agreed. "The next order of business is resupply of small-arms ammunition. We'll set that up for our next rest periods, have the ships gang-launch the resupply rockets while our Shrikes are out to keep the enemy from trying to intercept them. That way, maybe most of the ammunition will make it down intact. We'll want to have the men who are going to guide each rocket in out in the open to give them the best view for the work. Get the rockets in and get the ammunition distributed as quickly as possible. We'll bring in as much as we can. Any surplus will be used quickly, I think." Besides, no soldier ever complained about carrying too much ammunition when a fight was expected.

"No one's ever tried to resupply two whole regiments at one time," someone said on the circuit. Lon did not recognize the voice. It was one of 15th's battalion commanders.

"We're spread out enough that it shouldn't be a major

problem," Lon said. "There are more than enough control
frequencies to avoid having the wrong rocket respond to
commands. The men running the controls will have an
acquisition blip on their head-up displays. After that, it's
pretty much the same whether there's one rocket coming
in or a thousand, as long as the controllers are paying
attention. And bringing them all in at once buys us a mea-
sure of safety from enemy interception. There'll be too
many rockets in the air for them to have any hope of
targeting even ten percent of them."

It *sounded* good, and Lon had not been able to find any
reason why it might not work, but the anonymous voice
had been right. It was something that had never been tried
before. *Operations this large are so rare, the need has
never come up,* Lon consoled himself. It was, of course,
still one more thing to worry about.

His primary worry, at the moment, was forcing the enemy on the ground to fight. There was no guarantee it
would be possible. Both regiments pushed as hard as they
could through the day. The rocket artillery and, later, the
self-propelled howitzers forced the New Spartans to stop
three different times, and slowed their pace for nearly
three hours before the artillery exhausted the percentage
of munitions that Lon had allotted to the task.

There had been no answering fire from the New Spartans. If they had any mobile rocket launchers left, they
must certainly be out of ammunition—at least that was
what Lon tried to convince himself of. But there was a
nagging worry that the enemy might be reserving a few
rounds for a more desperate situation. *I would if I could,*
he thought.

Through the day, the only long stops the New Spartans
made were those occasioned by the artillery fire, when it
became simply too dangerous to advance. Other than that,
they took no more than five minutes every hour and a
quarter or so. "We'll take two breaks for every three they
take," Lon told 7th's battalion commanders. Fal Jensen
pushed 15th even harder. It was a questionable trade-off,

speed in catching the enemy against how tired the Dirigenters would be when they did.

"We have to take the risk," Fal Jensen told Lon. "We can't let these New Spartans evade us until their reinforcements land."

Lon had not tried to argue the point.

Still, an hour before sunset, both regimental commanders did allow a longer rest—time for a meal, time to let everyone get off their feet for an hour . . . and maybe get thirty minutes of sleep. "I think we're close enough to risk it, not that we have much choice," Jensen said when he and Lon conferred about the necessity. "The New Spartans are moving a lot slower as well. They'll have to take more time or have too many stragglers to be effective. We've already picked up a couple of them."

"The Elysians are almost on top of the New Spartans," Lon said, closing his eyes. He did not expect to get any sleep himself during the short stop. He doubted he would get a chance to try. A meal and coffee would have to be enough. "As soon as it's dark, they'll hit. That'll slow the enemy some more. The tanks will be in position to cover the fight by then as well."

"I've just had a report from one of my patrols," Jensen said, almost overriding Lon's final words. "The New Spartans have stopped and seem to be moving into a defensive perimeter. Maybe the chase is over. They're no more than two thousand yards out from my leading elements."

"The other batch of them, south of the river, are nearly to the ford," Lon said, after switching the view on his mapboard just long enough to check the latest position. Though none of those New Spartans were currently using active electronics, CIC had pinpointed the most recent sightings. That left room for error, or deception, but it was more reliable than guesswork.

"That still leaves them at least five or six hours away, no matter how hard they push," Jensen noted. "If we can handle the main force quickly, the troops south of the river will be pretty much irrelevant."

"Don't count on this being over that quickly," Lon said. "These *are* professionals, like us. They might still have a few surprises for us. I'll be surprised if they don't. We can't even be certain they don't have any rocket artillery left."

"Maybe," Jensen conceded, "but I think they'd have used that before now, while we were pounding them so hard before."

"Like they say, 'Don't bet the farm.' "

Lon made the rest of the calls he had to make, trying to keep each brief. The longest conversations were those with Jensen and Ives. Lon wanted each to be absolutely clear on what he planned. In case something happened to him before the night ended, there would be no lapse in command. Lon ate during the process, a mouthful here and there, spaced around the talk. Phip, Torrey Berger, Howell, and Dorcetti ran errands and brought messages as well.

Sunset came. In the next half hour Lon moved some of his companies nearer to their attack positions, closing possible avenues of escape for the New Spartans ... who showed no sign of trying to escape. The artillery was alerted against the possibility—probability—that the enemy troops south of the Styx might try to cross within the next hour.

Finally, Lon had an all-too-rare moment to himself. He leaned back, rotating his head to help ease a strain in his neck, then closed his eyes—just for a few seconds. He rested his head against the tree trunk behind him. There was an ache over his right eye, and he felt the beginnings of a tic—pure nervousness, tension. It couldn't be anything physical; his nano HMS would correct any physical problem quickly, automatically.

What am I missing? What do the New Spartans have up their sleeves? He had no idea how many times he had asked himself the same questions before. There had to be *something,* something perhaps vitally important. The New Spartans wouldn't just calmly put their collective head in the noose without some plan, some realistic hope of turning the tables.

"They're not acting desperate," Lon whispered. He opened his eyes again. "What's their hole card?" *What could it be?* He shook his head. More ammunition for their rocket artillery than he thought possible? More launchers that hadn't been spotted yet? Both? Or did they maybe have more men on the ground than he knew about, men who had been observing strict electronic silence since the Dirigenters arrived? *Maybe we're supposed to worry about the six hundred men south of the Styx, to keep us from looking elsewhere,* Lon thought.

He called CIC on *Peregrine* again, to ask about movements of New Spartan ships—especially the cruiser that was close enough to interfere. It was maintaining position; the transports were still well out on their highly eccentric orbits, apparently doing everything they could to stay out of reach. *Peregrine* and the rest of the Dirigenter fleet were continuing a close scan of everything within forty miles of the DMC troops. There were no anomalies, no hint of additional enemy units, but most of the ground was tree-covered. Forest canopy could hide hundreds of troops as long as they did not use active electronics. Even thermal signatures could be concealed, or disguised, with the right kind of insulation and discipline.

We could do it without much difficulty, Lon thought. *We have to assume that the New Spartans can.* But there was little, if anything, he could order done that wasn't already being done to discover any surprises the enemy might have. Patrols were being run. Electronic snoops had been set out in almost spendthrift fashion. The ships had the terrain under constant surveillance, from several angles, scanning from infrared through ultraviolet, and throughout the usable spectrum of radio frequencies. *If they do have anything, we'll get at least a few seconds' warning before anything hits,* Lon told himself. It was not much consolation.

I could bring Junior here and keep him close tonight, out of the way of trouble. That thought, unbidden and unexpected, was something of a shock. Junior had not been in Lon's conscious thoughts for some time. He shook his head. *I can't do that, for many reasons.* Junior would resent it, and too many people would see it for what it would be, an effort to keep the younger man away from the greatest danger.

Doc Norman would shake his head and cluck his tongue just at the suggestion, Lon thought. He shook his own head. *I guess I haven't completely put all my worries to sleep. I guess I never will, not as long as he's in the Corps and in harm's way. I'm still not completely a Dirigenter in my head.* Lon sighed, softly, and shook his head again. *But I wouldn't be a proper father if I didn't worry about my only son.*

Fal Jensen launched his attack, supported by 15th Regiment's tanks. At first the attack made some progress, but it was stopped three hundred yards short of the New Spartan line by concentrated—and extremely accurate—small-arms fire. *Too much fire for the manpower they have?* Lon wondered. Farther east and south, the companies of Elysian soldiers raced to join the fray. They had hardly begun to contribute when CIC relayed the news that the other contingent of New Spartans had started to cross the Styx. As planned, Lon committed most of the rockets his artillery still had to making the crossing as expensive for the enemy as possible.

Lon's 4th Battalion was the next unit to join the firefight. The rest of 7th Regiment remained too far away to participate. Lon had those three battalions on the move, though, heading for the northern flank of the New Spartans. The enemy had high ground behind him, and secondary positions, allowing them to withdraw into even better defensive posture, higher.

"We're about forty minutes from engagement," Lon told Fal Jensen. "Keep them occupied."

Lon did not hear Jensen's reply. That was when the New Spartans chose to spring their surprises.

20

That the New Spartans still had self-propelled rocket launchers and missiles for them to fire was not the most startling surprise possible. What Lon was *not* prepared for was the sheer volume of fire and the area where it originated—south of the river, and farther east than the area near the ford that had been under closest scrutiny. In less than a minute after the first crew-served rocket was fired, it appeared certain that the New Spartans had at least eight and perhaps a dozen or more launchers across the Styx, platforms that had not been spotted—or even suspected—before they started firing at the Dirigenter positions. The missiles came with profligate abandon, the launchers moving as they fired, following courses designed to be too random in appearance to permit successful counterbattery fire. Some of the rockets targeted the Dirigenter artillery, but most were directed at the infantry units pressing the attack against the main New Spartan force.

At the same time, obviously coordinated, the New Spartan cruiser in orbit launched all of its aerospace fighters on an attack against *Agamemnon* and *Odysseus,* ensuring that the Shrike II fighters could not be used for ground support.

"We've got to do something about that artillery!" Fal Jensen shouted into his radio connection with Lon. "They're right on target, tearing us to pieces."

"There's not much we can do, Fal," Lon said. "We don't have enough rockets yet to saturate the areas they're firing from, they're too far away for the howitzers, and it's going to take forty minutes or more to get the big guns close enough. The best we can do is close with the enemy infantry fast, get right in with them so their artillery can't hit us without hitting their own people."

"Can't we use what rockets we do have?" Fal asked.

"We've used almost every rocket to hit that short battalion of infantry crossing the river," Lon replied. "We'll put one or two rockets in the area where they're shooting from, but we don't have anything more. Keep your men down and dispersed until you can close with the enemy. As much as possible, passive electronics only. Don't give them anything they can home in on."

"They don't *need* electronics to home in on us. The New Spartans in front of us know exactly where we are."

"So don't help them. And we're not all in sight of the enemy. I'm going to make the order general. No radio or any other active electronics emissions unless absolutely essential," Lon said. "Pass that to your battalion and company commanders while I do the same for mine."

Lon had not finished passing that order along when the New Spartans unveiled their next surprise, an attack against the rearmost units of 7th Regiment. Since Lon's headquarters was, at the moment, very near the rear, he did not need reports to know about this attack. It seemed to be aimed directly at him.

Jeremy Howell almost bowled Lon over, trying to get him flat on the ground. The headquarters detachment had been on the move with the rest of the regiment, so they did not have slit trenches or any other cover available. The two men were scarcely down, and turned to face this latest threat, when a rocket-propelled grenade exploded eighty yards from them, quickly followed by several others along an arc, all at about the same distance.

"Maybe they're wasting rounds," Howell shouted near the side of Lon's helmet, "but there's no need to take chances. Give the rear guard time to deal with them, sir."

"I know, Jerry. Now will you kindly get off me?" Lon said, shrugging his entire body to move Howell's weight off his back and side. "I'm not so old I can't fall down on my own." Howell slid sideways.

"Sorry, sir," Howell mumbled, but both knew he would do the same thing again without thinking past the need to keep the Old Man safe. "Things sure went to hell in a hurry. Where'd they all come from?"

Lon didn't even try to answer. He adjusted his position, bringing his rifle to the ready, jacking a cartridge into the chamber and switching the safety to off. *At least I still know how to use this,* he thought. There was no need for him to start issuing commands to deal with the attack. The trailing companies of 1st and 3rd Battalions were already moving to isolate and eliminate the attack against the rear of the formation. Within three minutes he had a preliminary estimate of the number of New Spartans involved—no more than a single company, two hundred men, and more likely only half that number.

Those men did only minimal damage directly, but they were close enough to call in accurate ranging information to their supporting artillery, and rockets started falling by the time Lon knew how many of the enemy there were west of him. "That means we've got to move, and now," he told Howell before broadcasting the order to the affected commanders.

The two companies on rearguard duty would do what they could to hold the enemy in place while the rest moved north and east, hoping to escape direct observation. Lon's security detachment formed up around him—not a human shield, except for Howell and Dorcetti, but a properly dispersed infantry platoon adopting fire-and-maneuver tactics, using their rifles and rocket-propelled grenades to suppress enemy fire. The security troops were more heavily equipped with RPGs than line companies were, two per squad rather than one.

It was an orderly withdrawal and, since they were moving in the direction of an even stronger enemy force, it could not be properly called a retreat—an ironic thought that flittered through Lon's mind as he moved from one tree to the next, running bent low, zigzagging as erratically as he could. *Leaving others to do the dirty work.* There was no time to pursue that thought. He would be derelict in his duty if he *did* get involved in a minor skirmish at the edge of the main battle, distracted from his primary responsibilities.

After he had covered forty yards, Lon did stop momentarily, mostly to catch his breath. He sank to one knee, the trunk of a massive tree covering him from much of the enemy fire. Before he got up to start moving again, he did loose several short bursts of rifle fire toward the enemy, more for his own satisfaction than because he hoped to seriously contribute to the effort. He looked around, noting the positions of Jeremy Howell and Frank Dorcetti—never too far from him.

"I'll take care of this end of things, Lon," Phip Steesen said on their private channel. Lon noted Phip's position, by a blip on his head display, as thirty yards away, somewhat closer to the New Spartans. "You get out of the line of fire and worry about the other end."

"Just don't stick around too long. There are two companies back to handle this attack, so let them do it. Give me three minutes, then bring your people along. Let the rear guard do its job," Lon repeated. *I don't want to lose you the way we lost Dean on Bancroft.* There was no time for the pain of that memory to assert itself. There had been four of them originally, best friends as well as teammates, inseparable. Dean Ericks, Janno Belzer, and Phip Steesen had been the three musketeers of their platoon when Lon was assigned to their fire team. Lon had come under their collective wing, their D'Artagnan, a young officer cadet out to win his commission. Janno had quit the Corps and married. Lon and Phip saw him only infrequently these days, usually with his wife. Dean had died on contract.

Lon started moving again, his escort keeping pace even though they kept their attention more on what was behind than on where they were moving. *Use the terrain for*

cover and concealment. Don't follow a predictable pattern. Be as erratic as possible. Up and down. Side to side.
The New Spartans were too occupied with the counterattack by the Dirigenter rear guard to pay much attention to a few dozen men at extreme range and moving farther away. Still, an occasional round did come close enough to hear—or to see it hit. Wood splintered from the trunk of a tree just before Lon passed it, a little above head high. Some of the splinters bounced off the faceplate and side of Lon's helmet. He ducked instinctively, though it would have been too late had the wood been able to penetrate.

It was nearly ten minutes after the start of the attack on the rear before Lon was able to sink to the ground for more than a few seconds. The fight behind was dying away. He finally had time to turn his attention to the main battle again. There had been a few scattered reports before, but Lon needed to catch up . . . and quickly.

"At least we seem to have lost the enemy rocket artillery here, sir," Sergeant Howell said. "Moved too much for them to keep track of us, I reckon."

Lon took a moment to just listen. There was noise, including the explosions of heavy artillery, but none of it was nearby. "Maybe you're right, Jerry, but keep your butt down, just the same. Humor me. Now give me a minute to find out what's going on."

At first Lon did no transmitting. He simply shifted from one command channel to the next, listening for reports from those closer to the fighting, more concerned with getting a "feel" for the action than with specifics. The New Spartan infantry south of the river was still moving across the Styx—more than two-thirds of the men were already on the north bank and moving toward the rest of the fight. The rocket artillery had not managed to stop the crossing or—from what Lon could gather—make it as costly for the enemy as he had hoped.

"Brief me," Lon said on his link to CIC. While he moved, anxious to get away from the position he had—

briefly—revealed through transmitting, he listened, gaining confirmation of what he had gathered from his eavesdropping. Ninety percent or more of the New Spartan infantry might make it across the river—more than five hundred men. The Dirigenter heavy-weapons battalions had had too few rockets left to seriously impact the crossing and the enemy artillery firing from south of the Styx. As a result, neither attempt had been particularly successful.

"Our best estimate right now, Colonel," the duty officer in CIC reported, "is that you might not have much more than parity with the enemy on the ground, and that does not take into account casualties within the last quarter hour." He went on to give numbers—estimates—for both sides, along with updated position reports. The picture was not overly optimistic, but neither was it as bad as Lon had feared it might be.

"I'm going to move the tanks in as close as we can," Lon said. "Run them and the other heavy weapons until they don't have any ammunition left, then pull the crews to fight on foot." He closed out that conversation, then linked to Fal Jensen and the commanders of the heavy-weapons battalions and gave them the same orders. *It's a good thing we got the resupply finished,* he thought. There had been no incidents, and only one supply rocket had been lost—due to a fault in its guidance system. Then it was time for Lon and the men around him to move again . . . before the New Spartans could target their new location.

This time, the move was not as frantic. Lon and the people with him were not under direct small-arms fire, nor under direct enemy observation. The rearguard action had ended, with the few surviving New Spartans retreating, pursued by a single company from 7th's 1st Battalion. *Not Junior's company,* Lon noted. He wasn't certain whether he should feel relieved by that. No one was likely to escape danger for long this night.

It used to be so much easier, Lon thought, his eyes

searching a wide arc of ground in front of him, *back when I only had to worry about two platoons, or a single company. I knew everyone better, what they could do, what to expect.* The price of that intimacy had been that he had been closer to the men under his command. Every loss was a personal one. This operation was too big, spread over too much ground, for one man to stay on top of everything that was happening every minute. By the time he could get a complete picture from his subordinate commanders, the situation had changed. And there were too many men for Lon to know them as well, to feel as close to them.

Lon stopped moving and went down to one knee. There had been a hint of movement ahead, and a squad was investigating. Before they had gone far, the movement came again. This time Lon saw that it was a large bird that looked something like an owl, getting away from the advancing humans. *At least it's not one of those big lizards,* he thought. Then: *How can anyone keep track of this many people and what's happening to them?*

This was no time for philosophical pursuits. Inwardly, Lon shook his head. He blinked several times. He did not want to use his radio and give the enemy a chance to pinpoint his location. He listened, scanning the frequencies his officers would use. Those who were already in direct contact with the enemy had little reason to maintain electronic silence. And CIC was maintaining a constant update on a channel that the regimental and battalion commanders and staff could audit.

Before long, 15th Regiment would have to divide its attention between the main enemy force and the group coming north from the Styx. Fal Jensen was aware of that. He had started to space his troops accordingly. One of his short battalions was moving to establish a line, and to space land mines and electronic snoops farther out to give warning of the enemy's approach. The tanks of 15th's heavy-weapons battalion also were moving in that direction, hoping to get close enough to strike at the New

Spartan rocket artillery south of the river. Seventh Regiment's tanks also were moving that way, farther back. They would be able to take the enemy infantry under fire before they could touch the artillery. *It probably won't do much good,* Lon thought. *Those rocket launchers can pull back until they're out of range of the tanks and still be able to hit us up here.* But he did not countermand the order. The effort had to be made.

At present, the main New Spartan force was being faced on three sides. If they wanted to, they could still retreat east, over the crest of the line of hills they were on now. *If they're going to try moving, they're going to have to do it within the next half hour or so,* Lon thought, taking a moment to glance at the display on his mapboard. *They wait much longer than that and we'll have them effectively surrounded, able to cover the remaining gap with small-arms fire from either side.*

Lon shook his head. *If they were going to retreat any farther, they'd have started before now, not waited until we were close enough to make it too costly. They've got to be counting on that extra-short battalion and the rocket artillery south of the river. And any other surprises they might have left,* he added. There was still that possibility, that the New Spartans had not yet shown all their cards. *Still more than two full days before those new ships can get close enough to contribute anything. How do they expect to hold out on the ground that long? Do they even have enough rifle ammunition to hold us off if we keep pressing the attack?*

"That might be the key," Lon whispered. *Unless they cached ammunition and chose that spot for their stand because of its location, they'll run short on ammo before the new force can land.* He tried to focus on that, looking for flaws in his reasoning. What *were* the chances they had cached ammunition along that ridge? After a moment, Lon conceded they were pretty good. The New Spartans had not been *driven* to the site. *They* had picked it. In addition to the tactical advantages of the location, knowing they were sitting on a stock of extra ammunition might be a major bonus.

Just means we'll have to press that much harder, Lon thought. *We started action tonight with all the ammunition we could carry for our rifles and grenade launchers, and if we have to, we can get another resupply drop in before the new enemy fleet gets close enough to interfere.* He was glad that there had been no indication that the New Spartans had the capacity to resupply men on the ground by rocket. *We might find out soon enough if the intelligence on that is right,* he decided.

"Lon, this is Fal Jensen. I've got an idea you're going to think is totally insane, but hear me out."

"Go ahead, Fal," Lon said, getting up and signaling his detachment to get ready to move.

"The enemy rocket artillery isn't going to let our tanks sit north of the Styx and shell them. They can pull south, out of our reach, and keep on clobbering us. Why not send our tanks—from both regiments—across the river? The info I have is that the ford is shallow enough and has a firm enough bed to let them cross safely. Even if we can't destroy the rocket launchers, we can drive them out of range of our people up here."

"What about the time it takes them to cross the river?" Lon asked. "They'll be sitting ducks if the New Spartans are watching, and they probably will be."

"Three minutes, maybe four for the crossing," Jensen said. "They blow across at best speed and get out of the open before the New Spartans have time to target them and get rockets to the river."

Lon hesitated, for perhaps as long as thirty seconds. He closed his eyes. It would be a terrible gamble, but . . . "Set it up, Fal. We'll give it a try. Maybe it's just crazy enough to work. But keep me informed. If it goes bad, we may have to pull them back in a hurry." *If there's time,* he thought.

21

It was 0100 hours. The battle for what Lon had started to think of as "Spartan Ridge" had been going on for three hours. The New Spartans had been in position long enough to dig in. The Dirigenters had to scoop out what defensive positions they could under fire. At least the ground was wet enough to make that relatively easy, but not so muddy as to make the resulting trenches swampy. The earlier showers had, mostly, stopped. A few minutes of drizzle, now and then, were all that was left from the cold front that had crossed the area.

The shooting had progressed by fits and starts as the Dirigenters probed for weak spots in the enemy line. The battle had never been general, all along the New Spartan perimeter simultaneously. There were also occasional skirmishes away from that perimeter, patrol meeting patrol. And the New Spartans coming up from the river were met, ambushed, and stopped short of rendezvous with their main force on the ridge. Part of 15th Regiment was involved with that, and the EDF troops had been diverted to help. The radio reports Lon heard suggested that the Elysians were doing their best to exact revenge for the New Spartan invasion.

The New Spartan rocket artillery was no longer firing so heavily at the Dirigenters. They had used so many missiles in the early stages of the fight that they had to be running short of ammunition again. Just before 0100 hours, the Dirigenter tanks had crossed the Styx. Two of those tanks, near the end of the lines, had been hit by rockets. The wreckage stood in the river, still smoking. No one from the crews had made it out—six men dead. But the rest of the tanks were now on the south shore of the Styx, racing toward the New Spartan rocket artillery . . . which was moving farther away from the engagement, just what Lon and Fal Jensen had hoped. Soon, if everything went well, the New Spartan rocket launchers would be too far away to continue striking Dirigenter infantry at all. Lon tried not to think of the cost to the tank companies.

Half of Lon's 2nd Battalion had moved across the ridgeline and were sliding into position behind the New Spartans, forcing them to worry about their entire perimeter and not just the western and southwestern sections of it. Fal Jensen was attempting to edge a company and a half of his 3rd Battalion around the southern flank.

"If we can box them in, we've about got the issue settled," Jensen said when he and Lon conferred—just before the tanks crossed the Styx. "Pop 'em from all sides until their lines start leaking, then close in and finish 'em off."

"I hope it's that simple," Lon said. *But I still can't make myself believe it will be.*

It was now 0125 hours. The fighting heated up on the reverse slope of the ridge, east, as the New Spartans moved to keep from being surrounded. A full battalion of them came out and turned north, to face the stronger of the two Dirigenter elements trying to close the noose around them. Ten minutes later, a second battalion wheeled toward the south, engaging six platoons from 15th Regiment on that end. The rest of the New Spartans started moving uphill, to the ridge, to secondary positions that apparently also had been prepared in advance.

"Are they just taking new positions, or ready to try a breakout?" Lon asked. "I need information, *fast*." He was on a channel that connected him to CIC, Fal Jensen, and each of the battalion commanders. He left that channel open for replies, but switched to another channel to connect to Phip Steesen.

"We're moving in closer," Lon said. "Saddle 'em up and let's go." As soon as Phip acknowledged, Lon went back to the other channel. "I'm moving my CP closer to the ridge, between 7th's 1st and 3rd Battalions. If the New Spartans are trying to get away, I've got to be near enough to react." This time he did not wait for acknowledgments. His security detachment was up and ready to move, spread around their commander. Lon used hand signals to indicate the direction.

There was already a noticeable slope to the ground, climbing toward the east. The land rose at a gentle angle, no more than ten degrees. The tree cover started to get sparser, and within a few minutes Lon started to see the damage that the fighting had caused—trees felled or shattered by artillery; trunks scarred by bullets; a few small, smoldering fires and the ashes of others. The trees and grass were too wet to burn easily.

He also saw bodies on the ground, Dirigenters who had fought their last fight. Lon counted eight, within not too great a space. All were lying on their backs, with indications that each had been checked by one of the medtechs. Lon gritted his teeth and tried not to think how many more dead there already were, how many more might fall before the fight came to an end.

Ten minutes on the move: Lon and his security detachment stopped, taking what cover they could. The sounds of fighting were noticeably closer in the east, but the battle still was a thousand yards away. Lon asked for news, any indication that the New Spartans had tipped their hand: Were they taking new positions or trying to escape? There still was no answer.

What's it going to take to get them to quit? Lon asked himself as he got up and started moving east again. *How can we convince them they can't hold out until their reinforcements land?* The New Spartans were mercenaries, professionals. Surely they wouldn't make a futile "last stand." That was bad for business, worse than accepting an inevitable defeat and rebuilding, living to fight another day, on some other world.

We would never push it that far, Lon thought, though units of the Corps had in the past—at least on one regrettable contract. An entire regiment had been wiped out on a world known as Wellman, and the second regiment sent in also had been defeated. He squeezed his eyes shut for an instant as he knelt next to a tree. *If we can't finish this batch off, at least seriously degrade their strength before the new fleet reaches attack orbit, we may have to concede defeat ourselves.* That thought hurt, but Lon would not let his command be totally wiped out if there was no chance of success—or hope of holding out until another regiment and more ships could arrive from Dirigent. And *that* would take another four weeks, absolute minimum.

Lon took a deep breath. *Come up with something brilliant so you don't have to worry about that,* he told himself. *Find a way to end this in the next forty hours.* That would give him half a day to get ready for the incoming fleet. *Convince the New Spartans to surrender.* Lon snorted softly and shook his head. *Brilliant ideas seem to be in short supply. And the New Spartans aren't making any major mistakes.*

A call from Vel Osterman took him out of his thoughts. "I'm on the north flank," Osterman said. "Near the ridge, with a clear view down into the area the New Spartans were originally defending. I think they're pulling out completely, probably aiming to withdraw to the next ridgeline, five miles farther east. They're showing good discipline, an orderly move, covering their asses. Once they get clear of this ridge—in maybe ten minutes—the entire western slope will be wide open."

"Except for whatever mines and booby traps they're leaving behind," Lon said. "And maybe the occasional patrol or sniper."

"That's why I called, Lon," Osterman said. "I haven't

seen any preparations of that sort, and I'm in good position to. It might be nothing more than creeping paranoia on my part, but I think they *want* us to chase them straight over the hill, that maybe they've got more than the usual presents waiting for us, something they set up before we got here."

"You mean some kind of trap," Lon said.

"That's what I'm thinking. I could be all wrong, but this gives me an itch I can't scratch. If they wanted to, they could probably hold this ridge long enough for their reinforcements to land, and moving exposes them to dangers they can't be sure of accurately gauging. Unless. . . ." He let that hang.

Lon hesitated a moment before he replied. "I wouldn't put it past them, but if we detour completely around we're going to lose a couple of hours, give them that much more chance to put distance between us and settle themselves in somewhere new." Another hesitation. "I think we have to take our chances, Vel, but I'll put several squads out to cover the ground before the rest of us move through. Thanks for the warning."

Lon switched channels to call the commanders of his 1st and 3rd Battalions, Ted Syscy and Benjamin Dark. "Get your best scouts out to look for traps in the area the New Spartans have just vacated. Tell them to be especially careful. I know they always are, but even more than usual. There's a damned good chance the enemy has left something extra behind to catch us with our pants down."

Both of the battalion commanders acknowledged the order. "It might be nothing more than that they've had time to register every rock and tree on that slope for their rocket artillery, with spotters to pass the word where we are," Syscy added. Early in his career, before transferring to 1st Battalion, he had spent a year in the regiment's heavy-weapons battalion. He considered himself an expert on artillery. "No way to tell how many of the big rockets they've got left to dump on us."

"I hope there's nothing more to it than that, Ted," Lon

said, "but we've just about got their rocket launchers out
of range, unless they have even more they haven't used,
and that's unlikely. They've already shown a lot more
than they should have had. I'm guessing that it's something more like a thick screen of command-detonated
mines, concealed well enough that a casual patrol might
go past without spotting them. Something on that order.
Hard telling what they've dreamed up. Just tell your patrols to be alert for anything."

"How much time do we have to get the scouts
through?" Syscy asked.

"Not enough, I'm afraid. We can't give the New Spartans a minute more than absolutely necessary. I can't fun-
nel enough men around the flanks fast enough to catch
and hold them until the rest of us tiptoe across the ridge.
I'm going to move everyone as close as we can, then . . .
well, we'll give your men a few minutes. Not many."

"We'll do what we can," Syscy said. Dark clicked his
transmitter to agree.

Lon had kept moving during this conference. As soon
as it was over, he signaled Phip to change direction, angling southeast instead of north of east—to throw off any
enemy response if they had been tracking the detachment.
There were more orders to pass, and Lon had to apprise
Fal Jensen of what 7th Regiment was going to do. *Keep
the pressure up on both sides. Make sure the New Spartans have to withdraw slowly, under fire. Don't give them
time for anything else.* The New Spartans had come out
to north and south to hold off the Dirigenters, letting the
rest of their force withdraw through the gap. Then the
flanks had closed in behind, withdrawing in orderly fashion.

They're doing it awfully well, Lon thought with grudg-
ing admiration. An orderly withdrawal under heavy enemy pressure was one of the hardest maneuvers to
accomplish, and it could be extremely costly in lost men,
even if the withdrawal did not turn into a mindless rout.
And Lon saw no indication that this was likely to degen-

erate into a mad retreat. *That would be a major surprise,*
he thought.

He finally called a halt for his headquarters detachment,
no more than three hundred yards from the van of 1st and
3rd Battalions, which was near the foot of the hill the
New Spartans had evacuated less than an hour before.
There had been considerably more destruction to the forest here. Few trees were still standing and unmarked by
the fighting. There was a smell of smoke and gunpowder
heavy on the air, clinging.

Lon sat in the crook between two trees that had fallen,
one across the other. Snapped and bent branches, charred
and wilted leaves formed something of a canopy over his
head. He lifted the faceplate of his helmet, then took one
of his canteens from his belt. He splashed a little water
on his face and rubbed the water around. That helped
more than the sip of water he actually drank. That had a
slightly bitter metallic taste to it, the taste of gunpowder
and burned wood that was already on his lips and in his
mouth. The smell of fire was heavy on the air. Lon considered opening a meal pack for a couple of mouthfuls of
food but decided against it. Food could wait a little longer.

The scouting patrols from 1st and 3rd Battalions were
halfway to the ridge, near the second line of slit trenches
that had been dug by the New Spartans. So far the patrols
had not found anything unexpected. In fact, there was a
dearth of land mines, booby traps, and electronic snoops—
the very items that a well-equipped enemy would be most
likely to leave behind to slow pursuit. *Either they've run
out of everything or they* are *very anxious to have us follow as quickly as possible,* Lon thought, recalling Vel
Osterman's warning. *And we can't assume that they're
out of anything.*

He stared up the slope, squinting, as if that might help
him spot an answer from a distance when the men walking
the ground had not found anything. *Something.* He shook
his head, which was becoming all too frequent a gesture
for comfort. *If we can't find whatever they have in mind,*

maybe we can trick them into tipping their hand a little too soon.

Maybe. Lon signaled for Phip to come to him. "Listen closely," Lon said after both men had raised their faceplates. "I want to try something a little unusual." He spent two minutes explaining exactly what he wanted done, going back over everything a second time; then he made Phip repeat the instructions back to him, to make certain there was no confusion. "I don't know that this is going to do us any good, but I think we need to do something."

"Okay, I see your point," Phip said. "I think it's probably a crazy waste of time, but we're better off with that than maybe walking into something that'll kill any chance we have of finishing this job the way we want to. I'll grab Dorcetti and get started." Then he hurried off to implement Lon's instructions, hardly hearing the softly sardonic "Glad you approve" Lon sent after him.

Lon pulled his faceplate down and checked the time. *We've been on this world less than seventy-two hours,* he thought with amazement. It seemed far longer. All he could do now was wait to see if his ruse would work . . . *if* there was anything up there. Ten minutes. Phip would need that much time to get started, and the scouts high on the slope would need that much time to reach the ridge and take cover. Lon settled himself more comfortably behind the two tree trunks. *Maybe it is crazy,* he conceded, *but if it isn't, maybe this will save some lives as well as time.*

He took another drink of water, a little more than before. The taste hadn't improved. His mouth and throat remained dry. *If this doesn't turn anything, we're going to have to just go ahead and move forward. We can't take the time to move most of a regiment around on either side. And there's no guarantee the New Spartans didn't leave deadly surprises for us there.*

He glanced at the timeline on his visor display again. The seconds seemed to be marching in place instead of moving forward the way they should. *Time:* In perhaps as little as fifty-five hours, the New Spartans would have another regiment on the ground, or landing. *There's no way we can face what they have on the ground now and what's coming at the same time. They'll run all over us.* Lon closed his eyes and took a long, slow breath, as deep as he could, holding it before expelling it just as slowly, tried to ignore the bitter odor on the air. Even that spent less than a minute of the waiting time. Phip hadn't even had time yet to tell everyone what they were going to do.

I should have saved some of the work for myself, split it with Phip. That would have kept my mind busy and made the waiting shorter, Lon thought, but it was too late to change that. All he could do was suffer through the waiting. Another seven minutes to go, at least. Phip would give the signal to the chosen men once everyone had been told what to do. *I'll give the order for everyone else to get down and stay put once I see the blips light up for the guinea pigs.* Or sacrificial goats.

Lon looked around, pulling his faceplate down to take advantage of its dual night-vision systems. Phip was barely visible eighty yards away, off to the right, zigging his way through the trees—both standing and felled. On the other side, Sergeant Dorcetti was moving in similar fashion, carrying instructions to others. Dorcetti had been the first man Phip had talked to. They were splitting the notification. Altogether, Lon hoped to have fifty men taking part in the deception. *Limit the risk, but use enough men to make it believable.*

He switched channels to listen to the feed from CIC, the running commentary provided from what the ships could see through its own cameras and other sensors and through the cameras mounted in the helmets of officers and noncoms, and hear on the many radio channels available to the troops about the engagements on the ground. The fight on the other side of the hill had slackened off. The New Spartans were on the slope leading up to the next ridgeline, across an almost dry creekbed. The Dirigenters on both flanks were moving east as well, staying off to the sides, trying to pick up a little distance to give them a chance to eventually get behind the enemy. The fight against the smaller group of New Spartans, the men who had crossed the Styx earlier, also was continuing, moving gradually to the east as well, but 15th Regiment was making certain that those companies could not move north, closer to rendezvous with their main force.

One more sip of water. Lon quickly pulled his faceplate back down and glanced at his timeline. Two minutes were left of the ten he had estimated for preparations. He adjusted his position, getting farther down into the cover offered by the two fallen tree trunks. *I wonder where Junior is?* Lon wondered, glancing toward the north. Junior would be with 1st Battalion. *Or is he with one of the patrols up near the ridge?* Lon had not asked who was leading those. It would have been ... not quite proper. *I hope he knows to get his head and butt down at the right time.* Lon swallowed hard.

I could sure use a pint of Geoff's best lager right now, Lon thought, startled by the intrusion of memories of his father-in-law and the pub he ran on Dirigent. He could almost taste the beer, feel the muggy warmth of the pub. *Maybe it is time to retire and move to Bascombe East. Spend the next few decades tending bar. Be around to see at least one child grow up, not miss almost every birthday and Christmas the way I have with Junior and Angie.*

He blinked furiously for several seconds and looked at his timeline. This was not the time to think of home and the baby whom Sara was carrying. *Any time now,* he told himself. *Phip and Frank have had time enough to get the word out.* He stared at the head-up display on his visor, looking for the appearance of friendly blips along the line that the two noncoms had followed. Phip's would be the first to show. The rest should appear almost instantly after that.

Now! Lon saw the blips appear. In a ragged line they started moving forward. Some went out, then reappeared a few yards farther on in staggered sequence—the sort of display that might result from officers and noncoms giving orders and taking reports as their battalions started a broad advance. Lon switched to an all-hands channel that would connect him to every man in 7th Regiment. He spoke one word: "Down!" The men Phip and Frank had enlisted knew the command did not apply to them.

Lon got under one of the trees, squirming to get as much of his body touching the ground as possible. *Now we wait,* he told himself. *Again. And find out how foolish I'm going to look.*

The wait was not as long as he had feared. Little more than ninety seconds passed before the entire western slope of the hill seemed to explode at once.

22

First, there were two thin strips of dirty orange-red light, roughly parallel to each other on the slope, approximately following the lines of slit trenches and foxholes that the New Spartans had dug earlier. The orange-red glow drew Lon's eyes. He lifted his head—just a couple of inches—to see what was happening, an instinctive motion that might better have been suppressed. The sound of the explosions and the concussion wave swept down the slope and across his position as the line of light stretched into the sky—bulging, blossoming as it raised smoke, dirt, and heavier debris. It cast rock and soil up and out, broke off heavier chunks, and started them rolling down the slope, beginning a prolonged rockslide. Lon could feel the ground shaking beneath him, even after it had stopped. The initial concussion had knocked the air out of him, and recovery seemed infinitely prolonged. He could hear nothing but echoes of the explosion for most of a minute, and his ears continued to ring after that.

Lon, like most of the troops of the two waiting battalions, was far enough back that the heaviest debris fell far short of where he lay trying to cover himself as the sky fell, but dirt and small stones pelted him and the others, some of the objects with enough force to be painful. A shower of very small bits of rock and dirt rained on Lon's helmet, a staccato rattle that temporarily obscured the ringing in his ears.

The assault from above seemed eternal, but lasted less than a minute. The rockslide lasted longer, only gradually coming to a halt. The smoke above the slope dissipated, lifting, thinning, dispersing. The dust settled. Lon found that he was holding his breath and released it quickly, then inhaled deeply. The smells of explosives and dirt were almost overpowering, choking. He coughed several times, then shook his head to dislodge the grit and dust that had collected on his helmet. Finally, he cautiously lifted himself to his elbows to look out through a gap in the trees he had sheltered behind and below.

He looked up at the slope of the hill. There were a few small fires—grass and low shrubbery burning along the lines of the explosions—and the infrared display of his nightvision system showed alternating bands of hot and cool spots on the hillside—hot where the blasts had originated, cool where deeper layers of rock and soil were now exposed on the surface.

Only slowly did Lon become aware of talk on the radio, faint, almost unable to compete with the volume of the tinnitus that remained from the concussive force of the explosions. He adjusted the volume on his receiver until the voices were louder than his inner-ear static. There was still a jumble of sound, too many voices trying to talk at once, electronic silence forgotten. Still, Lon needed nearly a minute before he was able to respond, to say, "Can the chatter" on his all-hands channel.

It spoke well for the training of his men that silence came to the troop channels immediately. Lon switched frequencies. "Phip, are you there?" he asked on the channel that connected them directly. "Phip?" Lon held his breath while he waited for a reply, switching his head-up display to show vital signs. There was no indication of any signs for Phip. Lon looked for Frank Dorcetti's vital signs then. Something flickered across his display then, and vanished. It hadn't been a proper readout, simply static.

Damage to the electronics, Lon thought, fighting down the fear that he might have lost another friend—the closest he had ever had. *We'll probably have a lot of that, after a blast that strong.* That did not totally erase the agitated thumping of his heart, the edge of fear. He switched channels again. "We need medtechs and several squads to help them find the men we had out front," he said, speaking to the battalion and company commanders in 1st and 3rd Battalions. "Lead Sergeant Steesen and Sergeant Dorcetti were leading them. We'll have to find them to find out just how many people they had with them."

Lon got to his feet, leaning against one of the fallen trees that had sheltered him. He rested his gun across the trunk, the muzzle pointed vaguely up the slope. It was, perhaps, reckless to expose himself, but that never even crossed his mind. In the wake of such massive explosions, any other danger seemed unreal. His eyes scanned the terrain, which certainly looked like a war zone now, as stark as some of the old battlefield photographs he had seen at The Springs on Earth, images from the two global conflicts of the twentieth century. Several bands of low-lying smoke or dust clung to the hillside, slowly descending, only slowly being torn apart by the light breeze.

His men were out there, and two of them counted as friends. Resisting the urge to look for them personally was the most Lon could manage. He stood and watched as squads of searchers moved forward, weapons at the ready, eyes glancing nervously up the hillside, as if in anticipation of more explosions. A medtech moved with each squad, his medical bag over his shoulder, a folded stretcher on his backpack. But each medtech also carried a rifle and held it ready for instant use.

Lon called the commanders of 1st and 3rd Battalions. "Get a check from your companies. Make sure we don't have any other casualties from the blast. Then get ready to move out before the New Spartans have time to figure out that they didn't decimate us. We're going to the top of the hill. And beyond. I want us ready to start in five minutes." Five *long* minutes. Lon had been tempted to order an immediate advance. That was what he *wanted* to do, almost desperately. Cover the ground. Close with the enemy. Force the fight . . . and take some payback. But he could not order some mad charge. This had to be done properly, in military order.

Lieutenant Colonels Syscy and Dark acknowledged the order—indicating that they had already started checking for casualties among their men. Their voices seemed distant, hollow, to Lon, though the ringing in his ears had declined considerably. He shook his head, gently, trying to rid himself of the remnants, but it was not that simple. It would take time for the effect to end. This was something Lon had experienced before.

"I think our deception worked," he said, still on a link with the two battalion commanders. "Those blasts were meant to catch us all on the slope, in the kill zone. We got lucky."

"It would have done a number on us if we had all been moving, that's for sure," Dark said. "But I wouldn't call it all luck. That was fancy thinking, setting up decoys that way."

A little bit of occupational paranoia, maybe, Lon thought as the word "decoys" tied his stomach in new knots. Decoys were meant to be sacrificed to draw out the enemy. *How many men did I send to their deaths this time?* Lon closed his eyes for an instant. *It's time I start getting reports on that.* The first report came within seconds. Six men were dead. Twenty were wounded, half of them seriously enough to need time in trauma tubes. Frank Dorcetti was among the dead. Phip Steesen . . .

"His left shoulder is in pretty bad shape, Colonel," the medtech who examined Phip said, "but I don't think he'll lose the arm." Hesitation. "It's going to be close, though. The shoulder and upper arm were crushed, the joint pretty well shattered. I can't tell how much nerve damage there is—some, certainly. We've minimized the bleeding and got him on a stretcher. He'll be in a tube in three minutes. He's not completely conscious."

Lon called Lieutenant Colonel Dark to arrange for a security detail to stay with the medtechs and their charges when the battalions moved on. Then Lon gave the order to advance. He climbed over the fallen tree in front of him as the men of his security detail started forward in a ragged line. As always, Jeremy Howell was too close, a couple of steps to Lon's left.

Dorcetti's dead, Lon told himself as he put one foot in front of the other. Frank had been his driver since Lon had taken command of 7th Regiment. Lon had never felt quite as close to Dorcetti as he felt toward Jeremy Howell, but still, Frank had been there every day, always with a joke and a grin to help Lon along. *Not always good jokes,* Lon thought, *but he tried. He always tried.*

Lon tried to fight through the empty moment, the void of loss. The time for grief would come later, after the fighting was over and they were on the way home. For now, Frank was simply one man among many who had died on this contract. It was always the same, difficult to be that abstract about the inevitable cost of battle. The hundreds of men who had been killed in their shuttles trying to land on Elysium were less important—at this minute—than one man who had died a few hundred yards from Lon.

But even thinking about Frank served mostly as a shield to help Lon avoid worrying about Phip's condition. A full session in a trauma tube, maybe more, even if the medtech had not underestimated the extent of Phip's injuries. If there was serious nerve damage in the injured shoulder and arm, Phip might be out of action for weeks. *Left shoulder crushed,* Lon thought. *A few inches to the right and it would have been his head, and he might have been beyond help.* Lon stumbled as he closed his eyes against that thought.

The advance slowed as the lead companies started to cross the debris field at the base of the slope. Men had to pick their way over or around obstacles, and often a footstep started the man-made scree sliding again. *Turn big rocks into little rocks* swept through Lon's mind when he reached the raw gravel and dirt himself. There were sizable boulders among the debris, but most of it was smaller, loose. The footing could scarcely have been more treacherous if the men had been climbing an icy slope against a strong headwind. More than once Lon had a foot slide out from under him, forcing him to catch his balance awkwardly. Each time, Jeremy Howell moved closer, ready to help, moving back when Lon gestured at him.

It took twenty-five minutes before Lon reached the line of the first New Spartan defense perimeter, the site of the lower series of explosions. The fronts of the slit trenches had been blown forward, leaving raw gashes in the dirt and rock, reaching down to the heartstone of the hill in places. Behind, sharp rises of up to three or four feet that had to be clambered over.

Lon started paying attention to reports from Fal Jensen and CIC as well as from his battalion commanders. The smaller group of New Spartans was still being kept from moving north to rendezvous with their main force, which was establishing defensive positions on the next ridge. They were being harassed by Lon's 2nd and 4th Battalions and by most of what remained of 15th Regiment.

The New Spartans were still fighting as smart as they could under the circumstances—keeping good order, not allowing the Dirigenters to roll over or around them, and husbanding their ammunition, relying on accuracy more than volume. *They still think they can hold out until those ships get in with their reinforcements,* Lon thought. It was a discouraging notion. They might have good reason for their optimism. *What more can they do?* Lon wondered, but his mind was too numb to explore the possibilities. *Just hope they've run out of surprises,* he thought. *They have to, sooner or later.* That might be more wishful thinking than logical deduction, though, and Lon knew it.

The slope steepened above the line of the first explosions—more than Lon had realized from looking at the hillside from a distance. The blasts and landslides had taken the slope down to rock, stripping the thin covering of soil, and in many places the rock itself bore the scars of new fractures, areas where rock had broken loose and fallen. Much of the loose stone that had gathered in the few relatively level areas was sharp-edged.

The muscles in Lon's calves and thighs started to tighten. The advance slowed more. Lon stopped moving forward for nearly two minutes, rationalizing that he was getting too close to the van, closer than he should be. Jeremy Howell looked toward him, an unasked question about Lon's well-being clear in the tilt of his head. The rest of the squad charged with protecting the regimental commander took their positions around him, looking up and outward, vigilant . . . and nervous.

We're almost five miles from the enemy, Lon thought, noting the disposition of the men around him. *After those explosions, there can't very well be anything left to go off close.* But he did not say anything. His men were doing their job, and would continue to do so despite any protests he might make. All the more now that the regimental lead sergeant was out of action.

As he started moving up the hill again, Lon got on the channel that connected him to everyone in his security detail. "We'll take five just before we reach the ridge, give the rest time to get farther ahead of us." The squad leader voiced his acknowledgment. Lon saw a couple of heads nod, in either acknowledgment or relief. *They'd all feel a lot better if I never got within twenty miles of any fighting,* he thought, *and not because it would keep them that far from danger.* He shook his head in amazement.

By the time he got near the ridgeline, Lon was glad he had decided to halt there. The climb had him breathing hard, and he had slipped once, bruising his right knee badly, with a two-inch gash at the center of the bruise. The knee hurt, and had already started to swell. Once he settled to the ground, Lon pulled up the trouser leg and put a medpatch over the cut and bruise; that would help his body's health implants speed through the work of repairing the damage, and kill the pain.

The two battalions with Lon kept moving, scouts checking the eastern slopes for mines and booby traps. There were only a few, and even fewer electronic snoops. Apparently the New Spartans had concentrated their available explosives on the western slope, in what they had hoped would be a *coup de main. I hope they used everything they had,* Lon thought after hearing a report from one of the point patrols.

He glanced at the timeline on his visor display, then tilted his faceplate up and looked into the sky. There were still a couple of hours of darkness left, and the sky remained heavily overcast even though the rain had ended. There were no stars visible, nor any light from Elysium's moon. Lon couldn't even see a glow from lights in University City, off to the southwest. *It would be great if we were up against an enemy without nightvision systems,* Lon thought, but the New Spartans had gear as advanced as that of the Dirigenters.

"Colonel, why don't you have a meal pack as long as we're going to be here a few minutes," Jeremy Howell said. He knelt next to Lon and lifted his faceplate. "Got to give the body fuel to work, sir." When Lon chuckled, it startled Howell. He drew back a little.

"Sorry, Jerry, I wasn't laughing at you," Lon said. "You just triggered a flashback. Back in prehistoric times, when I was a cadet, everyone in the company seemed infernally preoccupied with making sure I shoved calories down my throat every time I opened my mouth. They weren't happy unless I was as stuffed as a Thanksgiving turkey." He hesitated. "Yes, I'd better have a little food while we're stopped. A nap for an old man would be nice, too, but that'll have to wait." *Maybe a long time,* he thought as he accepted the meal pack Howell handed him.

The New Spartan main force did not stay long in their positions on the next ridge, hardly long enough to dig minimal slit trenches, eat, and—perhaps—get a little rest. Once they saw the Dirigenters advancing again—obviously not destroyed or seriously weakened by the explosions left to catch them—they abandoned their new holes and started east again. According to the nearest Dirigenters, the New Spartans appeared to be moving slowly. They had been under constant observation this time, and it seemed clear that they had not booby-trapped those positions as thoroughly as they had the earlier lines.

North of the New Spartans, the Dirigenter 2nd Battalion, 7th Regiment was pushing east as rapidly as the men could—faster, perhaps, than was prudent. On the south, 4th of the 7th and half of 15th Regiment also were pushing east quickly, though not quite at the same pace as Vel Osterman's battalion. Osterman had his lead company as far east as the van of New Spartans, with the advance patrols starting to curve south, attempting to slow the enemy until the rest of the battalion could get in place to hold them. The rest of 15th Regiment was still engaging the smaller New Spartan force near the Styx. The New Spartans were finding it increasingly difficult to keep moving toward a hoped-for rendezvous with their main force.

"We've still got two days to bring this to resolution," Lon said, conferring with Fal Jensen and the battalion commanders from both regiments, "but we don't want to use every minute until those new ships get close enough to launch troops and fighters against us. We get that close to the end and there's little chance the New Spartan commander on the ground will surrender. They'll try to keep us occupied right up until the new force can get into the act. And if that happens, we're in big trouble."

"They can't have any rocket artillery left, not close enough to hit us," Fal Jensen noted. "Our tanks have driven the few launchers they had left out of range. If they had anything closer, they would have hit us by now. And our Shrikes are keeping them from using their fighters for close air support."

"And vice versa," Lon said. "We can't get Shrikes in to help us either. That end of it is a stalemate, at least until the new force gets close enough to use its fighters. Then our fleet is in trouble, too. Maybe the New Spartans don't have any rockets left for their self-propelled launchers, but we're also out of ammunition for our rocket launchers and artillery, and getting close to out of ammunition for the tanks as well."

"Is getting the New Spartan commander on the ground to surrender going to be enough?" Tefford Ives asked. "That new fleet might still attack our ships. We might end up being stranded without a way off. If that happens, the New Spartans can land whatever troops they're bringing and give us as much trouble as we can handle."

"One step at a time, Teff," Lon said. "The troops on the ground are the only ones we can do anything about. If we force them to surrender, strip them of weapons, ammo, and communications gear, we'll have a chance, no matter what the newcomers do. If the enemy can't provide replacement equipment, the men won't be much use. We'll get in another ammunition resupply before the new fleet gets close, maybe risk shuttles to bring in food and ammunition for the heavy-weapons battalions." He paused. "We'll have to risk that, as long as there's a possibility we'll have to keep fighting. After that . . . we'll do whatever we have to do."

23

Lon took time to visit the treatment center the medtechs had set up on the western slope of the ridge the
New Spartans had blown. Twenty trauma tubes were in
use. Another forty men were lying on blankets spread on
the ground. Those were men whose injuries were not serious enough to need time in a trauma tube . . . or who
had to wait their turn because their injuries were not as
critical as the men already in the tubes. Lon stopped to
say a few words to each of the wounded who were not
in tubes but were conscious—words of encouragement,
comfort. He asked the medtechs about each man in a tube,
and stopped hardly longer next to the tube holding Phip
Steesen than any of the others.

Get better fast, Phip, Lon thought, resting his hand on
Steesen's tube before moving to the next casualty.

"We're okay for the moment, Colonel," Major Norman
said during their tour together, "but I can't answer for how
much longer. One more major firefight and we could run
low on medical supplies, even critical components for the
trauma tubes—assemblers and controllers. I talked with
15th's acting SMO an hour ago, and they're much closer
to that point than we are. They lost a third of their medical
stores in the shuttles that were destroyed. And, of course,
the one thing there never seems to be enough of is trauma
tubes."

"We can't do much about the tubes," Lon said. "Set
things up to use resupply rockets to bring in consuma-
bles—whatever can survive a landing in one of those

225

rockets. We'll do double drops in case some of the rockets don't make it."

"Even if all the rockets are brought in on target, we'll probably lose some cargo, possibly thirty percent of the most delicate items," Norman said. "The molecular controller units are particularly fragile. They can't take a hell of a lot of hard treatment. That's why we've never really considered the resupply rockets as a routine means of bringing in medical stores."

"I know, but since we don't have any viable options, we have to use what we've got," Lon said. "I'll give CIC authorization. You get on with *Peregrine*'s SMO on what you want and any tips you can give him on how to pack it to minimize losses."

Norman nodded. "Lon, there's one other thing I have to bring up as senior medical officer. How long do you plan to push the men without sleep? We're not to the critical point yet, since a lot of our people had a chance to get *some* sleep yesterday afternoon, but we're on the move, heavily loaded, and looking for a major engagement at the end. If the chase goes on until dark tonight, with a fight after that, we'll be getting critical. Tired men make more mistakes, and mistakes in combat get men killed and wounded."

Lon hesitated before he replied. "I know the situation, Dan," he said, very softly, "but . . . we just don't have many realistic options. I hope we'll be able to get enough men behind the New Spartans that they won't be able to keep running, or that they'll get tired enough that *they* have to make a long stop to let their men sleep. But with that new enemy fleet coming in, we don't have time for luxuries like sleep. We can't stop until the New Spartans already on the ground stop. Once we get the enemy main force locked into position, I'll try to give us enough time to let everyone get a few hours' sleep. *If* possible. A lot depends on how long it takes us to force them to stop— and whether they try to force a breakout when we do."

"My concerns about sleep extend to you as well, Lon,"

Norman said. "You need enough to be able to function at your best as well. Maybe more for you than for the younger men in the line companies. You've been at this business since before a lot of them were born. If you're a glutton for punishment, I can get the exact percentage for you in about five seconds."

"I know how old I am, Doc," Lon said, his voice showing a harsh edge. "And I've already got a pretty good idea about the other. No need to rub my face in the obvious." He shook his head. "I do that myself every time I look in the mirror."

"Tell me, did you ever get a chance to meet Warren Greavy?" Norman asked.

Lon laughed. "Old Prune Face himself? Yeah. I was introduced to him at a Founders' Day ball, back when I was a fairly new lieutenant. Matt Orlis told me that Greavy was a hundred and thirty years old, and he looked twice that."

"He was fifteen years older when I met him, not long before he died." Norman shrugged. "I was surprised when I heard about that. Old as he was, he had looked fit enough to last another ten or fifteen years, and you couldn't get a bet that he wouldn't reach a hundred and fifty. My point is, he remained on active duty until he was well past ninety, set all kinds of records, commanded 4th Regiment twenty-three years, served three terms as General—and flatly refused a fourth term. He took his annual physical qualification test just before he finally retired, and passed it with numbers to spare, not a hell of a lot worse than you did on your last qualification. He was eighty-nine the last time he led a combat contract, and from the reports I read, it was no beer run. He managed to get himself shot on that one, but kept fighting for twenty minutes before a medtech got to him."

"So he was an ornery old goat. So?"

"So don't get yourself hooked on thinking about how old you are, or how long you've been in the Corps," Norman said. "Don't rub your own face in it, or beat yourself over the head with the calendar, any of that nonsense. With all the nanotech floating in our systems, age is more a state of mind than anything else."

Lon smiled. "Point taken, Doc."

When he returned to the ridge, Lon moved his command post into the valley between it and the next line of hills—which the New Spartans had already abandoned. His 1st and 3rd Battalions had already pushed past the creek that marked the lowest line through the valley and were climbing toward the next ridge. The point companies were within two miles of the enemy rear guard. The situation on the flanks was better. Dirigenters were level with the New Spartan point, closing in from north and south. Lon concentrated on getting updates from CIC, Fal Jensen, and the commanders of each battalion. They were making definite progress, as much because the New Spartans had slowed down as for the increased speed the Dirigenters were attempting.

"Unless they pull another rabbit out of the hat, we should have them pretty well encircled by sunset," Jensen said. "And the smaller force is just about taken care of. The reports I'm getting from my company commanders is that those New Spartans seem to be running critically short on ammunition."

"Critically short, or just saving it for when the situation gets critical?" Lon asked, noting the change in Jensen's tone. He sounded optimistic now, not worried that disaster was only moments away. He was growing into his command.

"That's the point, of course," Jensen said. "No way to be certain. I've got two eager young officers—one who's been a captain less than a year, and a lieutenant commanding half his company because the shuttle carrying the rest was blown apart before landing, with their captain and the other lieutenant—who think we can overrun the five hundred New Spartans they're facing without too much trouble. I've told them to continue as they have been, keeping our exposure to a minimum."

"And they want to charge right in and finish it off?"

"Isn't that the way it always is?" Fal said, almost a hint of humor in his voice. "If I could be anywhere near certain that their estimate of the situation is right, it might work. Both men are good officers, but—"

"Are you asking me to make the call?" Lon asked.

"You're the boss," Jensen said. "I've told them, for now, to keep pressuring the enemy without doing anything, ah, foolish. No empty heroics. Personally, I think it's a little soon to try to finish that batch. They haven't taken all that many casualties since they crossed the river and we diverted the tanks to handle their rocket launchers. There could be five hundred New Spartans left there, and I've hardly got that many men around them. It is, as I said, your call, if you want to overrule me."

"Who's your battalion commander on the scene?"

"Captain Jim Binnes is acting CO. Marty Turin and his entire staff were lost coming in."

"Binnes the captain urging a full-scale assault?" Lon asked.

"No. Binnes just passed the request to me without comment. Jim is adequate for the job for now, but. . . ." Jensen snorted. "If I had someone else I could move into the job. . . ." He didn't need to finish that statement.

"I think you've made the right call, Fal. We'll play it your way, at least for the next couple of hours. Put as much pressure on them as we can without forcing a last-stand brawl. We go in before those New Spartans are ready to call it quits, and it could come down to bayonets. Keep a watch on the situation and let me know if you see enough to want to go ahead."

"Right. My estimate right now is that another two or three hours of constant pressure might be enough, but I'll keep an eye on things there, as best I can."

Two or three hours. The phrase kept running through Lon's head as he hiked east. *If we could spring a couple of Shrikes loose, we could turn the situation over faster,* he thought. *But if we could spring Shrikes for close air support,* everything *would go a lot easier. We could finish the business on the ground in no time at all.* But bringing Shrikes in would draw the New Spartan Javelins as well, or put the ships at hazard.

If it comes down to it, we'll have to take the risk, Lon decided. *Soon enough to give us time to recuperate before the new fleet gets in range. Can we do it a little sooner, take out the smaller enemy force, then go right into the main force?* He kept walking east as he turned the question over in his head. A captain temporarily thrust into command of a battalion in combat might be excused for indecision, after a time. A colonel commanding a regiment—two regiments—would not. *I'm the contract officer. I'm the one who has to make the final call,* Lon reminded himself. *I've got to make a decision . . . and it had better be the* right *decision.*

Another fifty paces forward, with his security squad ranging in front and to either side, weapons at the ready. Lon continued to listen to the continuous updates from CIC, interrupted only when he received a report from someone on the ground. There were no surprises in any of the messages. The situation was moving—slowly, but in the right direction.

Just not fast enough, Lon thought. *This all gets down to timing. Hit at the right time, providing we can hold the New Spartans in place long enough.* Timing. Lon kept walking. *I'd like to have the situation on the ground resolved within twenty-four hours, soon enough to give us plenty of time to rest up for the new people coming in.*

Time to rest. *We need to rest our people before the big fight, if we can. And we'd better find a way.* Tired soldiers became casualties more easily. They made stupid mistakes. They quit *caring* enough to be careful. When things got bad enough, a bullet seemed a small enough price for the luxury of four hours of rest—even in a trauma tube. *If we can lock the enemy's main force in place, by sunset*

*or so, then move everyone into place and take a few hours
for sleep. Hit the New Spartans maybe an hour or an hour
and a half before dawn. And bring in a few Shrikes to
help, despite the risk.*

Lon felt as if he had shed half the gear he was carrying.
Tentatively, at least, he had made his decision, even if he
was not ready to start issuing the orders. *Now, if we can
just force the New Spartans to halt so we can implement
it, we'll be all set,* he thought.

24

Morning. Daylight. Unlike the day before, this one looked to be only partly cloudy. The weather front had pushed through, leaving only scattered high clouds behind. There was a moderate breeze coming out of the northwest, holding the temperature down somewhat. The local forecast out of University City was for a high in the mid-eighties, Fahrenheit. The temperature that night might dip into the fifties, away from the city.

At dawn, the New Spartan fleet bearing in on Elysium was still fifty-three hours out from a standard attack orbit. *A sword of Damocles,* Lon thought after receiving the latest update from CIC, *except we know when this sword is going to fall.*

By the middle of the morning, Lon was beginning to feel confident that his men would be able to force the New Spartans already on Elysium into battle before dawn the next morning. *If we can do that on our terms, I think the odds will favor us, at least a little, and we can force the issue before their reinforcements get in,* he told himself. *Even if we only have parity in manpower, we should have the edge in ammunition. After that, we trust that our men are better trained and that our officers are better leaders. Including me.* He felt a tiny shiver of doubt. In the end, it might come down to which side had the better commander.

Lon started slowing the pace of 1st and 3rd Battalions just a little, allowing ten minutes for the men to rest after each hour on the move, instead of five. "Half an hour for lunch about noon," he informed the battalion commanders at eleven o'clock. "We don't need to push so hard here. It's the units on the flanks that need to hurry to surround the enemy."

Fifteen minutes before noon, the smaller band of New Spartans tried to break through the ring of Dirigenters, aiming to cut the siege on a direct line to their main force. The units of 15th Regiment that had boxed the enemy had been watching for the maneuver—some of the men had been *hoping* for it—and they met the enemy spearhead with a volley of rocket-propelled grenades and automatic rifle fire. The New Spartans kept coming, and the fighting in the northeastern quadrant of the sector quickly became hand-to-hand. The engagement lasted more than an hour, and casualties were high on both sides.

Lon extended the lunch break for the two battalions with him, listening to reports from the battle to his south, wondering whether he might have to send a company from 3rd Battalion to reinforce Lieutenant Colonel Jensen's men. Then that fight ended, suddenly, not ten minutes after Lon had given the order for 1st and 3rd to resume their movement east.

"They surrendered," Fal Jensen reported, sounding almost ecstatic. "I don't have a firm count yet, but it looks as if we've got nearly three hundred prisoners. It's going to take a time to get things sorted out, but we can put everything to taking on the main enemy force when we catch them up."

"Good job, Fal, and pass that on to the officers and men involved," Lon said. "Get the wounded cared for, ours and the New Spartans'." He did not have to specify that Dirigenters came first, and had first call on trauma tubes. "Strip the New Spartans of weapons, ammunition, helmets, and any other electronics. Destroy the helmets and other electronics and do the best you can to make the weapons inoperable. Dig a pit and burn the ammunition. Just in case we have to face the reinforcements they've got coming in and lose our prisoners, I don't want to leave anything for them to use against us."

The electronics were incompatible with DMC systems. In other circumstances, Lon might have ordered the weapons and ammunition held as a reserve for his own men—he *had* done that before—but here, he decided that the greater danger was that the enemy might recapture the munitions, not that his people might run short of ammunition. Having workable resupply rockets erased any worry Lon might have had about running short.

"I'll take care of it," Fal said. "It's going to take most of the men I've got down there to treat the wounded, get rid of the enemy's gear, and guard the prisoners, unless we can turn the prisoners over to the Elysians. You want I should do that?"

"Not yet," Lon said after a very brief hesitation. "Maybe we don't have to worry about the Elysians mistreating prisoners, but they want to be in on the final fight, and all the soldiers they have available are moving around in front of the New Spartan main force." He had never *quite* forgotten about the companies from the Elysian Defense Force moving in on the southern flank, but they had not been at the front of his mind until Jensen mentioned them.

"I'd feel less nervous with us pushing the final attack and the Elysians away from the action," Jensen said. "We don't know how good they are, and we can't be sure what they'll do."

"I know the arguments, Fal, but this is their world, and they're our paymasters on this contract. They are good. We'll just have to keep an eye open. For now, just keep me informed on the progress your people make." Lon got to his feet and started following the two line battalions again, and his security squad moved as if they were physically linked to him.

"Hey, what's the big hurry?"

Lon stopped and turned at the sound of Phip Steesen's voice. Phip was hurrying toward him. Lon's eyes were immediately drawn to the sling Phip's left arm was in, the arm strapped tightly to his body. Phip also seemed to be limping a little, favoring his left leg. He carried his rifle in his right hand.

"What the hell are you doing here?" Lon asked when Phip finally reached him. "I know damned well Doc Norman didn't release you for duty with that arm strapped up like that. Why aren't you back at the field hospital, where you belong?"

"They got enough work without me hanging around. Never mind my arm. I can do my job, much as anyone ever lets me do it anymore. Nothing wrong with my mouth, or my brain," Phip said. "I'm not about to sit on my ass and let you do everything. And if it comes to it, I can shoot better one-handed than half these kids can with both. Any way you slice it, I can do you more good here than there. Besides, I've had my rest, more than I need."

Lon stared at Phip, clenching his teeth against the impulse to order his friend back to the field hospital. "Just what did the medtechs tell you?" he asked finally. "How much recovery time do that shoulder and arm need? Straight out."

"Only minor nerve damage—pinched, not severed. I've got a little tingling in the fingers. The bone is pretty well repaired—eighty percent, anyway. Another eight to ten hours and I'll be fully functional. And the big fight won't come before then, will it? I've been listening in on as much as I could the last hour or so, since they pulled me out of the tube."

"The big fight won't come before then if things go the way I hope they will," Lon said. He did not question how Phip had managed to replace his damaged helmet electronics. There had undoubtedly been casualties whose helmets had survived. "There's a chance the New Spartans will force the issue before then, though. They might be better off if they do."

"That smaller force waited until it was too late to try

to break out," Phip said. "Any reason to think that the main force will play it any smarter?"

"They can see what happened playing it that way," Lon replied. "That might be enough to make their commander decide to try something different. I would if the tables were turned."

Phip snorted. "If the tables had been turned, you'd have attacked soon as it got dark last night, anything to keep the enemy from playing it his way. Maybe charged in right after blowing that stupid hill down on top of them."

Lon shook his head. "I don't know what I'd have done if I had the other hand in this. I don't even want to guess. Whatever seemed to offer the best chance of holding out until help arrived, I expect. Right now, running looks to offer more hope for the New Spartans than sitting still, or turning and attacking us."

"How seriously you figure they take their name?" Phip asked.

"What do you mean?"

"I got to thinking about that fight the old Spartans had, back on Earth, that one we talked about."

"Thermopylae?"

"Yeah, three hundred men standing off an army of umpteen thousands, fighting to the last man."

"I don't think we have to worry about that," Lon said. "The New Spartans are mercenaries, not maniacs. No professional is going to accept a contract that requires a last stand." Lon shook his head. "There's no future in it." Phip's groan at the pun made Lon feel better—about both of them.

Lon kept Phip close through the afternoon, and made certain that Jeremy Howell and the members of his security detachment knew to look after the lead sergeant, no matter how much he tried to discourage the attention. As much as he could without being obvious about it, Lon kept a close eye on Phip as well, noting that the limp disappeared within a half hour even though they were hiking across rough ground. Not long after that, Lon noticed Phip flexing the fingers of his left hand, repeatedly making a fist, testing the arm as far as the sling and straps would allow. Phip kept the faceplate of his helmet down, so Lon could not see if he was in any discomfort.

It was after 1430 hours when Lon finally got a count on the number of New Spartans who had been captured by 15th Regiment. Three hundred twenty had been taken, seventy-three of them wounded. Jensen's men also had counted eighty-three enemy bodies at the site of their last firefight and the attempted breakout. Twenty-four Dirigenters had died in the fight, and there were forty wounded men, about a third needing time in trauma tubes.

A few minutes later the two companies from the EDF opened fire on the main New Spartan force, tying them down for twenty minutes before withdrawing to better positions—now right in front of the enemy, due east of their lead companies. The New Spartans made a few attempts to find a way out to the northeast, but 2nd of the 7th was in the way there.

"I think we've finally got them cornered," Lon told Phip when a report from Vel Osterman said that the New Spartans were setting up a defensive perimeter and digging in. "They don't have anywhere to go but through us now."

"If they realize that, they're liable to try it before we get everyone in place," Phip replied. "Right after sunset at the latest, I'd guess."

"If they wait until sunset, it'll be too late," Lon said, glancing at the sky. "Four hours from now we'll have all our people in place, a tight ring around them."

"But that gives them four hours to rest, while we're still humping around," Phip said. "*I'm* okay. I had all that rest in the tube, but most of our men haven't had the luxury. They've started to drag their butts along the ground."

I know, Lon thought. "We'll keep the New Spartans' minds occupied, enough to keep them from getting much rest, at least. I'm going to try to give our people most of the night to try for some sleep, plan on going in about ninety minutes before sunrise if the New Spartans don't do something sooner." *Go in with everything we can muster. Maybe it's not smart to put everything on one roll of the dice, but we don't have many choices if we want to hope to avoid facing them and all the reinforcements coming toward us.*

The New Spartans had no real advantage in the terrain they had been forced to defend. They were on a gradual slope, the ground rising to the east, not to another ridge but just into rolling prairie with waist-high grass and scattered stands of trees and brush, and the Dirigenters and Elysians were above them as well as below—but never by much. There was more soil and less stone away from the hills, though, which meant that the New Spartans were able to dig in easily.

"It's going to be a bloody mess on both sides," Phip said as he and Lon surveyed the enemy positions before sunset, passing powered binoculars back and forth between them. Lon had set up his command post a little more than two miles from the nearest point on the enemy line, on the slope leading down from the last line of hills, near the edge of a thick copse of trees that draped like weeping willows on Earth. The CP was a little higher than the New Spartans, dug in and camouflaged as well as the men of the regimental headquarters staff could manage. A few trees had been felled. Slit trenches and foxholes had been dug, with the dirt piled in front of them. Nearly all of the Dirigenter and Elysian troops were in position, surrounding the enemy, and Lon had already put his people on half-and-half watches, to allow everyone to get some sleep before the battle. Hopefully.

"I'm afraid you're right," Lon said, sighing softly. "Dark will make it a little easier, but not enough to suit me." He glanced at the sky. "Too bad we don't have the low cloud cover and rain any longer. That would have gotten rid of the starlight and moonlight."

"I hope we can do most of the job before we have to get close enough for those needle guns of theirs to be effective," Phip said. "Someone brought a captured needle gun and its ammo by the hospital before I left. Those slivers of metal are heavier than you'd believe possible. Must be depleted uranium." He shook his head. "It'd be better yet if we could hang way back and just use our beamers to thin 'em out. We've got more energy weapons than they do, I think. Or more power packs for the beamer rifles we *do* have. I've been checking around. We haven't lost anyone to a beamer in almost twenty-four hours."

New medical supplies had been received, along with ammunition and meal packs. There had been no losses, except for some of the delicate medical stores that had been jarred by too-rough landings. The New Spartans in orbit had not even tried to intercept the small rockets. Nor had they attempted to resupply their own troops.

"They have to be getting short on ammunition for all their weapons," Lon said after a lengthy silence. "Probably short of food as well. They haven't had any fresh supplies in since we hit the ground, and I doubt that they carried more than a couple of days' worth before we showed up."

Phip shrugged. "They had almost three days to build up their stockpiles on the ground between the time we came out of Q-space and when we reached attack orbit. Maybe they *are* short of food, but they won't starve before their compatriots arrive, even if their stomachs growl a lot. But if they haven't got bullets to feed their rifles, why the hell don't they surrender now and get it over with? Save a lot of lives."

"Maybe their commander still believes in miracles," Lon said. "And maybe he's waiting to see if we've got the balls to try to finish them off. There's a chance that once we start to press the attack they might show the white flag in a hurry."

"So *who* still believes in miracles?" Phip asked. "I thought you got cured of wishful thinking a couple of decades ago."

Lon laughed as he turned his head to look at Phip. "I *did* give up believing in miracles, but then you went and got married and I had to reconsider."

Phip shook his head, but he was grinning. "Hard to argue with that reasoning," he said. "Why don't you have a meal, then get some sleep? I'll keep my eyes open and let you know if anything important happens."

Lon hesitated. "I'm not really hungry, but I'd better try to get a little sleep," he conceded. Just the mention of sleep forced a yawn from his throat. "At least a couple of hours."

"Try, hell," Phip said. "If you can't get to sleep without it, put a four-hour patch on. We're neither of us kids. We need our sleep. I had mine in a tube, and that's better than sleep, but you've been on the go forever. You've got to have your head clear when the fight starts. Go on, use a patch. Anything happens, I'll pull it and put a stim-patch on to jerk you awake."

25

When Lon woke and opened his eyes, the timeline on his visor display informed him that it was 0225 hours— almost two-thirty in the morning. He took several slow breaths to help get rid of the slight tension headache that a sleep patch almost always left him with. *Almost two-thirty; I got the full four hours,* he thought. *That means nothing has gone wrong.* That was a relief, dampened when he next realized that it also meant that nothing had gone exceptionally well either—the New Spartans had not surrendered to spare themselves the bloodletting of battle. *I guess that was too much to hope for. If they were going to surrender that easily, they would have done it earlier.*

Lon could hear no gunfire, which also spoke loudly to the peacefulness of the moment. He stretched cautiously, almost as if he were afraid that someone would notice. He clicked his radio receiver on and turned to the channel that gave him the running commentary from CIC on *Peregrine*. With no activity on the ground, the talk was no longer constant. There was a pause of nearly twenty seconds before someone in CIC started repeating the latest summary. *Nothing new on the ground. No fighting at the moment between us and the New Spartan cruiser. The new fleet continues on course toward us; no change in their estimated time of arrival; they're still at least thirty-one hours away. We'll repeat this message in five minutes.* The dull tones of the sailor reading the report reinforced the bland nature of the message. There seemed to be a "ho-hum" behind each phrase, as if he had difficulty staying awake through it.

Several blinks. A more expansive stretch. Lon looked around him, subconsciously ignoring the slight greenish tinge that the infrared portion of his night-vision system gave to everything. That was so old-hat that it was extremely rare when he actually noticed. He saw Phip's figure about ten feet away, and knew it was Phip mostly by the way he sat, his head forward just a little, the sight movements of body and limbs. The sling was gone from his left arm. Lon needed a few seconds before he noticed its absence.

"Did Doc Norman approve that, or did you do it on your own?" Lon asked, lifting his faceplate when Phip turned to look at him. The night turned dark without the night-vision gear.

"I gave it all the time he told me to," Phip said. He only lifted his faceplate far enough to expose his mouth. Lon pulled his back down, to the same extent. "Feels okay, really, just about one hundred percent." Phip made a series of movements with the arm, flexing and stretching all the muscles, exercising the joints. "See? No pain, just the least little stiffness from having it immobilized so long."

"Any news I should know about?" Lon asked. He opened his canteen and took a long sip of water. That and several deep breaths banished the last traces of his headache.

"Nothing but routine, far as I know. Everyone's where they're supposed to be, getting what rest they can, ready to go when the time comes, or whenever the New Spartans decide to do something." He paused. "Whichever comes first, I guess. The skipper of *Peregrine* wants you to call him. I suspect he wants to gripe about how many Shrikes you want to pull down to support this operation."

"I suspect you're right. He'd prefer keeping all of them to defend our ships, even though he's got numerical superiority over the New Spartan fighters. Now, if there's nothing else I need to know about, it's time for you to shut your eyes and get a little rest before the attack."

"To tell the truth, I've already dozed a couple of times. Jerry and me been taking turns, making sure one of us is always awake and close by, listening to the radio and watching. Things are getting too close. Even if I could get to sleep, it'd be time to wake back up so soon it's not worth the trouble."

"Worth it or not, take the trouble," Lon said. "Humor me. You've already caused me enough worry for one contract. Besides, your medical nanobugs will work that much better while you're asleep, and I can see that arm and shoulder aren't quite all the way back yet. I'm awake and alert. Soon as I get a bite to eat, I'm going to be busy on the radio."

Lon spent nearly ten minutes talking with Kurt Thorsen, the captain of *Peregrine*. Thorsen made only *pro forma* objections—though he repeated them several times—to the use of four Shrike II fighters to provide close air support. They would rotate in and out, two at a time, minimizing the time when the troops on the ground would be without air cover. As each pair of fighters returned to the ships, they would be rearmed while another pair went out ... at least as long as the Dirigenter ships did not come under heavy attack. Four shuttles would come in under the cover of the first Shrikes, carrying ammunition for the heavy-weapons battalions. Lon decided to do that at the same time as the ground attack, rather than wait and try to slip shuttles in after the battle, before the next New Spartan fleet got close enough to interfere. *If this fight gets close, maybe they'll make the difference,* he reasoned. *One fight instead of two.*

Most of the conversation concerned various contingency plans, including the possibility of sending *Agamemnon* and *Odysseus* out to intercept the incoming New Spartan ships as far away from Elysium as possible—too far out for them to launch shuttles and reinforcing troops.

"We can only risk that if we win the fight down here," Lon concluded . . . to Thorsen's obvious relief. Any further debate on the topic could wait until later.

"Everything depends on how you people do this morning," Thorsen said. "I wish there was more we could do to help, but we've got our own problems up here, as you know."

"Be ready to launch an MR back to Dirigent once we know how the fight goes down here," Lon said near the end of the conversation. "If it goes badly for us, you may have to make the reports." *I may not be here to make them.* He tried not to think about that, but the thought kept sneaking past his defenses.

One by one, Lon spoke with Fal Jensen, Tefford Ives, and each battalion commander in both regiments. He asked each about unit strength and readiness, and gave the commanders personal briefings for the upcoming operation, asking each man if he had any suggestions—and giving each suggestion his full consideration. Still, the process did not take all that long—no more than half an hour altogether. There was, now, time for that. By the time Lon had finished, the last sleeping men were being wakened to give them time for breakfast and whatever reflections might come in the last hour before battle.

Lon thought about calling Junior, to have at least a few words with him before the shooting started, maybe the last words they would ever be able to exchange. The temptation to indulge himself was strong, but—in the end—he did not. *I can't fuss over him like a mother hen,* Lon thought. *Let him keep his mind clear for what's coming. Don't complicate things for him. He doesn't think about this the way you do. He's a Dirigenter by birth, not a transplanted Earther.* But it could not stop Lon from *thinking* about Junior, and the rest of his family, almost until it was time to give the order to start the assault against the New Spartans. Images drifted through Lon's mind, words and pictures, mostly of times when Junior was very small. And Angie, more when she was a toddler than now, almost a grown woman. Only briefly did Lon think about the baby who was coming, the third child . . . and the chance that he might not get home to ever see him or her.

Don't think about that, Lon told himself as sternly as he could. *Even if this turns into a disaster, there's no reason why you won't get home. Sooner or later.* That was one . . . courtesy one mercenary could expect from another. Prisoners would be repatriated eventually, though perhaps at a price. If the Corps lost the fight on Elysium—this one or a later battle with the New Spartan reinforcements—Lon might go home in disgrace, but there was every reason to believe that he *would* go home.

Sara. Lon mouthed the name silently, closing his eyes. He pictured his wife in his mind, imagining that she appeared farther along in her pregnancy than she was, seeing her as she had been just before she had delivered Angie, or Junior. She still looked almost that young, but Lon could *see* the differences in his mental image, vague overlays as through a lens whose focus was subtly changing . . . a few pounds, a few tiny wrinkles. *I hope she's not worrying* too *much about us,* Lon thought. *She doesn't need that kind of stress while she's pregnant.* But she would worry, though she always tried to hide it; that was the Dirigenter way. *Two of us to worry about now, and out on the same mission.* Lon shook his head and opened his eyes. *I've been a Dirigenter for almost thirty years and I still don't have the instinct to treat this as just a job, with risks that have to be accepted. Another day at the office.* Sara did not see those risks quite the same way Lon did, and Junior was even more . . . cavalier about them. *How much is real and how much is pretense?* Lon asked himself—as he had countless times over the years. *Do they really see this so much differently, or is it only an act they're conditioned to from infancy?*

Lon took his canteen out again, seeking the distraction of routine activity to try to rein in his thoughts. He took a mouthful of water, sloshed it around his mouth, then spit it out, over the front of his slit trench, too noisily. Then he took a slow drink and swallowed before he put the canteen back on his belt, focusing on each action. A few feet away, Phip shifted position, as if he had been disturbed by the activity.

Is he trying to sleep or just faking it to keep me satisfied? Lon wondered. Again: reality or pretense? *There's so much of that, masks over masks.* Even if Phip were asleep, it would not take much to rouse him, not in a combat zone—even though the enemy was a couple of miles away. *Either way, I can give him another five minutes,* Lon thought. He glanced at the timeline on his helmet display. He had told the commanders that the order to begin the assault would come at 0455 hours, and that was only fifteen minutes away. Already, the Shrike II fighters and the shuttles would be well away from their ships, more than halfway through their run in toward the ground.

Fifteen minutes. Lon closed his eyes for a few seconds, then opened them again. It would take a few minutes for the battle to be fully joined after that; the inertia of waiting would have to be overcome. Around the New Spartans, the Dirigenters with beamers—energy rifles—would be the first to open fire, invisible and silent death if there were any targets visible . . . if any of the New Spartans were the least bit careless about staying down. The time for the slug-throwing rifles and grenade launchers would come next, perhaps not until the New Spartans realized that they were under attack. When the first pair of Shrike IIs started strafing and firing rockets into their positions, there would be no doubt left.

There won't be many RPGs at the beginning, Lon thought. *We don't have that many units close enough for grenades to be effective. The Book* listed the maximum effective range for the grenade launchers at two hundred yards, and recommended that they be used at targets within one hundred sixty yards. From experience, Lon knew that a good grenadier could hit a target with a ten-foot diameter four times out of five from two hundred thirty yards, slightly more if the terrain and wind were to his advantage—and with a kill radius of twenty-five yards for fragmentation grenades, that was more target than a grenadier needed. But a sharpshooter could put a rifle bullet into a man-size target at near a mile's distance under optimal conditions, and a beamer could—*theoretically*—hit the same target at up to five miles before atmospheric dispersal of the twelve-millimeter beam rendered it ineffective.

"Okay, Phip, time to rise and shine," Lon said, the visor of his helmet up just a little. He did not speak loudly, but Phip rolled over immediately and raised up on his right elbow.

Phip groaned softly. "We're both getting too old for this crap, Lon. I wish I hadn't tried to sleep. I felt pretty good before. Now I ache in every joint."

"It's all in your head," Lon said. "If you're going to grab a bite to eat, you'd better get right to it. Another eight minutes or so and I give the word to start the assault. The first flight of Shrikes will hit about two minutes after that."

"I'm not hungry," Phip said, a rare statement for him. "I don't even want to *think* about food. You know something?" he added after a short pause. "War makes a lousy spectator sport. I hate sitting back and watching what's going on more than I hate being up close and having buzzards shooting at me." He got to his knees and looked over the dirt parapet in front of him, then reached for the binoculars and put them to his face. "Sometimes it feels like there's something vaguely obscene about this long-distance watching, a damned peep show. Makes me feel dirty."

"Well, your griping is back up to speed, so you must be just about recovered from your injuries," Lon said, fighting to hold back a chuckle. Phip had always been a masterful complainer. "I guess I can stop worrying about you."

"Now if I could stop worrying about *you,*" Phip said.

"You've never stopped worrying about anything in your life, once you get a bee in your bonnet," Lon's mother had told him—a year or two before, during a discussion about Junior's decision to join the Corps, a talk that had inescapably turned to Lon's childhood. "You were like that even when you were five or six years old, and I swear it got worse every year after that. If you didn't have something *real* to worry about, you manufactured something and fretted at that until something better came along."

The memory was obtrusive and the timing bad. Only four minutes remained until the time Lon had scheduled for the beginning of what he hoped would be the final battle of the Elysian contract. *Maybe I have worried too much about some things,* he conceded to himself. *But worrying about a problem is the first step toward solving it. You don't worry about a problem, you don't go looking for solutions. Even if they don't exist.*

The Shrike II fighters were on their way in, on schedule, already inside the atmosphere. Lon had an open radio channel to Fal Jensen and all of the battalion commanders in both regiments on the ground. Everyone was ready, waiting for *the word.* Lon watched the seconds tick off on his head-up display's timeline. Unless the New Spartans preempted him, he would give the order exactly on schedule . . . then watch what happened.

I know what Phip was talking about—war as a spectator sport. It's worse when you're the one who has to give the orders, knowing that people are going to die because of those orders. Lon swallowed hard, feeling a knot grow in his stomach. There was a different fear associated with giving the orders than there was in receiving them and going head-to-head with an enemy. Fear of dying versus the fear of making a mistake and causing too many of his men to die. And the latter was worse, in many ways. Dying was all too easy.

Two minutes. Lon took another drink from his canteen, more from nervousness than thirst. The waiting made his mouth dry, but he didn't want his voice to crack when he gave the order. That might show his fear to others, and *that* was something a commander needed to avoid at almost any cost. One drink. A second. The canteen was more than half empty now, and Lon had only one more on his belt.

Lord, don't let me fail my men. The prayer was old. Lon had used it every time he had led—or ordered—his men into combat.

Time! Lon clicked his transmitter open. He gave the order. "Go!"

The order was repeated, from battalion to company to platoon and squad. Men brought their weapons to their shoulders. Those with energy rifles started looking for targets, if they hadn't already been watching through the gunsights. In a few carefully chosen locations—determined by the lay of the land and the course the Shrikes would follow coming in for their first attack runs—squads started inching closer to the enemy lines, their goal to get their grenadiers within range.

Defenders had serious advantages in a tactical situation like this, and a thousand years of history to reassure themselves with. They were dug in. The attackers had to move, expose themselves, cross open ground, and those were invitations to casualties on an unacceptable scale. Lon hoped that the aircraft coming in would help negate the defenders' advantages. Men would move closer to the enemy while the Shrike II fighters forced the New Spartans to keep their heads down. If the fight went on long enough, the Dirigenter artillery would have a chance to get the ammunition being brought in by the shuttles, move close enough to get into range, and pound the New Spartan positions until they were untenable—*if* their commander let the fight continue that long.

The sound of gunfire reached Lon and Phip then. "They know they're under attack," Phip said. "That was coming out of the New Spartan positions. Our beamer boys must have hit something."

"Some*one*," Lon corrected, almost a whisper, a correction more for his own benefit than Phip's. The targets were human beings, not silhouettes on a firing range.

The first few scattered shots soon escalated into complete engagement all the way around the New Spartan perimeter, coming and going. Muzzle flashes winked like chains of Christmas lights. The noise built on itself, audible even over the two miles that separated Lon and Phip from the fighting, but at this distance it sounded more like a holiday fireworks display than what it really was. Lon saw the flashes of the first grenades that exploded before he heard their distinctive report. He glanced skyward, though he could see nothing through the leaves of the trees that sheltered his command post. It was time for the first pair of Shrikes to hit. One of the pilots had reported that they were within fifteen seconds of their initial points for the run.

Rockets first. Leaning forward, Lon saw the fiery trails of four missiles, though he could not—and would not—be able to see the fuselages and wings of the black aerospace fighters, or the rockets themselves. After the missiles—tipped with explosives and tightly wound coils of depleted uranium wire for fragmentation—were away, the pilots would start to pull out of their dives, braking to allow themselves perhaps a second and a half to strafe with their Gatling-style cannons. Once they were across the target area, they would climb and go to full power, to get out of danger—away from any shoulder-fired surface-to-air missiles the New Spartans might have.

The first run would be the easy one—comparatively speaking. The enemy might not have SAM launchers ready, or they might not be looking in the right direction;

they would have little time for corrections once the aircraft started shooting. The second time through, they would be waiting. The Shrikes would come in from a different direction the second time, and they would not come as low, or slow down quite as much, and they would be ready to deploy electronic countermeasures the instant their instruments reported that they were being targeted by SAM launchers. The pilots would be nervous but focused—as long as possible. They knew that they had less than two minutes before New Spartan Javelin fighters would catch up with them. CIC had been tracking the progress of a pair of the enemy aerospacecraft.

Four explosions, spaced along the New Spartan perimeter. The chatter of the Shrikes' cannon, a much deeper sound than that made by rifles. Lon could not see Dirigenters on the ground rushing forward in the seconds of maximum impact on the enemy positions, but he knew that hundreds of men would have taken the chance to get a little closer to the enemy. The men of the Corps were well trained, and obeyed orders as long as it was humanly possible.

The dying has started, Lon thought. He looked away from the battle—just for an instant—and shook his head, trying to force destructive thoughts out of his mind, and trying to settle his stomach, which was threatening to rebel. *Don't go morbid, idiot!* he told himself, feeling anger at the distraction. *You know what this business is all about, and you know what will happen if this attack doesn't succeed.* He forced himself to look back at the scene, scanning the front through his binoculars. Even with them, there was not a lot of detail he could see.

"It could hardly look less real if it was an old action vid on the entertainment nets," Phip said, talking over their private radio channel now. "Not even a whiff of gunpowder." He sounded angry, as if the lack of odor were somehow an insult.

Lon did not bother to reply. The first pair of Shrike IIs made their second run and burned for orbit. The second pair was about three minutes away. Lon scanned radio channels, stopping to listen whenever he heard anything from the men who were up close. The runs of the Shrikes had decreased the amount of fire the New Spartans could put out, but only briefly. Once the fighters were climbing away, the volume picked up again—increased, even, according to the report of one lieutenant to his company commander.

There were calls for medtechs, and reports of men killed. A little ground had been gained. In three different areas the grenadiers were finally close enough to go to work, dropping their loads of shrapnel in and around the foxholes and slit trenches of the enemy. If the New Spartans were short of ammunition, there was no sign of it in the early fighting. They were not stinting.

The New Spartan aerospace fighters came in, making one pass across the Dirigenter lines west of the perimeter, then climbing, rushing to meet the second pair of Shrike II fighters as they came in. Lon switched channels to monitor the Shrike pilots, to make certain they knew that trouble was heading for them. The talk between the two pilots assured Lon that they knew what was coming and were ready to meet it. They were receiving constant updates from their control room aboard *Odysseus*. The four fighters passed each other without anyone hitting anyone else with rockets or cannon fire. The time it took for the various craft to maneuver at high speed meant that the Shrikes were able to make their first pass at the New Spartans on the ground before they had to worry about the enemy fighters coming after them again.

When the competing pairs of fighters approached each other the second time, the situation was different. They were not moving head-on toward each other until the last couple of seconds. The planes launched missiles at each other and followed up with cannon fire. In an explosion that lit up the predawn sky like a premature sunrise, two of the fighters collided. There was clearly no chance that either pilot survived. The other fighters veered away, but both were caught by debris from the explosion. Lon listened as the pilot of the second Shrike II informed his controller that he was going to have to eject. The remaining Javelin was corkscrewing away, out of control.

"Get someone moving to make pickup on that pilot," Lon told Fal Jensen. "Your people are closest."

Lon lost most of Fal's reply because Lieutenant Colonel Ted Syscy broke in with an urgent report. "Colonel, we've got men to the enemy line, right on the northeast section. My Delta Company has closed in and the fighting is hand-to-hand."

That's Junior's company! boomed in Lon's head, almost overriding his reply to Syscy. "Push everyone you've got in after them, Ted. Try to widen the break. I'll get help to you as quickly as possible."

Lon immediately called Vel Osterman and Ben Dark to inform them of the breakthrough and to order them to push as hard as they could, sliding the companies they had flanking 1st Battalion in to follow the units that had reached the enemy perimeter. Then he keyed in the radio channel that the officers of 1st Battalion would use among themselves—simply to listen, hoping to hear his son's voice.

Then all he could do was wait, dreading every interminable second.

26

Ten minutes. Twenty. Lon found it almost impossible to concentrate on anything but listening for his son's voice, or some indication that he was still alive and well. *Hand-to-hand fighting. Anything can happen once it gets that close,* he worried. *Ability isn't always enough. Blind chaos, and no one can guarantee your luck, your survival.* Lon had been in that kind of situation more than once in his career, but the incident that came to mind was the first combat contract he had been on, still an officer cadet, on a colony world called Norbank. That was where his mentor, Arlan Taiters, had died, in hand-to-hand combat on a wilderness hilltop.

The fear of uncertainty was almost paralyzing. Lon scarcely noticed the flashes of gunfire or the first attack by the next pair of Shrikes that came down—this pair from *Agamemnon. Watch yourself, Junior!* Lon urged silently, projecting his thoughts to where his body could not go, as if willpower could perform some extrasensory miracle. His mind drew images from memory, populating a grassy slope with men in slightly different patterns of camouflage fighting with bayonets and fists, bullets and knees, in an impossible confusion—a waking dream . . . or nightmare that refused to release Lon from its grasp.

Reports came through. Lon managed to acknowledge most of them, though he continued to find it difficult to spare attention for anything but the fear that was gripping him, so real it became a physical pain in his gut, so severe it was all he could do to keep from doubling over in

agony. *I can't let this stop me,* he told himself. He sucked
in a deep breath and straightened up, forcing himself to
confront the pain and . . . slowly, ignore it. He consciously
straightened up without exposing too much of himself.
Another deep breath. He lifted his faceplate long enough
to wipe the sweat from his face. A quick sip of water. *Do
your job!*

Two companies of Elysian troops, starting with three
hundred eighty men, forced a second breach of the New
Spartan lines, but at the cost of seventy men dead and
another hundred wounded. Lon warned away the next
flight of Shrikes. They could no longer be certain of a
clear field of fire, and Lon did not want to risk friendly-
fire casualties.

Dawn—a rising line of light in the eastern sky—
brought a reddish glow to the horizon as precursor to the
appearance of Elysium's sun. A dirty yellow haze hung
over and around the oval territory—less than a mile long
and three-tenths of a mile deep—that the New Spartans
were defending, dirty air from gunpowder and the blasts
of grenades and rockets.

Lon heard a voice—no more than two words—and
strained at the memory. *Was that Junior?* He wasn't certain, and nearly called back on the channel to ask. *Nearly.*
He did not, though the effort caused him to bite his lower
lip, drawing blood. He leaned against the dirt piled up in
front of his foxhole and searched the battlefield through
his binoculars, as if he might somehow be able to pick
out his son from the hundreds of other soldiers wearing
identical helmets and battledress . . . at a distance of two
miles.

"Colonel?"

How long can the fighting go on now? Lon asked himself. *We've been inside their lines for more than half an
hour, pouring more men in every minute. Don't they know
they've lost? Why don't they give it up?*

"Colonel Nolan?"

Lon blinked rapidly and shook his head a little. "What

is it?" he asked, not even certain who had called him. There was something. . . . Lon blinked again and raised up a little more. He couldn't hear gunfire any longer.

"Colonel, this is Ted Syscy."

Oh, no! Lon thought; his heart started to pound almost out of control at the fear that Syscy was calling to say that Junior had been killed. His vision dimmed, almost as if he were ready to black out.

"It's over, Colonel. The New Spartans have surrendered. Their commander is being escorted to my CP to make it formal. We've won, Colonel."

Lon's mind needed a few seconds to grasp what Syscy had said, an instant of vertigo that left him hanging onto the ground in front of him.

"Your son is partly responsible for this, Colonel," Syscy continued, oblivious to Lon's momentary difficulty. "While the rest of his company opened a way, Junior led his two platoons through until they were within a hundred yards of the New Spartan headquarters. That's when their colonel surrendered. Junior is leading the escort bringing him to me now."

"Thank you, Ted," Lon said, finally finding his voice. "I'll get everyone notified. Get help to the wounded. Start collecting the weapons and electronics of the New Spartans. You know the routine. Destroy or disable anything they might be able to use against us later. I'll be there to meet the New Spartan commander as quickly as I can. I suspect I'll need at least forty minutes, maybe fifty to reach your position." Lon had signaled for Phip. Jeremy Howell also had moved closer.

"We won?" Howell asked after Lon lifted his faceplate.

"This part of it, at least," Lon said, wiping his face with his sleeve. He was drenched in sweat. "The enemy on the ground has surrendered. I haven't heard anything about their ships, especially about the new fleet coming in. Phip, we've got to get our skates on. The New Spartan commander is being escorted to Ted Syscy's CP. We're going there to accept the formal surrender."

Phip nodded. "Junior?" he asked.

"He's okay." Lon let out a long breath. "Better than okay, I guess. Ted says it was Junior who got through to the enemy headquarters and forced the surrender."

"Jerry, go get everyone ready to move out," Phip said, gesturing to Lon's aide. "We've got a two-mile hike ahead of us, and the sooner we get started, the sooner we get done." He waited until Howell moved away, then stepped closer to Lon. "How about you?" he asked. "You okay?"

A smile tried to climb onto Lon's face but failed. "I will be," Lon said very softly. "I've never been so damned scared in my life." He turned and leaned against the edge of the foxhole, his back to the east, toward the enemy and the bulk of his own troops. "I'm not sure I could have taken much more of it, Phip," he whispered, so softly that he was not sure he could hear his own voice.

"You'd have managed, Lon. You always have."

"I don't think I can risk putting myself through something like this again, Phip. Not . . ."

"Look, I know what you mean. But, well, once we get home, you'll get over it."

"Maybe," Lon allowed, mostly to avoid continuing the discussion. "Come on, let's get moving. I want to know if it's *all* over or if we're going to have to go through it again when that new fleet gets here."

The meeting was civil and very reserved. The New Spartan commander introduced himself as Colonel Armond Kaye. Lon guessed that he might be sixty years old. Kaye was about six feet, three inches tall, thin, with washed-out blue eyes and a deeply tanned complexion. He had a field dressing around his left biceps, with a little blood that had seeped through showing. "Nothing, a scratch," Kaye said when Lon inquired about the wound and whether Kaye needed the attention of a medtech.

"It is a difficult thing to do, this," Kaye said. "I thought we could do the job, either alone or by holding out until our reinforcements could arrive." A shrug. "Events proved otherwise, Colonel Nolan. I compliment you." They were sitting on folding chairs, and Lon wasn't quite certain where *they* had come from. Jeremy Howell had found them somewhere, and made sure they made it to the site of the meeting.

"About those reinforcements, Colonel Kaye," Lon said. "That is something we do need to discuss."

"As mission commander, my surrender is binding on all New Spartan forces participating in the mission, including those now on their way. As soon as you permit, I will transmit orders to the incoming fleet to avoid engaging, or whatever you require."

Lon looked over Kaye's head. Junior was standing about twenty feet away, his rifle at his side, looking as if he expected the enemy commander to stage some sort of nasty surprise, even though Colonel Kaye had been relieved of his weapon and electronic devices. His words could carry no farther than he could shout.

"We would want all fighting ships to bear away from Elysium, Colonel," Lon said, bringing his attention back to his opposite number. "And we will discuss arrangements for bringing your transports in to pick up your soldiers—with suitable precautions, you understand."

"Of course, Colonel," Kaye said, nodding. "Now, if you require assistance with your wounded . . . ?"

The rest was details. And waiting to make certain that the commander of the incoming New Spartan reinforcements would abide by Colonel Kaye's pledge.

Epilogue

After discussion with the president and chancellor, Lon approved an amendment to the contract. Seventh and 15th Regiments would be relieved, go home, and the regiment on its way to reinforce them would complete the six-month contract—surety against a New Spartan decision to come back, or another effort by the Confederation of Human Worlds to force Elysium into its fold.

It was the twelfth of April when 7th and 15th Regiments returned to Dirigent. The dead, those whose bodies had been recovered, were the first to land, their shuttles carrying them directly to the port within the confines of the Corps' main base. The living landed at the civilian spaceport and made their usual parade through Dirigent City. Casualties had been high, primarily because of the shuttles that had been shot down before they could land their troops, but the contract had been successfully fulfilled. Of the 974 Dirigenters who had died on the Elysian contract, 605 had died in the shuttles.

Colonel Robert Hayley retired from the Corps for medical reasons—the unbridgeable gaps in his memory. Fal Jensen was promoted and given command of 15th Regiment.

New recruits were brought into the two regiments from the training battalion. A few score men, mostly commissioned or noncommissioned officers, were transferred from other units. It would take nine months to bring 7th and 15th Regiments back to full strength.

The Corps went on. It *always* went on.

• • •

On the last day of July 2830, Sara Nolan gave birth to identical twin daughters, Amanda and Ariel, without difficulty. All four grandparents were on hand to help Lon through the birth and the first days at home of his new children.

Elysium proved to be the last combat contract that Lon Nolan, Senior, would participate in. Twenty-three months after his return, he was—to his great surprise—elected General. The vote was thirteen to one. His had been the only dissenting vote. Three days after the end of his year in office, Lon retired from the Corps—to the surprise of his peers on the Council of Regiments and many of his own officers and men. Phip Steesen retired the same day.

Lon, Junior, waited six weeks before resigning his commission. He had served on only one combat contract after Elysium. Two months after he left the Corps, Junior left Dirigent to attend the university on Elysium—a week after his sister Angie married . . . a civilian with no intention of ever becoming a soldier.

That was not, however, the end of the Nolan family's connection to the Dirigent Mercenary Corps. Even after Lon and Sara moved to Bascombe East with the twins and gradually took over running the Winking Eye, Lon went off on a couple of diplomatic missions, including one to Buckingham, the capital of the Second Commonwealth, that lasted nearly six months. He also continued to serve as an adviser to the Council of Regiments.

In the next six generations, twenty-seven descendants of Lon and Sara Nolan served in the Corps, and three of them became General—one great-grandson serving three terms. And, more than three thousand years later—long after the Dirigent Mercenary Corps, the Second Commonwealth, and the Confederation of Human Worlds had all passed into ancient history—a direct descendant of Lon and Sara Nolan commanded the security detachment aboard the *Exoprise,* a converted asteroid fitted out to be the first ship to try to reach the great galaxy in Androm-eda, hoping to find, *finally,* another sentient species in the universe.

Turn the page for an exciting excerpt from

HOLDING THE LINE

The first book of
Rick Shelley's thrilling new military series

Coming in paperback from Ace Books
August 2001

I needed twenty-three minutes to reach the battalion orderly room on main base. Fritz looked apprehensive as he got up from his desk and moved toward the door to Major Wellman's office.

"He's waiting for you. I'm to usher you right in."

"Level with me, Fritz. What's up?"

Fritz shook his head. "Honest, I don't have any idea." Then he knocked on the old man's door, opened it far enough to stick his head in, and said, "Sergeant Drak is here, Major."

Wellman's "Send him in" was muffled, but didn't sound happy. Fritz swung the door open all the way and gestured me through. He closed the door behind me.

"Sergeant Drak reporting as ordered." I braced to attention and saluted. Since I didn't know what was up, and figured I was in trouble for *something*, I made it all as crisp and proper as I could, acting like I loved all the routine bullshit.

Major Wellman looked up slowly and returned my salute as if he were trapped in gelatin. Then he stared with his watery blue eyes. Staring was one thing the major was excellent at. He had made it nearly an art form. Wellman looked me up and down, then back up again. There was no steam coming out of his ears, but I didn't need much imagination to picture it. I remained stiffly at attention. Maybe I don't look much like a recruiting poster soldier—I'm too short and stocky for that—but I do know my job; I'm damned good at it, if I do say so myself. I can handle any weapon in the inventory and I can take care of myself without any weapons but those I had when I entered the world.

"At ease, Sergeant," he said after what felt like two or three minutes—but was probably less than thirty seconds. I moved my feet apart and put my hands behind my back.

"I have good news for you, Sergeant," Wellman said. He leaned back so he could stare with less discomfort. "You have volunteered to be part of a new unit, the 1st Combined Regiment."

"Sir?"

Wellman scowled. That was the other thing he was good at. If there were more than those two, I hadn't seen them.

"The Combined General Staff of the Grand Alliance has decided—in its infinite wisdom—to attempt to integrate the armed forces of all the species in the alliance down to the battalion level. And *our* Chief of Staff has decided that we need to contribute the, ah, most capable soldiers available, especially combat veterans, and *most* especially decorated heroes." At this point, his scowl got so deep and convoluted I thought he was about to puke. "Personally, I don't see how a soldier deserves a medal for somehow surviving when damned near his entire platoon was killed around him."

"Sir, maybe you'll see how if you ever manage to get in combat yourself. And survive. Sir." Okay, I was way out of line, even though his jibe was a dig at me, but I couldn't stop myself. It wasn't the first time I had sounded off out of turn, and I wouldn't make book on it being the last.

Wellman got to his feet slowly, leaning on his desk with his long, pickpocket fingers until he was nearly all the way up. He didn't have to get all the way up to be taller than me, but he stretched out to his full six feet four inches—eight inches taller than me. I could see his face go from its usual pasty white to a brilliant crimson. "You've got three hours to report to the flitter port for transportation to West Memphis. You are not to discuss your orders with anyone while in transit. Have fun playing with the lizards and monkeys. Now, get out of here before I have your orders rewritten to send you out as a corporal."